DEFENDERS
OF THE
BREACH

DEFENDERS OF THE BREACH

DOUGLAS J TAWLKS

MOVEMENT PRESS
CALIFORNIA

Defenders Of The Breach
By Douglas J. Tawlks
Copyright © 2016

The Defenders of the Breach Series
Book 1   Defenders Of The Breach
Book 2   Sword Of Deliverance
Book 3   Coming Soon!

History and Background
For more information about names of characters, roles
and history depicted in Defenders Of The Breach, go to...

www.defendersofthebreach.com

Third Edition October 2016
Published By Movement Press, California
ISBN 978-0-98198-411-7

DEDICATION

To my amazing wife Shari, you are my lover
and best friend. To my incredible kids Kyle,
Krysta and Jarrod, your heartbeat is found on
every page of this book. Honorable mention goes
to my mother Lena Tawlks, a member of the
intercessors hall of fame; her faith and prayers
have carried me through the years. Above all this
book is dedicated to the Ancient of Days who is
known by many other names.

Praise for Defenders of the Breach

Doug Tawlks' DEFENDERS OF THE BREACH has the "magic" and "wizardry" of HARRY POTTER and the high adventure of LORD OF THE RINGS. Tawlks' places his characters in situations that we face today. The hero, Cyle, is confronted by evil and must decide what to do on his quest for the "Ancient of Days".
-Howard Kazanjian, Executive Producer Raiders of the Lost Ark,
Return of the Jedi.

In Defenders of the Breach, Doug Tawlks presents the classic story of good versus evil in a page-turning, fast paced, action fantasy reminiscent of Lord of the Rings and The Chronicles of Narnia.
-David E. Bixby, Ed.D. Executive Vice President, Azusa Pacific University.

I really enjoyed the book. I don't know if it was meant to, but it spoke to me where I was at spiritually…in a battle. It captivated me from beginning to end. I will be getting some copies for my friends.
-Dr. Samuel Huddleston, Author, International Speaker & Church Leader.

Amazon Reader Reviews

I read this book shortly after its release. I loved it. I could relate to the main character, Cyle. He wanted to be "somebody", and make a difference in the world, yet he was full of fear, lacked confidence and felt he had neither skill nor opportunity. I really wanted to spend more time with Cyle, Lena, Bixby and the others I had come to know and love.

My 11 yr old said it's the best book he's ever read, full of action and adventure with many surprises, amazing creatures and characters. There were lots of details making it full of life.

My name is Parker and I am 12 years old. This is one of the best books I have ever read. The characters struggle with real life problems in a mythical setting. Non-stop action keeps you on your toes and at the edge of your seat -waiting for the next battle. We've already purchased several copies for our friends and donated one to the school library. I made my own staff to imitate the main character and practice with it everyday.

This book caught my attention from the very beginning and held it the entire time. Although the book's storyline is fantasy based, the messages embedded in the story are absolutely true and applicable to current time. Each character and scene is so eloquently detailed and yet not overdone to the point of losing sight of the story's message. One cannot help but get involved with the book because it's filled with adventure, laughter, pain, suffering, and most of all it connects to our own lives.

ACKNOWLEDGEMENTS

Special thanks to my editors, Annette Anderson
and Marie Reid, whose pursuit of excellence and
commitment to the task was a great inspiration to me. Also
to my good Friend and associate Dave Miller and the rest of
the team at Life Bridge. I honor your relentless commitment
to restoring hearts and releasing desinty in countless lives.
A very special thank you to my Graphic artist and content
manager Rose Campodonico for her excellent work on the
cover art and her tireless efforts toward unleashing this series.

PROLOGUE

The streets of the walled city were entombed in silence, broken only by an occasional dog barking or the distant sound of a lone rider's horse clopping down the rock-imbedded streets. A mist drifted lazily along the ground creating a haunting appearance.

She often walked these streets late at night, a lone watchman carrying a heavy burden. Her robes were wrapped tightly about her in a desperate attempt to fight off the relentless night chill. She was growing old and she wondered how much longer she could keep up her late night vigil. Aching bones and shortness of breath grew stronger with time. She was an intercessor, and her purpose here on these empty streets was to pray for her people and her kingdom.

There was a time when many joined her, but she was alone now and she had been for some time. So much had changed in the walled city. The hearts of her people had grown fat with prosperity and years of peace. The temples of worship were empty now except for the ones that had been taken over by beggars and thieves.

Her name was Lena. Many thought she was a crazy old woman who had lost her mind. They would call out to her in sarcastic taunts from their windows. "Go home, old lady. Prayers are for the unfortunate, and we don't need them." As she walked along she heard a familiar voice in her head, calling to her from a distance. Heartache comes for many, you must continue to pray. They will weep for their children and their husbands. There will be great sorrow and suffering. You must continue to pray.

Growing weary of heart and tired of body, she remains faithful and presses on in her prayers. As the morning light begins to rise above the horizon, she turns her weary body and heads for home, until the next time when she will come to this place again to pray for those who don't need her prayers, and those who don't know they have them.

DEFENDERS

OF THE

BREACH

Defenders Of The Breach Saga

CHAPTER 1

The cellar was dark and cold, dripping with the moisture that provided nourishment for the patchwork moss that hung from the rock walls. Cyle had made this trip to the lower regions of the castle many times before to retrieve wine for the King and his guests. This time he had to hurry. He was running a little late due to his habit of daydreaming, a common problem among sixteen-year-old boys.

He made his way to the back of the wine cellar where the air was cold and stale. A chill danced upon the back of his neck until a shiver flashed through his whole body. He hated going down there; it wasn't that he was afraid or at least that's what he told himself each time he had to make this trip to the wine cellar deep beneath the castle. It was an unavoidable duty that belonged to him as the cupbearer to the King. It was a responsibility he both loved and hated.

There were other jobs a sixteen-year-old boy found more appealing than fetching and pouring wine for the King. Cyle's restless spirit churned within him as he battled with the thoughts that had haunted him countless times before. Sure, it was considered a position of great honor and the King trusted him completely, but he would rather be serving in the King's military or protecting the outer realms of the kingdom as a border guard. Fighting for and defending the kingdom was the kind of honor Cyle dreamed about. So many times he had watched the Talinor warriors return from the outlying areas, marching in military formation or riding atop their warhorses, as they arrived home from battle for a well-deserved rest. They were strong and confident in their strides. Years of training in military skill and tactics had shaped them into the kingdom's finest warriors. Stories abounded of the great courage and valor of the fighting warriors of Talinor. Their dedication to the King and his kingdom was unsurpassed.

Cyle heard a stirring behind him, and then there was a crash as the cellar door slammed closed. His heart leapt into his throat, as he was jolted back to reality. Shaken instantly from his daydream, the room became as black as coal with the door shut. His heart pounded violently as fear paralyzed him. Unable to see through the blackness, he knew beyond a doubt someone was in the cellar with him. Soft scratching and then breathing came from the other side of the room. Someone or something was definitely on the other side of the wine cask, waiting in the darkness. Sensing the danger, Cyle's mind raced to find something to protect himself. He thought of the tales he had been hearing lately about dark magic and evil beings appearing in his homeland. The stories had been circulating out in the streets and among his friends. He tried to push down the rising panic so he could think more clearly. Then the scratching grew louder and the breathing deeper, finally changing into a low guttural moan.

Then it stopped all together, and once again the room grew completely silent. Only the trickle of water from the rocks on the cellar walls could be heard. Cyle slowly inched backward, fear still choking off his breath as he tried to calm his racing heart. He reached out slowly into the darkness, desperately feeling for something to defend himself. The laughter started softly at first, and grew louder as it echoed off the stone walls. Frozen in place, his knees started to tremble. The laughter grew louder as a wave of embarrassment rushed over him. He recognized it now; he had been tricked. The door latch moved and it swung open. Light flooded the room and Cyle saw the silhouette of three figures laughing and giggling with abandon.

"Micah!" Cyle yelled as loud as he could through his panicked breathing, "You guys scared the life out of me."

"We really got you this time, Cousin." Micah said, laughing with glee.

"Did you think it was an evil presence from the great beyond?" Devin, the other boy, was laughing as he taunted with his words.

Cyle stood there flushed with embarrassment, feeling angry and wishing he could think of something smart to say back to the jokesters. He knew that if he said anything he would just sound foolish. The third boy, Cree, was standing there with a smirk on his face. Cyle could tell he was about to say something to rub it in even deeper, but before he could say anything Cyle grabbed the broom in the corner and started after them.

"Whoa! Let's get out of here," one of them yelled, as they turned in flight and headed up the stairs with Cyle close in chase.

As the three cleared the top of the landing and disappeared through the door, a taller figure appeared in the entryway. Suddenly Cyle remembered what it was he was supposed to be doing…getting wine for the King and his guests. It was Darius, one of the King's chief advisors and Cyle's tutor. "Oh great," Cyle thought, "I'm in trouble now."

"Hard at work I see, young Cyle." Cyle hated the tone in Darius's voice when he was in trouble. He instantly started through his usual list of excuses but Darius lifted his hand to stop the flow of his prater. Cyle halted his discourse immediately. Darius looked almost ghostly in his long robes as the light behind the entryway created a silhouette of his frame in the doorway. It always amazed Cyle the way Darius could show up at just the wrong time. "Young Cyle, the King's guests are about to gather; it would reflect poorly on the King if his cupbearer arrived late with the wine."

"I won't be late," Cyle mumbled as he turned and headed back to the cellar. He was angry and he wasn't sure why. He knew Darius was right, but he hated what had just happened, and he hated appearing irresponsible, especially to Darius. Darius was always riding him to be more responsible. Cyle wanted to be thought of as a man, not a child. The struggle to become the person he perceived himself to be and desired to be was very difficult at this age.

When he entered the King's council chambers, the guests were already gathering. Cyle could tell by the garments they wore that many of them had come from different parts of the surrounding territories. Some of those assembled were recognizable to him, but he was sure of one thing, many of them were military advisors and governors; he could tell by the way they adorned themselves.

The King would enter the room shortly. Until his arrival it was Cyle's job to make sure that the other servants kept everyone's cups filled with wine. He carried with him a bottle of wine that he would not let out of his sight from the time he removed it from the cellar until he poured it into the King's chalice. It was his responsibility to insure that it remained untainted. Cupbearers were given the key to the cellar, and they alone were responsible to protect the King from the possibility of poisoned wine.

As far back as Cyle could remember he had been in training for this position. Chosen at a young age and raised as a cupbearer, he was taught the high value of trust and honor. Darius was the overseer of his education, and had done a thorough job of instructing him in the art of trustworthiness. There was the time when he was only five and Darius had taken him out in a field and made him stand on a boulder. "Turn, and face away from me," Darius commanded him in a cold and distant voice. Cyle felt an uneasiness rise up within him. He started to argue, but Darius was unmoving, "Do it now, or you will be cleaning the horse pens for the next three days." He struggled inside to obey this cold and distant command. Cyle resented these lessons that were designed to instill a sense of trust between them, and he often wondered where his tutor came up with these torturous ideas.

"Turn around." Darius's voice was more persistent than before. "Turn around, face the other direction and close your eyes." Sensing the futility of resistance, Cyle obeyed reluctantly. "Extend your arms out from your side and keep your eyes closed." Darius ordered. Now Cyle knew for sure that he wasn't going to like this. "When I say so, fall back and I will catch you." Cyle hesitated. "Do it," commanded Darius. Closing his eyes and taking a deep breath, he did as he was commanded, and Darius caught him. Another lesson learned.

There was a large wooden table in the center of the War Room where the guests were gathering. At the center of the table, inlaid with gold, was the symbol of Talinor, a majestic eagle with wings spread wide. On the wall behind the King's chair was a gold carving of the same image. Just below where the eagle hung on the wall were the words, "One Faith," inlaid in gold. The words had always stirred Cyle's emotions. They stood as a reminder of what his grandmother had taught him about the faith on which the kingdom of Talinor had been built.

The meeting was well attended by many of the King's allies. Bernard, of the Dwarves, a great warrior and leader of his people, sat quietly against the wall. Worry lines creased his brow. Nephli, of the Mountain Elves, and Graybeard, the prophet, were talking to each other in the corner. Cyle had not seen the prophet for a long time and wondered where he had been hiding. As soon as everyone was seated, Darius entered the room. He announced the arrival of King Shandon. As a sign of respect, everyone who was not standing rose to his feet and waited for the King to be seated first.

The King entered the room with Somuel, the Captain of the Guard, and Gerrid, the Chief Commander of the Tal military. He smiled regally to his guests as he seated himself at the head of the table.

When King Shandon spoke, the room grew suddenly quiet. "Nobles, governors and fellow countrymen, sadly what brings us here today is a matter of grave concern to us all. As most of you already know, Drashkar, ruler of the Boogaran nation, is at this very moment sending forces from the north to invade our lands."

"We have suspected for some time now that he was up to something. It was almost twenty years ago when Drashkar's father, Ashkron, attacked our territories in an attempt to take over our kingdom. It comes as no surprise to any of you that they want our lands and always have. In the last battle we were much stronger, and our military was better equipped to defend our kingdom."

"Now after many years of peace much has changed. We have grown soft, and our military force is not the size it once was. I have called this meeting at this dark hour in the hope that we may bind together our resources to defend ourselves from the Boogarans."

"Your Majesty," Bernard's deep voice boomed from the back of the hall. "May I speak?"

"Of course you may speak, good friend Bernard of the Dwarves. What have you to offer?"

"Good Sir, you will always have the allegiance of the house of Gartoff in any matters that would threaten safety. We have always been your allies, and as far as I am concerned, we always will. I was wondering if you knew what has become of Drashkar's father, Ashkron?"

"Unfortunately," the King offered a deep sigh, "all though bedridden and ailing, he is still alive. We have been told that he counsels his son in this current treachery against us." A muffled roar filled the room as looks of concern and anger appeared on everyone's faces. Cyle noticed that Graybeard the prophet stood in the back of the room, statue-like, showing no emotion.

Bernard spoke, "Good King, it has been years since we have engaged in a battle the size that this one would bring. The Tal army has not been seriously tested in years, and the Dwarves have lost many of their warriors to the farms. We would have little time to raise the army it would take to defend and turn back the armies of Boogara. But my greatest concern is that of Ashkron. If he gives counsel to his son, Drashkar, then we can be assured of facing the same principalities of darkness that challenged us the last time they attacked us. As we all know, Ashkron is in league with the Shadow Wraiths of the dark magic. How can we stand against this kind of evil without the assistance of the Gap Warriors?"

"There are no more Gap Warriors," one soldier yelled from the end of the table. Cyle knew who the Gap Warriors were.

He had heard stories about the mystical warriors of long ago who fought against Ashkron with weapons not of this world in the Great War to defeat the Shadow Wraiths.

Bernard spoke again. "Majesty, I know little about doing battle against Shadow Wraiths and the magic they bring with them from the realms of the dark void. There is one thing I am sure of, if we face Drashkar and his father we will be forced to face the Shadow Wraiths and their sorcery. We will have little defense against their powers without the aid of the Gap Warriors."

Darius broke in, "Allies and countryman, the Gap Warriors have not been seen nor heard from for many years. After the last great battle they disappeared. They have either long departed from our lands or have died away. It will do little good for us to fret over what we do not have. We must now focus on what we do have and come up with a plan for our present crisis. There are other ways to resist the dark magic of Ashkron."

"And what would those ways be?" demanded Bernard of the Dwarves. "Our temples sit empty and in ruins, and it has been years since the people of Talinor have entered those temples to worship in the old faith." Bernard looked toward the back of the room at the old prophet Graybeard. "With all due respect Graybeard, most of our prophets have died or left for other countries to find hearts that were more willing to receive their messages. Talinor's faith has faded like the colors on an old garment, with the exception of a few elderly women and children who still cling to the old beliefs."

"Bernard, you are a great and mighty warrior;" Darius interrupted, "there is not a man among us who would not welcome you at their side in the day of battle. You are not only skilled in the art of combat, but you are also known for your wisdom in the ways of war. We are grateful to count you among us. However, in the matters of battling the dark magic we must seek out those who are better schooled in such matters."

Cyle noticed that up until this point Graybeard had offered no counsel in these matters. "And what do you propose we do?"

asked Nephli of the Mountian Elves, "My people are a people of faith. We still follow the messages of the prophets, although our knowledge in the matters of dark magic is limited."

"I propose we seek out those who have had to deal with this dark magic," said Darius.

When he finally spoke, the prophet's voice resonated from the back of the room as he stepped forward, emerging from the shadows into the light.

"And who would that be, Darius?"

"The Priests of Zarish," Darius wasted little time in responding. "They have dedicated themselves to the study of the realms of magic. I have visited with them recently in the mountains of Zarish; of course, I did so at the request of the King," Darius was quick to add. "They are well-studied in the ways of magic and very willing to assist us if we decide to request their services."

"I have heard of these Priests," said Graybeard, "and I know little of their ways. How do you know they will be able to help us?'

"We have reliable records and eye witnesses of their assistance to others against the dark magic. Their success is well spoken of in the north and parts of the west."

"It has been our way to depend on the Gap Warriors in the past. We do not know for sure that the Gap Warriors no longer exist. Why should we risk looking elsewhere for help, and how can we be sure these Priests can be trustworthy?" asked Graybeard.

King Shandon broke his silence, "Graybeard, old friend, we have little time to sit and debate a course of action. Every day brings us closer to Boogaran hoofbeats and the ensuing battle; however, your concerns are noted. We will be welcoming the Priests to our city in a few days. At that time we can meet with them and see for ourselves what they have to offer. If we find them trustworthy, then we can ask for their assistance."

"At what price Majesty?" asked Bernard.

"That is unknown at this time. We will meet them on the

morning after the morrow, and we will know more then."

Cyle observed nods of agreement, as an air of relief seemed to fill the room. He also observed Graybeard standing with his arms crossed and a distant look on his face, and wondered why he did not say more. The King seemed uncharacteristically unsure of himself. Cyle thought of how much he admired him; he always had. They had spent countless hours together. The King on many occasions would share his thoughts with Cyle regarding the state of the kingdom. For some reason, the King trusted him completely and they shared a great affection for one another. His own son had died at a young age, and in a limited way, Cyle had replaced him.

He couldn't wait to get home to share this news with his grand-mother, knowing that she would have something to say about all of this.

The assembly spoke of their plans to gather as many as possible from the outer territories to strengthen their own forces. Bernard suggested they send some of his men along with some of the Elfin warriors to assist the border guard battalions to the east. Drashkar's forces would come from that direction since the mountains were passable at that time. This would allow them to send reinforcements to help fortify the troops at the smaller citadel of Easthold.

Easthold was built in the likeness of its predecessor, Talinor, just after the last war with the Boogarans. It was strategically located at the mouth of the eastern pass of the Valley of Talinor, designed as a first line of defense against any possible future invasion by the Boogarans.

In the event that Easthold falls, Talinor's second line of defense would be on the valley floor, several hundred yards in front of the city walls. If the lines on the valley floor should falter, then the army would retreat to its last line of defense, the city walls of Talinor.

Easthold would pay the highest price with loss of lives. It was no secret that the smaller citadel of Easthold would eventually fall to a military force as large as the Boogaran army. Talinor would need them to hold their position for as long as possible. This would give them the time they desperately needed to prepare the city for battle. Ramparts could be built, gates would need fortifying, and it would also give time for all the surrounding villages to make their way to the safety that Talinor's walls provided.

Cyle thought he saw something move above the crowd at the other end of the hall. Something shifted in the shadows above in the rafters. Startled at first, he made his way through the crowd to where he could get a better look. As he moved closer, he knew for sure that someone was up in the wooden beams above the War Council room. He was about to point it out to one of the guards when he realized who it was. It was Choppa, his friend. What was he doing up there? He had a way of showing up in some of the strangest places. Choppa motioned with his finger to keep quiet. Cyle had to laugh at his friend. He had that mischievous grin on his face that Cyle had seen so many times in the past when Choppa knew he was pulling something off. Choppa always seemed to know what was going on in Talinor and Cyle was not surprised. Cyle smiled at his friend's ability to just show up almost anywhere at any time unnoticed.

CHAPTER 2

The War Council meeting went on for most of the afternoon before Cyle was able to leave for home. As he made his way through the streets of the walled city, he passed by one of the temples that lay in ruins. The sun was beginning to set as the afternoon shadows stretched across the streets and buildings, creating a ghostly appearance.

There was a sense of sadness mixed with feelings of emptiness that seeped into his heart as he surveyed the remains. He knew only what his grandmother had told him about the former places of worship, and what they were like before the "falling away" as she called it. The temples had been simple and yet beautiful to behold, full of worshipers and seekers hungering for meaning and purpose. It was difficult to understand how this could have happened to them, but he desperately wanted to grasp it.

He had always been interested in the stories about the history of Talinor. There were so few like him that shared that interest anymore, except for his Grandma Lena. She did her best to help him understand the history of the temples and the faith behind them, but it was hard for a young boy to grasp things that were no longer a part of the world he lived in.

"Cyle," someone shouted from behind him, "where are you headed?" It was his friend Choppa running toward him, his short squatty frame bouncing along the street.

"Choppa, what are you doing out here?"

"Greetings," exclaimed Choppa as he approached him, a little short of breath and full of anticipation, "I am going to the street festival tonight. Do you want to come with me?" Cyle smiled to himself. Choppa was easily taken by the prospect of something exciting to do.

"I would like to, but my grandma needs me. I told her I would head straight home tonight to help her with some things."

"Come on, Cyle, there's going to be some great food and some of the members of the Tal army are going to put on a sword fighting performance. Can't you come for just a little while?" Choppa pleaded with him. He was good at that. Cyle had gotten himself into trouble a number of times by letting Choppa lure him into doing something when he was supposed to be elsewhere.

"Why don't you go on without me? Maybe I can meet you later."

"All right, Cyle," he sounded a little disappointed, "but try to come. It'll be great."

"Hey, wait a minute, how did you end up in the rafters at the King's War Council meeting today?"

Choppa grinned from ear to ear. "Hey, that was pretty good, huh? As you know, I have my ways of getting around." Choppa started backing up, avoiding the question all together. "I have to get going or I'm going to miss all the fun. Maybe I will see you later."

The meeting of the War Council had left Cyle feeling anxious. All the talk about dark magic and Ashkron's army was enough to give anyone the jitters. Running into Choppa had helped him forget about it for awhile. Choppa was probably Cyle's best friend. He was a few years older than Cyle, but in many ways he seemed like the same age.

Choppa had grown up in the palace with his father who was a Dwarf, and his mother a Mountain Elf. It was a very unusual combination, and as a result, Choppa was a small person, short and stocky with curly hair and slightly pointed ears. He had endured his share of teasing when he was younger, but he was older now and most folks seemed to like him for his good-natured personality. His father and mother had died during the last great battle with Ashkron. His father was a member of the King's Guard and had died saving the life of the King. His mother had fallen victim to a stray arrow.

King Shandon was indebted to Choppa's father, so he allowed Choppa to live in the palace and grow up there. He was given free run of the palace, and grew up with few responsibilities and a lot of free time on his hands. There were times when his carefree spirit and absence of focus would irritate Cyle, but for the most part, he had been a good friend. Tonight he would try to get away to the street fair to spend some time with him if he could.

As soon as he opened the door and walked in, the smell of homemade bread greeted his senses, and he realized how hungry he was. The food at the street fair would have been good, but it was hard to beat Grandma Lena's cooking. The warmth of the little stone house melted away the chill from his skin as he savored the smell of the bread. "Grandma, I'm home."

She appeared in the doorway immediately. "Hi, Cyle, how's my big boy?" She gave him a long warm hug and patted him on the back. "Are you hungry? I made you some homemade bread and venison stew, one of your favorites."

"I'm starving. I feel like I could eat the whole deer!" Cyle exaggerated. Her eyes brightened a little more at the prospect of feeding her hungry grandson and bringing him some delight.

Suddenly Cyle remembered the meeting from earlier today. "Grandma," he said excitedly, "I have to tell you what happened today; you won't believe it."

"That's fine, Cyle, but first I need you to split some wood and fill the water pots. Dinner will be ready very soon."

"All right, Grandma." He sounded a little disappointed in the delay, but that didn't slow him down. He was out the door in an instant. It only took him a few minutes to cut some wood and fill the water pots. When he had carried the wood and water into the house, it was time for dinner.

The two of them sat down to eat, and as was her custom, his grandma said a prayer of thanks before they ate. For just a moment Cyle's hunger caused him to forget that he wanted to tell his grandma about the War Council meeting. She filled a big bowl with hot venison stew, carrots and thick savory sauce. He tore off a piece of bread from the loaf, and as he took the first bite he savored the fresh salty taste of the meat. When he was almost finished eating he smiled and said, "Grandma, that's the best bread you have ever made."

"I'm glad you like it, Cyle; maybe you can take some with you tomorrow when you go to work at the palace."

"Grandma," Cyle interrupted, "that reminds me. I wanted to tell you about the War Council meeting today at the palace." She stood up and began cleaning off the table as Cyle continued excitedly, "There's going to be a war, Grandma. Bernard of the Dwarves and Nephli, the commander of the Elves, were both there, as well as the King's military leaders."

"And just who is this war supposed to be with?" she asked as she turned from cleaning the dishes.

"Someone named Ashkron and his son Drashkar of the Boogaran nation." He was going to continue his story, but a change in his grandma's mood caused him to hold his tongue. She slowly turned from the washbasin to face him; her face appeared ashen. She said nothing at first, staring at him for a brief moment with a mask of fear replacing her more familiar look of warmth.

"Ashkron! Are you sure?"

"Yes, Grandma, I was there for the whole meeting. Ashkron's son is the one who is leading the Boogaran army. They may be marching to Talinor already."

"No wonder there has been a storm in my spirit."

"What do you mean, Grandma?" Cyle was confused.

"Oh nothing, don't worry about it. Now tell me what else did you learn?"

"They spoke of the last war with Ashkron and the Shadow Wraiths. Bernard was concerned. He says we are defenseless against the dark magic. They even spoke of the Gap Warriors, Grandma, and said they no longer existed, and if they did, they were nowhere to be found." She sat down at the table and mumbled something about the Gap Warriors as sadness crossed her face. "What is it, Grandma? What's wrong?"

She hesitated before she responded, "The last Great War between Talinor and the armies of Ashkron was a costly one. Many lives were lost." She shook her head.

"I'm sorry, Grandma. I didn't mean to make you sad." Cyle felt so sorry.

"No, it's not you, Cyle. You never knew your parents, but as I have told you before, they fought in the battle against Ashkron. It was a few years after the war had ended when it happened. You had just been born and your mother and father had to leave on a diplomatic assignment to the Boogarans. They never returned. Your parents and the military escort that accompanied them were attacked just before they reached the Boogaran capital. No one survived. The Boogarans blamed it on bandits." She took a deep breath and continued, "My concern now is your safety and the safety of our city."

"Did they say what they would do about the dark magic?" she asked. "If it is true that the Gap Warriors are all gone, how can we possibly stand against the Shadow Wraiths? Their magic is evil and cruel; we will have no chance without a way to defeat them. Surely it won't be by the prayers of our own people whose hearts have grown cold and dark."

"Grandma, Daruius spoke of the Priests of Zarish. He said that they were well schooled in the magic, and have a reputation for dealing effectively with its ways. They have helped others before."

"I know so little of them," she said sounding a little angry, "I have tried to find out what they believe and stand for, but it has been difficult. What does Graybeard say about all of this?"

"He said very little. He asked a few questions, but for the most part he was very quiet."

"That concerns me. If ever we have needed his direction and counsel it is now." She turned and walked over to a chest in the corner of the room. After withdrawing something from it, she slowly walked back over to the table and sat down across from him. In her hands was a small leather pouch. "I have something I have wanted to give you now that you are older." She played with the pouch nervously in her hands. Finally she opened it and poured the contents of it into her hand. Cyle could make out a small metallic object attached to a chain. "Cyle, this was your father's. He always wore it when he went into battle."

"What is it, Grandma?" She reached across the table and placed it in his hands. The minute it touched his skin there was a slight momentary vibration. It was a circular medallion attached to a chain, and on its surface was the graven image of the eagle of Talinor.

"He would have wanted you to have it," she said thoughtfully. For a moment Cyle didn't know what to say. He thought she was trying to tell him something, or that there was some deeper meaning to what was happening.

"Could you tell me again about the meaning of the eagle?" He knew well of its importance, but he liked hearing his grandmother talk about it.

"Long ago, way before your father and mother were born, and I was just a small child, our family came to this region looking for a place to call home. Before long the people of this land grew into a kingdom with laws and governors. The people appointed their first magistrate, who after a time became our first king. His name was Kem Fellnar. He had come from a faraway land, and like most of us, he was looking for a new home. He brought with him a strong faith, something most of us did not have. We followed whatever gods were available or convenient to us at the time of our need. Kem Fellnar was different. He followed only one god. At first the people did not understand him and his limiting belief system, but with time he proved to be a benevolent leader who earned great respect from his people.

"He called his god the "Ancient of Days," and before very long many of the people came to believe in Kem Fellnar's God. He had taught them that the eagle that flies the skies and watches over the land was a symbol to remind the people of their God. Whenever they saw an eagle soaring upon the wind currents it was to remind them that they too were being watched over by the Ancient of Days.

The people of this land grew in their faith and started building shrines and temples to worship the God they had come to honor and serve. This is why the kingdom of Talinor flies the banners that carry the emblem of the great eagle. However, the eagle, as well as the Ancient of Days, has long been forsaken by most of Talinor. Its image is only a tradition. You and I, Cyle, may be the last two people in the kingdom who truly believe."

"What about Graybeard; doesn't he believe?"

"I cannot say for sure," she paused thoughtfully before starting again. "It has been so long since Graybeard has had anything to say in favor of the ancient faith. As for you Cyle,

16

you must stay strong in your faith. I know you are young in your understanding of things, but in time you will grow in that understanding."

Just then a knock sounded at the door. When Cyle opened it, Choppa was standing there out of breath and very excited. "Cyle, are you coming to the festival or not? You have already missed half of the competition. Your cousin Micah is going to be competing soon. Come on, let's go."

Cyle turned to his grandmother with a pleading glance, but before he could ask she responded, "Go ahead, just be back before it's too late.

There were street performers, clowns and the smell of meat roasting on open fires. An elderly farmer was roasting a pig on a spit that you could purchase by the slice. The air was filled with the sounds of laughter and merriment. Children were running everywhere with bright colored ribbons and little flags. The crowd packed the street making it slow moving for Cyle and Choppa. At the center of it all was the arena where the competitions were held. Two Tal archers were just finishing a contest with the bow and arrow when the two boys arrived. Cyle was filled with anticipation, hoping he was not too late to see his cousin Micah compete.

"Over here," Choppa yelled above the noise. "It looks like Micah is about to start." Cyle could see his cousin across the arena. He was suiting up with chain mail and armor. His heart started pounding as he watched his cousin getting ready. He would compete at his own level of skill with someone of similar experience.

Cyle would give anything to be in Micah's shoes right now. This is an exciting time to be part of the King's army. His frustration swelled as he thought about how he would be stuck at home serving wine to the King, while his friends and his cousin were fighting to protect Talinor. Soon these competitions would be real. Not just a matter of entertainment, but a true measure of skill. Cyle wondered if his cousin even knew about the War Council meeting or any of the danger he would soon be facing. Micah had never fought in a real battle before. Cyle's stomach churned inside at the thought of what might lie ahead for his cousin if this war became a reality.

Choppa grabbed him by the arm and yelled above the crowd. "Come on! I found a great place to watch the contest."

CHAPTER 3

Drashkar, son of Ashkron, was young and confident. His relationship with his father was strained, to say the least. The business of running a kingdom that was committed to the pursuit of conquering other kingdoms left little time for family bonding. All his life Drashkar had wanted to be like his father, strong, powerful and confident. His father ruled with an iron fist and commanded the respect of all of his subjects. He had one driving purpose as king to rule over and control as many people and as much land as possible. "When you control the land, you control the people," he would always tell his son. Gold and riches were important, but not for the purpose of leisure or extravagance. Ashkron was in it for the power. He was addicted to the power of controlling others through fear and manipulation. He had done it for so long it had become who he was, and now his only son was following closely in his footsteps. Drashkar wasn't trying to prove anything to his father; he just wanted the same things his father wanted. From the time he was very young he was able to observe his father and learn. And learn he did. Like the time he saw him order the death of one of his commanders. He had not come back with the head of a king from a warring nation. The battle had been won and the land had been secured, but the commander in charge had failed to return with the head of the fallen king. Ashkron was fond of both trophies and beheadings. They both accomplished the same thing. Mounting the head of a conquered foe in front of his military palace was a symbol of his power.

There was one other memory he would never forget. His father had suspected his mother to be flirting with one of his military advisors. He never questioned her or the advisor. Then one day she was gone along with the advisor. He never asked his father what happened; somehow he knew better. Sometimes silence was the best path to take in matters with his father. He found out later from others in the castle that his father had ordered them bound, tied in sacks and thrown into the river. Everyone was forbidden to speak of them ever again.

"The citizens of Talinor have grown weak and aimless in their prosperity." Ashkron's cough rattled through his lungs as he spit out the words in a venomous tone to his son. "This time we will conquer Talinor and gain the stronghold we were once denied." His breathing was heavy and labored. "Once Talinor is ours, we will be in a position to take the rest of the lands beyond." He coughed and sputtered through his words, his passion to seize Talinor growing ever stronger.

"Father, we will not lose this time. The warlock, Drok Relnik, has read the signs. He says they look promising. We also have the alliance that you have maintained with the Shadow Wraiths." Drashkar spoke with great boldness and conviction as he stepped closer to his father's side. "As you have said, Talinor and its people have grown pathetically weak in purpose and vision while the dark magic grows stronger in their midst."

His father looked at him with a piercing gaze. "Do not grow over-confident, my son. Invading their lands will give them a purpose that will unite them. We must never underestimate Shandon. He is a worthy adversary."

"That is true, Father, but King Shandon grows old and soft. His kingdom has suffered little hardship to keep them strong, and most of their battles have been small, insignificant skirmishes over boundary lines. It has been too long since they have worshiped in their temples and paid homage to their god. They have become a kingdom without a vision." Drashkar's words came with a passionate fury. "How can any kingdom stand with such an emptiness of purpose?"

"They cannot," Ashkron paused as he grimaced in pain against his sickness, "but we must not take lightly the task before us, for we will become their purpose."

"I won't, Father. Even now our soldiers are ready to march while Talinor's forces have yet to be gathered and organized for battle. By now he knows we are coming, but his attempts to organize his troops and bring them in from the surrounding areas will fall short. With any luck we will reach the fortress of Easthold, their first line of defense, within a week."

"My son," Ashkron's voice sounded tired, "what have you heard from Gizshra, leader of the Shadow Wraiths?"

"According to one of his messengers, some of his demons are already at work within Talinor, as well as the surrounding villages and strongholds. He was unwilling to give me any of the details; you know how Gizshra is about secrecy."

"Yes, I know, and it haunts me to not know all the details. I suppose it's a small price to pay for such a powerful ally," Ashkron mused. "If I know Gizshra, he is already working his magic into the land and twisting the minds of the people of Talinor. His hunger for conquest is even stronger than mine. I want the land; he wants the souls. We both need each other to win this battle."

"Father, you must sleep now; I must go to make final preparations for my departure tomorrow. I leave at first light. In the morning we will speak before I leave." Drashkar left the room and softly closed the door behind him. He walked down a long dimly lit hallway until he entered a large room lit by a single candle. Closing the door behind him he felt a chill wash over his body. Across the room, he saw a dark figure clothed in a hooded robe standing in the shadows. Cloaked in darkness, its face was hidden in its cowl. Drashkar forced his words out. "What is your name and why have you come here?"

"My name is of no concern to you. I am here at the bidding of my master, Gizshra." His voice was deep and guttural. Drashkar stood silent for a moment, still feeling the cold chill. He was not expecting the Shadow Wraith this night, and it caught him off guard.

"What is your purpose here? Does Gizshra send news?" Drashkar sounded unsure of himself as the Wraith moved ghost-like away from the candle on the stand. "They are more comfortable in darkness," thought Drashkar.

"Gizshra is concerned about the depth of your commitment to the task that lies ahead. He knows of your father's commitment, but as for you, you have little experience in the matters of war." The demon paused as if waiting for a response, and then it continued. "He wants assurance of your undying allegiance to this battle."

"My allegiance is to my father and my kingdom," barked Drashkar. "I will avenge my father's former loss to Talinor; you can assure your master of that." Drashkar felt repelled at the questioning of his competence by anyone, especially a demon.

"The master has little faith in family loyalty. He wants more than sentiment as a guarantee that he can depend on you in this campaign."

"Who are you or your master to question my loyalty or my ability in these matters? After all, we are the ones who have called upon you to help us with this task."

"Silence!" the demon screeched, appearing to grow in size. The candlelight cast ghost-like shadows across its robes, causing it to appear as an apparition from the dead. Drashkar recoiled as fear and loathing were threatening to overtake him. The demon raised its twisted hand as a clawed finger pointed at the King's son. His eyes glowed crimson red through the darkness as a pulse of unseen evil lashed out against Drashkar, and panic almost overcame his senses. "If your commitment to your father and your kingdom is as real as you say, then you must prove it.

You must give something of yourself as evidence of your loyalty to Gizshra." The demon hissed the words as they spewed forth. Drashkar did not like where this was going. He knew they could not win without the help of the Shadow Wraiths, but he loathed the idea of depending on them.

"What is it you want from me?"

"Only a small piece of your soul, that's all," whispered the Wraith while changing his voice to a more friendly tone.

"And if I refuse?" The words came out of his mouth before he could stop them.

"If you refuse, I cannot guarantee victory. If you agree, then the victory will most certainly be ours."

Cyle was exhilarated from watching Micah's competition. After congratulating him on his victory, he watched more of the matches and then headed for home. Choppa decided to stay longer; he was having too much fun to go home now.

For the second time that day Cyle found himself walking home. The sounds and the lights of the street fair grew dimmer in the distance behind him. His thoughts drifted back to the conversation he had had with his grandmother earlier that evening. Sadness gripped his heart as he thought about his parents whom he had never known. His grandmother had told him many stories about them and their service to Talinor. They had been great warriors; even King Shandon had told him that. If only he could be like his father. Most sons had the honor of following in their father's footsteps. In Cyle's case, he was a cupbearer because King Shandon wanted to protect him from the same fate his father and mother had suffered. Cyle knew Shandon had meant well, but it left him angry and frustrated. He had often wondered if his grandmother had had anything to do with his situation.

Suddenly he was aware of how tired he was feeling. Looking upward to the canopy of shimmering stars overhead, he thought about his soft bed at home, wishing he were already there beneath the warmth of his blankets. Then the thought struck him, tomorrow everyone would know about the Boogarans and the coming war. The city would be buzzing with the news. Troops would be gathering with their different commanders and making final preparations for battle. Shandon would stand on the balcony of his tower while all of the King's military and most of the city's residents would assemble below him. The royal banners of Talinor would flutter in the wind as they displayed the great eagle. His announcement of the threat of Ashkron's attack would be read from a parchment. Mothers would weep and young men would step forward to volunteer for military service.

Cyle wondered where Micah's assignment would take him. Some would stay behind to fight and defend the city; some would be sent out to scout, while others would be sent to fight in Easthold. He longed to be counted among those going to battle to defend the kingdom. Instead he would be stuck here at the King's palace doing the menial work of serving wine to the King. A wave of shame washed over him as he thought about how he would feel when the other young men his age left for battle while he stayed back in Talinor. He imagined how others would look at him and talk behind his back. He would have to live with this disgrace hanging over him for the rest of his life. Feeling the weight of discouragement press in on him, he reached the door of his home, entered and went straight to his room. He flopped down on his bed and drifted into a restless sleep.

The creature came at night. Not because it had to, but because it loved the darkness. The creature slithered through the night like a panther stealing upon its wounded prey, grotesque and twisted in form, a loathsome child of the dark magic. It entered through one of the smaller city gates. Talinor was asleep and unaware of its new visitor sent by its master, Gizshra, to work its deception upon the unsuspecting citizens of this faltering kingdom. The Shadow Wraith was hungry to consume human souls, but for now it would have to stay its lust. With the dawning of tomorrow's light it would take on the form of a human, enabling it to blend in unnoticed by others. Tomorrow it would begin subverting the minds of the foolish, and spying out any information that would be helpful to Gizshra. It was only the first. There would be many more of them to come later.

The creature headed up the street toward the palace until it came before a broken-down structure. Inside a fire blazed, and the sound of cutthroats and thieves could be heard drinking and gambling away their booty. Its eyes fell upon the dilapidated image of a statue in front of the building. When it realized that it was once the statue of an eagle, it started to laugh, a deep and hideous laugh. They no longer serve their god, it thought, we will give them new gods to serve, fear and devastation. It relished the thought of the souls it would consume, souls that would fall captive to it and others like it.

Something moved in the distance. The demon turned to see what it was. It sensed something was wrong, terribly wrong. Out of the shadows at the far end of the street a lone figure walked toward it. Covered in robes to stay warm, the person moved slowly in its direction. The demon shuddered as fear coursed through its black spirit; recoiling as if to protect itself, it turned and fled into the darkness.

She continued her prayer walk as she did every night. Something stirred within her. She prayed harder and walked a little longer. Tonight her heart was heavy and her prayers had a sense of urgency. As she imagined the days ahead, she saw a terrible darkness.

CHAPTER 4

There was a loud knock at the door wresting Cyle from a deep sleep. "It's time to get up," his grandmother's words were soft and loving. "I need you to go into the square to get me some supplies at the market." Cyle shook the cobwebs from his head. He didn't want to get up, but he knew he had to. It had been two days since he and Choppa had been to the festival and a lot had happened in that time. With King Shandon's announcement, the whole city was in a state of unrest. Outlanders from other villages were already flooding into the city in droves to find shelter from the threat of coming war.

His grandmother walked over to separate the curtains; bright sunlight flooded the room as she pulled them back. The light invaded suddenly as a rude reminder of a new day. Squinting to block the rays, he plunged his head beneath his pillow in one last attempt to recapture the fleeting comfort of darkness.

"Grandma, you know I don't like that," he groaned in muffled tones from beneath his pillow. She reached over and playfully shook him.

"If you don't get up pretty soon it will be tomorrow before it's today," she teased. "Come on, Cyle, Choppa's here waiting for you, and if you don't get going he's going to eat everything in our cupboards. You know how that boy can eat. I'm convinced he has a hollow leg."

Cyle stumbled from the bed, "I'll be out in a minute, Grandma."

After eating some bread and porridge, Choppa helped Cyle with a few morning chores; then they headed for the market. It was a clear sunny day with a soft breeze, which brought a mild chill. The streets were cluttered with people everywhere going to and from the marketplace. "Looks like everyone is stocking up," said Choppa. "No one wants to be left without supplies just in case this war goes on too long."

"King Shandon's announcement shook up a lot of people just like I thought it would," Cyle said as someone with a cart bumped into him, obviously in a big hurry. Another elderly lady weighed down with vegetables and a bag of beans almost ran into the cart man. "Watch where you are going, old lady," the man yelled. "Next time I will run you over." She scowled at him and moved on her way.

As they approached the vendors they could hear them yelling out to those who passed by. "Get your beans, flour, fruit and vegetables. Best price in town." Cyle couldn't remember a time when it was this crowded except right before the spring festival celebration, but this was no celebration. Everyone was edgy and impatient, showing little respect for each other.

"Look, sugar cream cakes." said Choppa, as his eyes widened. "Come on, let's get some. I'll buy."

"Don't you ever get full, Choppa?" Cyle couldn't believe he was hungry after all he had just eaten. "Let's wait until later, around lunchtime. We can pick up my grandma's supplies and then we can come back after we take them home." Choppa agreed reluctantly. They wasted no time in completing the shopping list. There were a few things he was unable to buy because the vendors were out. After taking the supplies home, they hurried back toward the market to satisfy Choppa's endless craving for sweets.

"Cyle," someone yelled over the noise of the crowd. Cyle looked around to see where it was coming from. He glanced at Choppa to see if he had heard it, but he was too busy eating his cream cake to notice. Cyle thought he was imagining things; then he heard it again. This time he thought the voice came from behind him, and when he turned around he saw his cousin, Micah, and his friend, Cree, running toward him.

"Cyle, we got our assignment this morning." Cyle's heart sank within him. He tried to appear excited for his cousin. "We'll be leaving tomorrow morning with a small company of soldiers to scout the outer villages," Micah said excitedly. "Then we head to Easthold to join with the outlanders and other forces to help defend against the first wave of attack."

"I can't believe it, Micah, you're going to battle." The reality of his cousin's assignment gave him great concern. Easthold was a death sentence. "Are you ready for this, Cousin?" he asked tentatively.

"We're ready," said Cree, cutting in with the answer, his voice filled with confidence. "What about you, Cyle, are you ready?" Cree's question was filled with the poison of sarcasm. Cyle felt a flush of embarrassment wash over across his face. Not knowing how to respond, he mumbled something and stared at the ground.

"That's what I thought," said Cree coldly.

"That's enough, Cree." Micah scowled at his friend. "Everyone has his job to do, and Cyle will be here doing his." Cyle appreciated Micah's effort to stand up for him, but it was little consolation for the shame he felt.

"Hey, Cousin," Micah stepped forward and grabbed Cyle by the hand, "we have to report to our commander now. I just wanted to let you know what was going on before I left. Wish me luck."

Cyle looked him straight in the eyes. "I wish you the best, Cousin."

"And I you, Cyle," said Micah warmly. Cyle wanted to say more, but the lump in his throat held back the words. As he watched the two of them walk away, a hollow pit opened inside of him and he wondered if he would ever see his cousin again.

Things were changing quickly and Cyle could feel the weight of that change bearing down on him. Fear was on the faces of everyone in Talinor. Already today he had come across women fighting over goods they were trying to buy before they were sold out. People were angry and impatient with one another. He had never seen or felt so much animosity before. The only one who seemed to be unaffected by it was Choppa. Then he realized that his friend was nowhere to be seen.

Cyle scanned the crowded streets to see if he could locate him. No telling where he might be. It was nothing new. Choppa was always wandering off. After searching the area for a while, he found him finishing off the last of some sugared fruit. He wanted to comment on the size of his friend's growing stomach, but he held back his thoughts. Together they made their way to the palace yard to see if they could learn more about any recent developments.

The Priests of Zarish had arrived the day before to meet with the King and his advisors. In an effort to find out about their meetings, Choppa had gone inside the palace, while Cyle spent time in the King's courtyard talking to some of the servants and guards. He wasn't having any luck. No one he spoke with knew any more than he did. The courtyard was busy with both citizens and military men coming and going. One of the servants came out declaring that the King would be making an announcement in a few minutes.

Trumpets sounded from the tower above. When they finished their resounding harmonies, one of the King's chancellors stepped forward to make an announcement. "Citizens of Talinor, at the time of high sun today the King has an announcement to make. Gather all citizens to the courtyard to hear His Majesty's decrees." The noise of the courtyard crowd increased as it began to fill in anticipation of the soon-coming announcement. Just then Choppa came running out into the yard looking for Cyle.

"Choppa, over here," Cyle tried to yell above the crowd, but it was no good, so he made his way over to where he was. After getting pushed and shoved in every direction, he finally reached his friend. "What did you find out?" He was sure Choppa had learned something; he was good at that.

"Cyle," Choppa was out of breath, "the Priests have convinced King Shandon of their ability to deal with the dark magic. Our old beliefs and traditions of faith must be set aside, and full allegiance must be given to the Priests. They say it's the only way they can help us. I spoke with Bernard, the Captain of the Dwarves; he is the one who told me. The Priests said that nothing must divide us, not even our old beliefs, if they were to defeat the dark magic. They said something about the beginning of a new era. Dying to the old, and embracing the new. It was some nonsense like that."

"What does that mean, 'renounce the old beliefs'?"

"I don't know for sure. I'm just telling you what I heard."

After waiting for the sun to reach the middle of the sky, the trumpets sounded again as the King stepped forward to make his pronouncements. The crowd grew silent as Darius spoke. "Attention, citizens of Talinor. Hear now the declaration of King Shandon."

When Shandon stepped closer to the edge of the balcony to speak, he appeared to be ill at ease. Cyle knew him well and could sense it.

"Good citizens of Talinor, in times past certain traditions have been established, and they have been an important part of our history as a people." The King's words echoed through the courtyard from his balcony above the street. "We began as a small root and have grown to a mighty oak. However, with the passing of time, people and kingdoms change, and with that change we must be willing to let go of the old, and embrace the new. We as a kingdom face a terrible threat from our enemies to the east. Those we once depended upon to protect us from those enemies no longer exist. Therefore, we must look elsewhere for help." The King paused for a moment as he looked out over the sea of faces below. They were afraid, and they needed his leadership more than ever.

"It has been our good fortune that help has found us. Like a gift on the wings of the wind, our neighbors, the Priests of Zarish have come to our aid." Just then three of the priests stepped into view. A great cheer erupted from the crowd below. The priests appeared humble and sincere in their white robes with hands folded in front of them.

"As your King, I want to assure you that they are very capable of protecting us against the threat of the dark magic. In preparation for the assault that is to come against us, the Priests have asked that we forsake some of the old ways in order to strengthen our faith in the new hope they are bringing us against the approaching darkness. I, along with my Council, have agreed to this." A soft rumble of voices passed like a wave over the crowd. "Therefore, I hereby decree that from this day forth the eagle shall no longer fly over Talinor." The King paused as two soldiers cut the ties to the great banner of the majestic eagle that hung upon the tower. Cyle watched in horror as it floated to the ground like a wounded bird. The crowd was silent.

Then Cyle saw him. Graybeard, the prophet, was standing in the square. He looked over at Cyle, but his face was unreadable. Then without a word, he turned and disappeared into the crowd. King Shandon spoke again. "The old ways and beliefs can no longer help us. It is time to build a new faith and a new hope. If we are to stand against our enemies we must put our trust in the new magic, the magic of Zarish." From the top of the tower a group of men appeared as a new banner unfurled over the edge of the tower. Its design was that of a shooting star. The demon that stood in the midst of the crowd, unnoticed in his current human form couldn't help but smile. He was the first to clap. Others slowly joined him. Then the demon cried out, "Long live the King!" The whole courtyard erupted with cheers and applause. "Long live King Shandon!" the crowd cheered. "On to victory!" one man yelled. The demon cried, "By the magic of Zarish." Until they were all chanting, "On to victory by the magic of Zarish!"

Nausea rose in Cyle's stomach. Everything was changing too fast. Choppa just stood there gazing up at the King; then he looked at his friend, Cyle, with a look of confusion. In the spirit of the moment, a group of men pushed over the statue of the eagle that stood at the base of the palace. It fell to the earth and shattered in a cloud of dust. Cyle's heart raced with panic setting in; he suddenly felt alone in the world.

"I've got to talk to the King," Cyle thought to himself. "If I could get to him, maybe I could get him to change his mind." It was a long shot, but he was willing to give it a try. After all, he had a special relationship with his King, and with a little luck he might convince him to reconsider. They had talked many times about the affairs of the kingdom, and though the King may not want others knowing that he discussed such things with his cupbearer, he did indeed confide in him on many matters. On more than one occasion, he had taken Cyle's simple advice on things they had discussed.

Cyle grabbed Choppa by the arm and motioned toward the palace. They entered through the door Choppa had come out of earlier. They made their way up the stairs through the dimly lit hall. Then Choppa stopped him suddenly and asked through shortness of breath, "What are we doing? Where are we going?"

"I'm going to talk to the King. He's making a big mistake. It's wrong; it won't work," Cyle's words flowed passionately.

"How do you know it won't work? We have to do something," replied Choppa.

"I just know it won't. This kingdom was founded on faith in the Ancient of Days. I may not totally understand it, but if we turn our back on that faith now, I know it will be our undoing. Besides, I don't trust these Priests."

"Cyle," Choppa cut in, "are you sure you're not just clinging to the past? Maybe this is what we need, a fresh start." He tried to sound convincing.

"Are we to throw away everything we have fought for in the past?" Cyle asked as anger rose in him. He was suddenly aware of the anger he was venting at his friend who rarely committed himself to anything. 'Take the easy path and don't rock the boat.' It had always been that way for Choppa.

"Not everyone has the comfort of having everything handed to him on a silver platter." said Cyle, glaring at his friend, "Some of us have to work for what we have."

Choppa stepped back with a look of surprise on his face. He started to offer a defense for himself, but Cyle spoke before he had his chance. "This is something I need to do on my own."

Then he turned and ran up the stone stairwell and disappeared around the corner. Choppa was left standing there, stunned by his friend's harsh words.

It didn't take long to reach the King's tower. He entered the room off the balcony where the King had just finished making his speech. The room was full of the King's advisors including Darius and the Priests of Zarish. The sounds of the crowd outside had faded. Cyle noticed the poles in the room that once carried the banners of the great eagle had already been replaced with the shooting star. Panic increased as he thought, "It's too late." Brushing the thought aside, he gathered his courage to approach the King.

It was a bold and desperate move, but he felt it was necessary. "Your Majesty," Cyle yelled above the noise in the crowd. The room stilled as every eye turned in his direction. When the King saw him, a smile of affection crossed his face, "Cyle." He spoke his name in an endearing tone.

There was a stirring in the room as one of the Priests stepped forward. "Your Majesty, forgive me for the interruption, but I couldn't help notice that the young man wears the image of the eagle around his neck." Cyle had completely forgotten that he had it on. Suddenly he could feel its weight; his heart raced as his plan crumbled before him. The room grew deathly silent as all eyes fell upon him.

"Your Majesty, this young man must renounce the old faith or be imprisoned just as you have ruled," one of the Priests spoke, breaking the silence.

"Cyle," Shandon spoke softly, "what he says is true. I made this ruling earlier today. It has not been posted yet because I wanted to make the announcement on the morrow."

"Your Majesty," Cyle broke in, "I cannot renounce the old faith. It is all I have." He stood alone against the crowd in the King's Council Room, fear threatening to paralyze him. The thought came to him. "Run, and get out of here while you can." So he did. He turned and bolted through the doorway past two guards and was gone before they could react.

"Arrest him," Darius cried above the startled crowd. The guards started after him.

"Wait," Shandon commanded.

"Your Majesty," Darius spoke again, "it is what you have decreed; you must honor your own law."

"Do not speak to me as if I am ignorant of such matters, Darius. I do not need you to tell me how to obey my own law." Shandon paused and looked around the room before continuing. "We have asked our people to take in a lot in a short amount of time. Young Cyle needs some time to think about what has happened today. I believe he will come around. Tomorrow at midday I want the new law posted. We will give him until then to change his mind. If he does not, then it will be to my great sorrow that we will have to arrest him."

It had been months since his last dream. This one, like most of them, was a little unclear. The sky was filled with dark clouds and swirling winds blew with a vengeance. Upon those winds flew a lone eagle. He saw Talinor in the dream, and when the eagle flew past the great city he knew he was to travel west toward Talinor. He was filled with a sense of urgency as the dream unfolded before him. Through darkened skies and powerful winds the eagle flew as hard as it could to reach its destination. Then he saw another eagle coming from another direction, and then another appeared in the distance, flying to join the other two. The three eagles had joined to follow the lone eagle which was the smallest of the four. Something was drawing them to the land of Talinor.

It had been years since he had been to that part of the known lands. Most of his time had been spent in the regions beyond the great White Mountains. His services and skills had taken him to places far from Talinor. He looked forward to returning to the kingdom; he carried fond memories of that place. Even though it had been many years since he last gazed upon her hills and valleys, his memories were as though it was yesterday.

Something was wrong; he sensed it as he thought back on the dream he had had the night before. These dreams rarely gave him the details, but he had learned a long time ago to trust them. When he followed their leadings, they had always led him to where he needed to be. Questioning and analyzing them in an attempt to figure them out was a waste of time.

When he was younger it nearly drove him to madness not knowing the details. Now he just followed them as best he knew how. He was older now, and he hoped a little wiser. Time had been good to him. His body was still strong, and his spirit grew stronger still. The many battles he had fought had made him a better warrior, and his wounds had healed favorably.

There were times that he would find himself wondering what it would be like to have a home with a wife and children. He had a lady once. She wanted to marry him and settle down, but his life was on a different course. Maybe some day, he thought, as the loneliness pressed in upon his reasoning. For the most part he had grown accustomed to the direction his life had taken. Constantly moving from one city to another, like a wandering mercenary, he never knew for sure when he would be summoned to move on to the next place.

The roar came suddenly and without warning, tearing him from his thoughts. Its hideous cry echoed through the trees and brought the hair up on the back of his neck. His horse reared and started to spin. He steadied him with the reins.

There were many strange creatures that made Farlagg Forest their home. It was a place twisted with the blending of magic and the natural. Traveling here was risky, but he was in a hurry. Going around would have added two days to his journey, and he knew that was unacceptable. The sun was already down behind the trees, and it would be dark soon. This only complicated his situation further. The trees around him were beginning to look like towering monsters as the twilight shadows settled upon the forest floor. Darkness was now his enemy, putting him at a disadvantage to whatever it was that was stalking him. He had heard similar howls before, and had no desire to become the next meal for some bewitched forest monster.

The howl came again, only this time at a fevered pitch. It must be moving toward him, he judged. His horse whinnied and rose up on its hind legs; he spoke to him to soothe his fear. Again he heard the howling screams echoing through the trees. Rearing on its hind legs again, he feared losing control of his mount. Gripping the reins, he pulled back hard to steady the anxious creature.

Riding for the high places was out of the question. With his horse exhausted from the day's ride, it would fail him trying to make the summit. No, that would not do. Instead, he would try his luck with the lower part of the valley even though the terrain would be a little rougher. His horse was used to that, and it would give him a better chance of losing the thing. Loosening the reins, he turned his mount and started to ride. Erupting against the darkness, the howl was louder and closer this time.

A swift kick to the flanks and they surged forward in a gallop toward the lower meadows. Leaves and branches whipped against his face making it difficult to see. He didn't care. He just wanted to get as far away from that thing as he could.

When the roar sounded this time, it seemed to come from every direction. Hope was fading fast when suddenly he broke free of the trees and into a meadow. This would give him a fighting chance. It was a full moon and there was enough light to give him better vision to take a stand against his stalker. In a full gallop he rode to the far end of the meadow and dismounted. Standing with his back to the forest behind him, he steadied his nerves as he prepared to face the beast. If necessary, he could always make a retreat into the forest. Scanning every inch of the tree line for some movement, he waited, breathing heavily as his heart pounded within. Then it appeared from out of the undergrowth of the forest. Its basic form began to materialize under the light of the moon.

He was sure that it was a gargenmall that stalked him, a creature formed long ago by the dark magic to serve in a time of war. He had never seen one of these creatures, but he had heard its bloodthirsty howls while sitting by the campfire late at night when he had last visited the Farlagg Forest. Like most creatures of its kind, the gargenmall was a ruthless killer that craved flesh and blood. They were used mostly in battle where great strength was needed to demolish buildings or large city gates.

Huge and foreboding, it lumbered toward him in complete silence, no longer howling that scathing sound, sensing that its hunting was close to an end.

Pulling his sword from the leather holster tied to his back, palms sweating, heart pounding, the lone traveler held his blade high above his head long enough to utter a quick prayer beneath his breath. As the great beast lumbered into the full glow of the moonlight, its features grew more discernable. It was a grotesque combination of fur, scales and claws, rearing up on two legs at almost three times his height.

Fighting the temptation to run for the trees, the swordsman held his ground. The running was over; he would have to make a stand. Maybe by some small stroke of luck he could wound one of its legs and then make a run for the trees to regain his mount. He knew that he alone would have little chance of killing it. Sweaty hands gripped the hilt of his sword as moonlight reflected off the long blade. He stood as tall as he could, legs evenly spaced apart, steadying his breathing and calming his racing heart as he prepared himself to strike out. The beast was upon him now, howling again, lashing out with its claws, flailing deadly strokes in his direction.

Suddenly, above the haunting cries of the gargenmall, he heard a thunderous sound. Beneath his feet he felt the ground vibrating, softly at first, and then stronger like an approaching storm. He judged it as coming from behind him, but he dared not look back now. The roar sounded as if it would engulf him when in a sudden flash of movement they passed him, riders upon their mounts, weapons drawn, yelling and whooping as they closed in on the monster.

The one with the bow struck first. The arrow lodged deep within its grizzled neck as the gargenmall shrieked in agony. There were three of them circling the creature on their horses, appearing ghostlike upon their mounts against the moonlit sky.

With his sword drawn, one of the attackers swung his blade in a wide arc slashing through one of the beast's limbs. In a blind rage it lashed out with its good arm, knocking one of the riders to the ground while the one with the bow circled around behind and dismounted. Pulling a long knife from its sheath he bounded up from behind the beast while the other two battled from the front. The one behind was on its back now, long knife high overhead he brought it down into the back of the beast's head. Screaming in a blind rage and flailing helplessly at the thing on its back, the creature tried to swat the man off. Twice he came down with the weapon trying to penetrate its thick scaly hide, and then the third time the long knife found its mark. When it entered the back of the creature's head, it let out one last death scream and fell to the ground. The meadow was silent.

Then the three attackers let out a victory cry and raised their weapons over their heads. One of the three turned to look at the lone man who had stood and watched the whole thing. They peered at each other through the darkness until the one of the three said, "Bixby is that you?" They all turned to see his response.

CHAPTER 5

Lena was exhausted from her prayer walk the night before. She had stayed out later than usual due to a growing sense of urgency. Today she was paying the price for it. It was at times like these when she felt the physical drain of her prayer walks that she would begin to doubt their effectiveness. Things seemed to be getting worse, not better. Decisions were being made by the high court that lacked the wisdom of the past. Crime was on the increase, and the streets were no longer safe for children. She had prayed faithfully for a change, but change only seemed to come for the worse. She tried not to take her own doubts too seriously because she knew she had a tendency to grow negative when she was fatigued.

The sun was beginning to set outside as a refreshing breeze blew through the house. The knock at the door startled Lena. She wasn't expecting anyone this early. "I hope it's not Choppa looking for Cyle," she thought to herself, "I don't have enough to keep him full until Cyle gets home." When she opened the door she was startled to find Graybeard standing there.

"Graybeard, what brings you to my home?" She could feel the anxiety building inside of her. It wasn't every day a prophet came knocking at your door. But it was more than that, she sensed something was wrong.

"May I come in?"

"Of course, come in and I will get you some tea."

"Please, Lena, don't bother. I have something I need to tell you and we don't have much time." Graybeard's tone was serious as he proceeded to tell her of the events of the day. He told her of the King's decree renouncing the old faith, and how the Priests of Zarish had requested it to be so.

"I don't understand," Lena looked confused and angry, "didn't you speak to them and challenge their decisions?"

"The Zarish priests have convinced our magistrates and

the King that they need full cooperation in order to defeat the dark magic. I attempted to reason with them, but they are not interested in my words. Fear and urgency rule them now. As the time of battle draws closer their need for answers grows more desperate. They have no time to make wise decisions. Wisdom moves too slowly for the desperate."

"Why do you come to me with this news? All I know to do is pray, and even that seems to offer little at this time."

"I am here to talk to you about your grandson."

"What about my grandson?" she asked defensively, "What does Cyle have to do with all of this?"

"I had a vision two days ago. There was a small grouping of eagles flying in different directions. Then one smaller eagle came from a distance and flew into the sky nearby. The other eagles gathered around the smaller one, and then it broke away from the larger group. As it flew away the others pursued it. Then I saw them from a greater distance away. They were flying together toward Talinor."

"What does this have to do with my grandson? If this vision has something to do with him, then tell me," she demanded, fear rising in her.

Graybeard paused a moment before speaking. "Today when I saw Cyle in the palace yard, I knew that he was the smaller eagle."

"What?" she gasped, "What does this mean?" A look of terror crossed her face.

"It means that your grandson must go in search of the Gap Warriors and bring them back to Talinor."

Bixby stood in shock as he moved closer to see who was calling his name. Then one of the others who stood farther back yelled out, "Bixby, it is you. I don't believe it!" All three of the men started to move toward him, and then he recognized them.

"Greggor, Duggan, and Marcos, I don't believe it. What in the name of life and death are you doing out here?" said the lone

one to the three others as they embraced one another with hugs and slaps on the back.

"We were passing through this area on our way back to the northern Highlands," said Greggor, the eldest of the three brothers. We had just set up camp when we heard the gargenmall howling in the woods. We had never seen one before so we decided to track it down to get a look. When we saw you standing alone against the thing, we decided you might need some assistance. Of course, we didn't know it was you standing there, but that makes the kill all the sweeter."

"Tell me something," Bixby asked. "Why is it that Marcos always gets the most difficult job? I noticed when you were fighting the beast that he was the one who climbed up on its back to strike the final blow."

"It seems that such honors often go to the youngest," said Greggor.

"Besides," offered Duggan, "Greggor and I are getting too old for such heroics."

"If the truth be known, I have always been the one to take the dirty jobs. The fact that my aging brothers are getting too old and feeble has had little to do with it," stated Marcos in an attempt to make sure his opinion was heard. They all responded to his comment with laughter.

"It all depends on how you look at it. Greggor and I had to face the vicious beast head on, claws and teeth bearing down on us. I thought it was charitable of us to let Marcos approach it from the rear. After all, we have to protect our little brother," Duggan teased. Bixby had always enjoyed the way the brothers worked one another. He knew that Marcos didn't need protection any more than the other two did.

The four of them made camp together that night and caught up on the lost time between them. They had been friends for years and had fought together in the battle against Ashkron many years ago. From time to time Bixby would cross paths with the three brothers, and their chance encounters were always a welcome interruption in his life.

"So where is it you said you were headed?" Duggan asked.

"I am headed for the valley of Talinor. My services may be needed there," answered Bixby.

"Is this another one of your dreams that summons you?" asked Greggor.

"Yes, but the dream tells me little more than what I have told you. I have learned not to question the details. Things seem to fall into place if I just follow the dream as far as it instructs me."

"We have heard scattered reports from Talinor. It seems there may be a possibility of war between Ashkron of old and Talinor," said Duggan. "We have been away from home for half-a-year in the land of Tereshon, serving in the Tereshon military. When word reached us in that region of the threat to Talinor and our own people, we decided we should return home to the Highlands to test the truth of the reports. If what we have heard is true, we will be right behind you."

The three brothers were members of a mountain clan known as the Highlanders. Their home was only a one-week's ride from Castle Talinor. Talinor and the Highlanders had enjoyed several years of strong trade, as well as a steady military alliance. A threat to Talinor was seen as a threat to the Highlanders and most of the other smaller clans in the region.

The three brothers, along with many others from their clan, had fought in the war of Ashkron. The Highlanders were a tough and rugged bunch. Their horses were well suited for battle as well. Mountain horses raised in the high country were not handsome to look at, but their mountain breeding had made them powerful beasts.

The Highlanders' military methods were unconventional compared with the organized military of Talinor. They were reckless and less systematic in their way of attack. They had built a reputation for taking on the difficult assignments in battle. Though they were often outnumbered, Bixby had seen them turn the tide in a battle more than once when the odds were against them. He had fought with them side-by-side and had grown to honor and respect them.

The following morning the chill in the air greeted them, as did the sounds of the forest creatures calling to one another in their unknown languages. The four of them shared a meal of jerky and stale bread before the sun came up, and then they were on their way.

They traveled together for most of the morning before their paths took them in different directions. The three brothers would head north toward the Highlands to join the rest of their clan for the journey to Talinor. Bixby would take a southern and more direct route toward the Valley of Talinor.

Lena was reeling from the prophet's words as her heart sank within her. She was afraid for her grandson. He could never survive such a mission with the lands outside the walled city growing increasingly hostile. He was young and had little experience beyond the palace walls. It was a completely different world out there, and with the coming war it was even more treacherous. "Are you sure about this, Graybeard? Could there be a mistake?"

"There is no mistake," responded Graybeard confidently, "and you must be the one to convince him. He will listen to you." Just then the door flew open and Cyle rushed into the room, out of breath, with fear swelling in his eyes. He started to speak, but when he saw Graybeard he decided to hold his tongue; instead he turned and ran into his room.

After the prophet had left, Lena sat alone in her home pondering the things that Graybeard had said. She wanted to argue with him, but she had learned long ago that it does no good to argue with a prophet. How could she send her grandson on such a quest? There would be no one to protect him, no one to guide him. The thought of it was overwhelming, but deep within her heart she knew she must do it.

The door to Cyle's room opened slowly at first, and then

he stepped through in full view of his grandmother. "Why was Graybeard here, Grandmother? Was it to tell you about the King's new ordinance?"

"He came to tell me about that and more," said Lena ruefully. Then she told him everything the old prophet had told her. She described the vision of the eagles and the quest for the Gap Warriors. Cyle listened as his stomach churned.

"The Gap Warriors!" He exclaimed, "But we don't even know if they exist."

"According to the prophet's vision they do still exist, and I believe they are out there somewhere."

"But Grandmother, how can we trust Graybeard? He has been almost completely silent for so long." Cyle held out his hands in frustration. "When the King made his decree today, Graybeard said nothing. He just walked away."

"Graybeard told me they are no longer interested in his words. He says their hearts grow desperate, and they have little patience for waiting."

"Even I tried to persuade them, Grandmother. Today I went to the King and spoke to him."

"No, you didn't!" Lena was afraid. "What was his reply?"

Cyle's head dropped. He wasn't sure he wanted to answer with the truth. "I don't know, I left before I could discuss it with him." Cyle didn't want to reveal to her what really happened. He knew she would just worry. Tomorrow he would go to the King when he was alone and try to reason with him. He had talked to the King before about these kinds of matters. He was sure he would be able to get through to him. It would all be over soon, he tried to assure himself.

"It's late. We can discuss this tomorrow after a good night's sleep. We will both have clearer heads, and maybe then we can decide what to do about the prophet's vision."

Cyle lay in bed for hours trying to go to sleep. Finally, when he started to doze off, he heard something. He sat up in bed so he could hear the noise better. It was coming from outside his window. He jumped out of his bed and carefully made his way through the darkness over to the shutters to look out. Slowing his breathing, he mustered enough courage to look though the crack. A shadowed figure moved into view.

"Cyle, it's me, Choppa. Open up, I need to talk to you." Cyle breathed a sigh of relief and opened the window. Choppa stood there out of breath with his eyes wide with excitement.

"What are you doing here?" whispered Cyle.

"Cyle, you are in big trouble. The King is sick, and they are blaming you. They're saying you poisoned the wine he drank before he went to bed. They will be here any minute for you. You have to get out of the city now."

For one moment the world stood still. At least it seemed that way. "Now, Cyle! You don't have much time!"

Cyle ran for his clothes and after changing, he climbed out the window into the night air. The two of them ran down the street away from the house and ducked into a dark corner between two buildings.

Choppa grabbed Cyle by his tunic and whispered, "Listen, we don't have very much time. You need to get out of the city as soon as possible. I will get some supplies and meet you later this afternoon at the old mill near the lake where we like to fish."

"All right, but do me a favor and let my grandmother know what is going on. I don't want her to worry any more than necessary."

"I'll do my best, but you need to get going. The sun will be coming up in less than an hour."

With his head spinning, Cyle took off for the South Gate. If he moved quickly enough he would make it there with plenty of time to leave the city and reach the woods before first light.

CHAPTER 6

Darius was enraged as he paced back and forth in front of the soldiers who had returned empty-handed without the cupbearer. This meant he would have to form a search party to track him down, and it would take some time to pull all that together. No doubt Cyle had left the city by now. It was difficult to guess where he might head. The men had questioned his grandmother, but she seemed just as surprised as they were. The trackers and the hounds would need to be organized as quickly as possible before he could slip away for good.

Cyle had made it to the mill just as the sun was coming up. He felt sure no one had seen him take that direction when he left the city. The old mill was empty and there was no one in the area as far as he could tell. It seemed like the perfect place to hide.

Now he had nothing to do but wait. He sat in the window of the upper level of the mill and looked out over the rolling hills and the oak trees. A rabbit scurried through the bushes below and then disappeared into some tall grass.

From where he sat, he could see the uppermost towers of Castle Talinor above the trees. The spires that seemed to reach above the clouds glowed majestically in the early morning sunlight. He couldn't help thinking to himself how things had changed so dramatically in the last few days. His thoughts were still reeling from the incident at the castle with King Shandon and his talk with his grandmother. He still didn't trust Graybeard. He had little reason to. In the time he had known him, he couldn't remember his ever doing anything to earn that trust. If he was a prophet, why didn't he speak up and defend his own faith? How could he trust someone who was not even willing to do that? His story about the vision of the eagles was a little too farfetched for him to believe. Besides, if the Gap Warriors existed, surely they would have been here by now. Why would they need someone like himself to fetch them? Surely there were other means of notifying them.

What would he do now? Where would he go? As the questions pressed him, there were no answers. He was beginning to feel tired from a lack of sleep. There was some straw on the floor of the mill that looked like it would make a soft bed. His body ached to lie down so he curled up in a ball, but he was afraid to sleep. The King's Guard might come looking for him. Within minutes he surrendered, and was still.

When he woke up, he wasn't sure what time it was. His head was still groggy as he climbed the ladder to the upper level of the mill. The sun still sat low in the eastern sky, so he guessed it was around mid-morning. He wondered where Choppa was and what was taking him so long. Then he heard dogs howling in the distance. They were tracking him. There was no doubt in his mind. With no time to waste, he slid down the ladder and started to sprint for the woods.

The dogs sounded as if they were only a few minutes away. Then it occurred to him that he might be able to buy himself more time. Wading into the water, he picked a spot down shore to exit the lake, and then he headed for the woods. It might be just enough to throw their scent off and give him a few more minutes to put some space between himself and the dogs.

Staying near the edge of the woods until he could reach the northern end of the Valley would offer him cover from the open spaces. This would also allow him to avoid the marsh. There were creatures in that place he wanted to avoid at all costs. Recently some unfortunate hunters had gone in and never returned. It was common knowledge that only escapees from the castle dungeons entered that place in a desperate attempt to elude their captors. When they were foolish enough to go in there, the prison guards didn't bother to follow because they knew there was little chance of their ever coming out alive. His plan was to head north to the seaport city of Kenna. He had relatives there he could try to find.

Cyle had left in a hurry and he was ill prepared for a trek of any length through the wilderness. He had counted on Choppa to bring supplies, but he could no longer depend on that. With the howls of the dogs signaling their swift approach, he could not wait for his friend's return.

As he ran through the trees he could feel the thick forest undergrowth beneath his feet as branches and twigs cracked under the fall of each step. The smell of the forest filled his senses, and its thick canopy offered shade from the noon sun. He set his running at a steady pace so that he would not tire too quickly. The barking faded for a while until the dogs picked up his scent at the lake and found his trail; then their howls grew with frantic delight. If they were on horses, he knew it would be difficult to elude them on foot. By nightfall he would be nearer to the marsh area, but that was still hours away. He would need to come up with something to gain an advantage over them.

A fox darted across the path in front of him causing him to jump. After climbing a small ridge, he came upon a deer trail and took it heading in the direction he wanted to go. His energy was beginning to wane, as the howls grew louder behind him.

He thought of his grandmother and how she would be worried sick by now. Her grandson was both a fugitive and a runaway. The thought of his situation made him angry, and he hoped that his grandmother would not believe the accusations that had been made against him.

He had always wanted more adventure in his life, but this was a far cry from what he had in mind. Someone had poisoned the King. Someone on the inside was either setting Cyle up or they just wanted to harm the King. It was hard to tell. So much had happened in the last few days. Getting caught was not an option for him. It would be difficult to prove his innocence. Even if he could prove he was innocent concerning the King, he would still be arrested for not renouncing his faith. He worried about his grandmother. She would never renounce the old faith even if it meant getting arrested.

The woods were getting thicker as trees grew closer together and many of them had fallen on the forest floor making passage a little slower. He was hoping that it would help to slow down the King's Guard, especially if they were on horseback. It would make his travel slower as well, but not as much as the horses. When he came upon another small creek bed he took it upstream for a couple of hundred yards, hoping once again to slow the dogs down. After leaving the stream, he found a ledge of large rocks that he climbed and then traversed along a hillside. Horses would have a difficult time crossing these rocks. After another hour of maintaining a steady pace he was beginning to feel the strain in his body. He had always had good stamina and it had served him well on this day, but his energy was running out. He listened for the dogs and they seemed to be farther away than before. A smile crossed his face as he felt a sense of accomplishment when he realized that his attempts at slowing them down must have worked.

A small waterfall emerging from the rocks beneath a clump of ferns provided him with some needed refreshment. After sitting down for a short rest he could feel his strength slowly returning. It dawned on him that he had no idea where he would sleep tonight or how he would keep warm. The nights could get cool, but not unbearable if he could find some shelter. With fall approaching, the weather could be unpredictable at times. He hoped it would stay as warm as it had been the past few weeks.

Beyond the ridge he had left behind him he could hear the baying sound of the dogs growing louder again; it was time to get moving. Staying high on the rocks seemed like a good way to go for now, so Cyle continued to scramble, goat-like, over the boulder field.

So far he had been lucky in eluding his captors. He thought of some of the hunting trips he had been fortunate enough to go on with the King and some of his guests. He was never allowed to hunt, but he learned a good deal about the woods and the tracking involved in the pursuit of game. It was giving him a slight edge right now and he couldn't help but feel proud.

Suddenly the rocks ended in a sharp vertical drop-off.

Cyle saw that he would have to take a lower course at this point to avoid the possibility of falling. This would force him to move closer to the edge of the forest where the trees met the valley floor and the marshlands below. The sun was creeping lower in the sky and soon it would be dusk. The trackers would hesitate to continue once it got dark. A nighttime pursuit would put them and their dogs in a vulnerable situation. A horse could break a leg or a dog could get lost.

As he reached the base of the rocks and made his way to where the trees thinned out, he was surprised to see how dark it was getting. Ahead he could see the valley through an opening in the trees and the patches of marshland. The dogs still threatened in the distance as they continued their endless pursuit. For the first time today he felt like he might not make it. If they continued to track him he would not have enough strength to continue at the pace he had been moving. A crescent moon appeared on the horizon as a soft breeze whispered through the trees, and the sounds of the marsh surrounded him. It was almost dark and by the sound of the barking, the dogs were showing no signs of giving up their pace.

He glanced nervously about, searching out his options. The cliffs were out of the question. They were too steep in this area. On the other side was the marsh, and he knew he wouldn't survive in there. Straight ahead was his only option, and not a very good one at that. As he turned north to set his pace he saw something ahead through the trees that caused his heart to jump. The forest cast ghostly shadow as the light from the moon and stars filtered through the trees. At first he thought his mind was playing tricks on him, but when he looked a second time he was sure he saw something move. What could it be? The forest was no place to be alone at night unarmed. He had heard many stories about the strange and twisted creatures that lived here. Then the thing moved toward him, ghost-like amidst the shadows, its features cloaked by the darkness of the forest. Without thinking clearly, Cyle panicked and ran as fast as he could toward the marsh. He was now closed off in three directions, and it was the only choice left for him to take. Water and vines threatened to drag him down. Suddenly he tripped and fell headfirst into the murky marsh waters.

When he came up out of the water, gasping for breath, he saw that the dogs were almost upon him. Behind them he could see the King's men standing back on the edge of the marsh watching and waiting through the darkness. Yelping and splashing the dogs narrowed the gap between them. With his heart racing and his energy nearly spent, he thought maybe he should just give up. Going back to face the King's court would be better than entering the danger of the marsh and the things that live there.

The water stirred not too far from where he stood. It was dark but he could see well enough to make out the motion that created a wake. Something was moving toward him below the surface. The dogs were almost upon him, howling in a fevered pitch. Something shot up parting the waters and sending a spray in all directions as a serpent-like creature rose before him, scales glistening in the moonlight. With its yellow eyes gleaming, the thing let out a hideous scream that pierced his ears. Paralyzed with fear, Cyle willed himself to back away from the creature trying not to be noticed. Then it struck out, lightning fast, and attacked one of the dogs. The poor animal yelped as the serpent's jaws latched onto it. The other dogs turned to run back to the shore, whimpering in fear as the beast wrestled its prey beneath the water level. In one last desperate attempt to escape, the animal thrashed beneath the surface, and then the water grew still.

Cyle turned and ran deeper into the marsh. It was the only route he could take with the serpent between him and dry land. His situation had gone from desperate to impossible. He heard yet another scream from behind him. It was the serpent moving in his direction. Cyle was waist-deep in water, and finding it almost impossible to move as his feet were being sucked into the mud on the floor of the marsh. He tripped again and plunged headfirst, swallowing the murky water and then coughing it out. The serpent was upon him, and just as he turned to look back at it something grabbed him from behind. A wet and slimy hand covered his mouth.

There came a strange gurgling and a voice that spoke into his ear. "Don't move." He struggled to free himself, but it was no use. The serpent's head recoiled as if to strike out at them. A hand shot forth from behind Cyle. It was holding a ball of putrid-smelling moss that almost caused him to gag at the stench. The serpent screamed in defiance as it hesitated for one brief moment, and then to Cyle's surprise, it turned to retreat back into the darkness.

"Are there any followers of the old faith left in the city?" Gizshra's voice echoed through the darkness of the meeting chamber, as he demanded an answer from his sentry.

"Master," the demon spoke with an air of confidence, bowing before Gizshra's demonic form. "Those on the inside tell us that there is only one old lady and a forgotten prophet. The rest of Talinor has pledged its allegiance to the new way of enlightenment and renounced the old faith."

"I know of the old prophet," said Gizshra thoughtfully. "At one time he was a force of considerable concern. I believe his fire has grown dim with the passing of time and a shortage of followers. It has been a long time since his faith has been stirred against us. I don't think we will have to worry about him. It is the woman that concerns me. What do you know of her?"

"The power within her runs like deep waters. Our spies on the inside cannot get near her. She remains strong in her faith even though her world crumbles around her."

"Does she p-p-pray for her kingdom?" Gizshra had to force the word out. He hated saying it.

"Yes, every night, Master."

"Arggh!" choking in disgust, Gizshra spat something green from its mouth.

"But Master, she prays alone," said the sentry with a look of pleasure on his face, "and she is continually mocked for it."

"Silence!" screamed Gizshra, the sound of his voice struck terror in the heart of his sentry. "We can count ourselves to the advantage that she prays alone, but do not discount her influence. See what you can do to hinder her prayers."

"Yes, Master, right away." The Shadow Wraith bowed and then it turned and exited the chamber.

CHAPTER 7

"Listen now," the words were spoken in a harsh whisper, "us two cannot stay here any longer, it is unsafe." Cyle turned to see his rescuer who had finally released his hand from his mouth. To his surprise, he was covered in moss from his head to below his waist.

"Who are you?" Cyle asked, gasping to find his breath.

"No time for words. Quickly, you follow me," said the mossy form standing before him, as he turned to lead them deeper into the marsh.

Cyle obeyed without argument. He felt he had no other choice in the matter. This person or thing had saved his life, and he knew he didn't stand a chance of surviving without his help. They walked a little further through water almost waist-deep until they came to an area where the water level dropped to their ankles. Cyle found himself having to hurry to keep up with his mossy guide. The pace was very difficult to maintain because he was feeling spent from the day's journey.

Soon they came to a rise in the ground where there was a clump of moss-covered branches. The moss man pulled back a door made of vines to an opening, and motioned Cyle to follow him in. They crawled on their hands and knees for a short distance through a dark and damp tunnel until it opened into a larger room lit by a small torch. The minute he entered the room his head started to spin. He stumbled backward against the wall, as the ground seemed to move beneath him. Everything went black and he began to dream.

The forest was alive with the sun's rays sparkling off of the green grass that covered the open meadow. Someone appeared at the edge of the meadow in a woodsman's garb, holding a staff in his hand. He motioned Cyle to follow him. He did not feel afraid and obeyed without hesitation. The tall figure turned and entered the forest. Cyle was curious, so he followed him to a small open area. In the middle of the clearing there was a huge boulder over twice the size of Cyle.

The man wore a hood over his head so it was difficult to make out his features. Cyle vaguely saw a beard closely cut to the man's face.

When he spoke his voice was deep and rich. "See if you can climb the rock." The stranger motioned toward it. Cyle tried without question. He circled the rock more than once trying to find the handholds that would give him the support he needed to pull himself upward. At times he would make a little progress, only to find that he was running out of knobs to hold on to. Then he would slip back to the ground and move to another part of the rock and try again.

"I can't do it," he said to the man, frustration rising and patience wearing thin. "There is nothing to hold on to."

"Try again," the man's words were almost void of emotion but contained a measure of firmness in them.

Cyle tried again. This went on for some time until the woodsman said calmly, "There are no rules here for getting to the top. You must look beyond the rock to find your way." Cyle wasn't sure what the stranger meant by his statement. It sounded like some kind of riddle, and he hated riddles. The thought occurred to him to look around the clearing, out beyond the giant boulder.

Noticing the staff the man was holding, he asked if he could see it. The man said nothing as he reached out to give the staff to Cyle. Cyle took the staff and used it to push himself upward against the rock. He found that with the help of the staff he was able to reach the higher handholds that he had been unable to grab before. Once he reached the top he lifted his arms in victory and shouted out loud, "I made it! I made it!" When he looked down from the rock no one was there.

When Cyle woke up he had no idea how long he had been asleep. His body ached all over from running the day before. He struggled to remember how he had gotten here. Slowly he began to remember the events of last night in the marsh. He remembered the moss man bringing him into the shelter. Looking around the room, he noticed the walls were made mostly of clay and thick branches. There was a small rock stove in the corner with wood burning in it. Gourds hung from the ceiling and various animal skins covered the walls. The musty smell of the room was unpleasant, but bearable; his rescuer was nowhere to be seen.

There was a shuffling noise that came from a small doorway across the room. A strange looking man suddenly appeared in the opening. The sight of him took Cyle by surprise. His skin was a deep green color and his hair had the appearance of river moss. He was no longer wearing his mossy disguise from the night before. Cyle noticed that his eyes were larger and rounder than an ordinary man's. They were mostly a dark yellow color and when he blinked his eyelids appeared as fish scales. His clothes were made of snake or lizard skin. Cyle had never seen anything like it.

"I have brought water and something to eat. Here, take." When he spoke, Cyle noticed the same gurgling sound coming from his throat. The little man seemed eager to please his new guest, and Cyle was beginning to realize how hungry he was as he took the gourd with water and the food his host was offering.

The food was salty to the taste with the smell of fish and the appearance of jerky. The water soothed his parched throat as it went down. In a matter of moments he gulped down the jerky-like meat. His hunger was so intense he thought anything would taste good right now. His host seemed pleased that he was enjoying his meal.

Cyle thanked the man for the meal and then asked him his name. "I am Gruber," he responded in a friendly tone, "and what they call you?"

"I am Cyle."

Gruber bowed in an awkward way. "My joy to meet you Mister Cyle. I have few visitors to my home."

Cyle was beginning to feel at ease with the strange-looking moss man, sensing that he was in a safe place. "How did you scare away the serpent?" Cyle asked.

"Gruber live in marsh for many years. Many seasons ago much fighting happened at Castle. They put Gruber in a room with bars. Gruber not like that. Gruber escape and run away to marsh. Gruber almost die many times, but learn to survive. One day Gruber discover that serpent hate smell of yellow mud. Gruber rub mud on body and carry mud ball everywhere."

That would explain the color of his skin. Years of rubbing the stuff on his body had turned it to a brackish green color. Living in this environment has allowed him to adapt and survive. Gruber seemed to be a very kind and simple soul. He was also the one who could help Cyle get out of the marsh safely. "Gruber, I need your help. I must get out of the marsh. Can you show me the way?"

"Gruber know marsh very well." Cyle thought he seemed excited to help. He turned to take something that looked like a sack from the shelf on the wall. "Cyle need water and food for trip," said Gruber as he scrambled about the room to gather supplies, placing them in the pouch.

After tying a rope to the pouch he gently hung it over Cyle's shoulder. Cyle had no idea why Gruber was so willing to help him. Maybe after being alone for so many years life had grown simple and uncomplicated. Possibly being cut off from the harshness of the outside world may have contributed to his simple and kind ways.

Outside Gruber's shelter the marsh was thick with low hanging branches covered with moss. The canopy of trees that loomed overhead prevented the sun's rays from reaching the floor of the marsh. The sound of birds and bugs filled the air in a symphony of sounds that seemed to play perfectly together.

"First, we must put mud on Cyle," he said. The moss man pulled mud from a pot that had a strong smell of sulfur to it. They both rubbed the smelly mud over Cyle's body from his neck to his knees. The process was an unpleasant but necessary one. At first the smell made him queasy, but he found the effects diminishing after a while. "Gruber will carry mud ball to protect from serpent." He also grabbed a spear to take with him, and handed a small stone-carved knife to Cyle. "You take. Gruber have more."

"Thank you, Gruber," Cyle said awkwardly.

"Gruber happy to help Cyle. Cyle have good spirit." His comment surprised Cyle. Only his grandmother had spoken words like that to him, and he just assumed that was what grandmothers were supposed to say. He wondered what it was that the moss man saw in him. "Come, follow Gruber. Stay close."

Gruber headed into the thick underbrush where the water was just above their ankles. The dense branches and vines made the going slow at first until the area began to thin out, and then they were able to pick up the pace considerably. From time to time Gruber would motion to Cyle to stop, and then they would change directions suddenly. On more than one occasion he fished snakes out of the water with his spear and threw them out of their path. Cyle was amazed at how skilled Gruber was at navigating through the marsh. He seemed to know what to do at every turn.

Years of surviving in the swamps had taught him the skills he needed to live comfortably out here. Throughout the day as they walked along their course, Gruber would stop and explain to Cyle some of the secrets of navigating the marsh. It was late afternoon by the time they reached dry land. Cyle took a few minutes to wash the mud from his body. It felt good to feel the slimy stuff slide off his skin. For the most part their trip had been uneventful, with the exception of a few snakes and the screams of swamp serpents in the distance.

Cyle would miss the company of his new friend. He wasn't looking forward to traveling alone again. When they said their good-byes, Gruber looked at Cyle with his saucer-like eyes and said, "Cyle on quest."

Cyle felt confused and intimidated at the same time. "What do you mean?" Cyle asked. The moss man was a strange person in many ways, but he seemed to be able to see beyond the natural world into another place.

When he turned to answer Cyle, he seemed to look right through him. "Cyle have special spirit. Cyle on mission. You must go now. Goodbye, Cyle, my new friend." Gruber turned and walked away into the marsh without looking back.

Cyle suddenly felt alone in the world. He looked around at his surroundings and realized he was alone again. He missed his grandmother, and he missed Choppa. He was even starting to miss his position as the cupbearer, although he didn't want to admit it to himself. Tears welled up in his eyes and he concentrated to force them back. Cyle didn't like to let those kinds of feelings out. He had always felt more comfortable holding them in, and besides, he knew he had to stay focused. The forest had thinned out considerably and by looking at the sun in the sky he could tell where north was. He worked at pushing aside the emptiness he felt within himself and pressed on.

CHAPTER 8

The Priests of Zarish would eventually restore all of the temples of Talinor. For now they would focus on the main temple near the front of the palace courtyard. Their leader, Orom, had insisted upon it. The Priests would need a place to practice their own faith and to teach the people about the new way. Of all the temples in the city, the palace temple was the largest with the most spectacular design. Its steps rose above the courtyard as they ascended to the entrance level where huge pillars lined the portico in front of the temple. The entryway into the main sanctuary was accessed through two brass-inlaid doors as least thirty feet tall.

On both sides of the entryway, high above the ground level, stood two eagles that had been engraved into the stone pillars that framed the entrance. The Priests had covered them with huge banners displaying the shooting star symbol. The main temple had suffered the least amount of neglect due to its close proximity to the palace grounds. In just a few short days the temple was ready for the Priests to move in and begin their worship practices.

The streets of Talinor were filled with activity. Laborers worked day and night building scaffolding along the city walls in preparation for the coming battle. The four city gates needed to be reinforced in order to resist the battering rams of their enemies. Food was being packed away in the storehouses to maximum capacity.

The Rainbow River flowed through the middle of the Valley of Talinor along the edge of the marshlands and into the heart of the city. It was Talinor's primary water supply. Workers were busy filling pots with water to last the duration of the siege. The river entered the north end of the city through a series of enclosed aqueducts, covered by screens to prevent the entrance of unwanted intruders. It ran through the center of town past the palace yard and exited the south end of the city through a similar series of water channels.

The Palace Guard stayed busy patrolling the outer walls of the city both night and day. It was important during times of war to keep a close watch for spies trying to enter through the smaller gates. Surrounding villagers were beginning to trickle slowly into Talinor through the main entrance. Guards were posted at all of the gates to inspect those requesting access to the city. In the coming days the number of those entering the city would increase dramatically. Some of the men would foolishly stay in their villages to defend their homes, while sending the women and children into the city where they could find refuge behind Talinor's walls.

The sun was dipping low on the horizon creating an orange glow over the hills and valley. An afternoon breeze stirring in the trees brought a refreshing coolness to Cyle's skin after a warm day of hiking. With the evening shadows closing in, there came the familiar cadence of the crickets and frogs sounding their approval of the falling sun. Light would be gone soon, and he knew he needed to find shelter before it grew any darker. He wanted to find a place that was safe from the danger of predatory animals or any other creatures that made the forest their home. After a brief search he found a large tree that had been struck by lightning. Just above his head there was an opening that looked big enough for him to climb into. With very little effort he was able to climb up into an area that was just about the right size for him to stay the night.

It was too early to sleep so he sat in the opening of the tree, watching the last rays of the sun disappear through the canopy of leaves. Something about the sunset contributed to the feeling of loneliness he had been feeling since he left Gruber earlier in the day. The thought of traveling alone in a land strange to him left him feeling empty and discouraged. He was one who had always enjoyed the company of others, but for now he would have to go it alone.

He found himself pondering the words Gruber had spoken to him earlier. "Cyle on mission," the words kept repeating themselves in his mind over and over again. Then he connected the thought with what Graybeard had said about finding the Gap Warriors. Cyle tried to push the thought away. Going on a quest to find the Gap Warriors was just too unbelievable for him to wrap his mind around. All he wanted to do was find his cousins in the city of Kenna and hide out from possible arrest. He had no interest in running around in dangerous unknown lands during wartime, trying to find a group of warriors who hadn't been seen or heard from in twenty years. Besides, even if they did exist, finding them under these circumstances would be impossible. He was a fugitive from justice; he didn't have any idea where to begin looking even if he had a mind to.

His thoughts rambled into a blurry haze until he fell into a fitful sleep. Once again he dreamt of the stranger from his last dream. The two of them were standing in the center of a ring surrounded by a rock wall. Each of them had a staff. The stranger was giving Cyle instructions on how to fight with it. They sparred together using the staffs as weapons. The stranger moved catlike; his motions were fluid and sure. At first Cyle's maneuvering of the staff was awkward and tentative. As the dream progressed his skills appeared to improve. Then the dream ended suddenly.

Cyle was up at first light and ready to move. The only way for him to keep his bearings was to track the sun's movement across the sky. Sometimes that was difficult because of the canopy of trees blocking its view over head. There were times he would walk for hours before finding an opening overhead allowing him to get his sense of direction again. He stopped worrying about the trackers hunting him down with the dogs. He hoped they thought he had become the serpent's dinner.

He found a stream and stopped to refill his water flask. The water was cold and refreshing, both to drink and to splash on his face. Scooping up the water in his hands he lifted it above his head and let the cool liquid dribble over the back of his neck. Then he ran his fingers through his sandy brown hair and pushed it back off his brow.

Crack, he heard something behind him that sounded like a twig breaking. His heart jumped and he turned to look in that direction. He saw nothing. Quickly gathering up his few belongings he turned to move on. He had no intention of waiting around to see what it was. At first he moved slowly, not wanting to draw attention to himself. He reached to find the knife Gruber had given him and pulled it out of the sack. It gave him little comfort, but it was better than nothing at all. After running several paces through the trees, he stopped and ducked under some ferns hanging over a huge cluster of rocks to wait and watch.

Whatever it was he had heard back there could still be following him. Then again, it may have been nothing more that a squirrel chewing on a nut, or some other creature crawling through the undergrowth. His thoughts were straining to bring up hope when he saw something back in the direction he had come from. The forest shadows made it difficult to see anything clearly. He froze where he was, sweat gathering under his tunic and on his brow. The figure he was looking at seemed to be moving in his direction. Cyle's mind raced to make a decision. Make a run for it or stay hidden behind the ferns. If he ran now he might be seen. If he stayed hidden a good tracker would find him. He decided to run. He moved slowly at first staying, close to the shadows. Once he was out of sight, he picked up his speed.

After running at a steady pace for several minutes he slowed down to a fast walk, making sure to look back regularly. He had not seen anything since he had left his hiding place. He was starting to feel as if he had escaped whatever had been following him when he heard more noises. It sounded like the voices of people, mixed with various other sounds. Through the trees ahead he saw where it was coming from. It looked like a small village. Excitement stirred within him. People, he thought, and food. Surely no one this far away from Talinor would have any knowledge of his alleged crimes.

The town's people were out in full force, milling about the market place. Street vendors, shoppers and common folk were everywhere buying and selling food and trinkets. Children ran in and out of shops and alleys playing tag. One mother scolded her young child for wandering too far away from her. No one seemed to notice Cyle in the midst of the busy crowd. He was suddenly aware of his hunger and thought he might buy some bread and jerky with some of the money he was able to grab before he left home.

The bread he bought wasn't as fresh as he wanted, but he couldn't complain about the price either. A little further down the street he went into another shop to buy some jerky. There was a man with a potbelly and a balding head at work behind the counter. The shop was cluttered with baskets and bottles. Hanging on one wall was an assortment of animal furs, most of them in poor condition. A thin layer of dust covered everything including the counter.

"Excuse me, sir, how much for a square of jerky?" asked Cyle hesitantly.

"Two silvers or a barter," the man behind the counter said in an irritated tone as if Cyle were bothering him. Cyle thought the price was a little high, so he hesitated to consider it. "What's the matter, can't you pull for that much?" said the storekeeper, his irritation rising.

"Maybe I should go somewhere else," said Cyle sheepishly.

"I have the best prices in town and the best jerky. Who do you think you are coming into my shop and insulting me?" growled the fat man, his double chin jiggling.

"Of course not, sir, the price is just a little higher than I was expecting and I am trying to conserve my funds; hard times you know." Cyle was trying to be diplomatic, but the shopkeeper just seemed to get angrier.

"You're not from around here are you, boy?"

"No, sir, I'm just passing through."

"Well, why don't you just pass right on through that door over there and be gone from this place?" The veins in his forehead were popping out as he growled and then cursed through a long list of obscenities. Cyle was more than happy to leave, so he turned to walk toward the exit. Just as he got to the door the shopkeeper started yelling, "Thief, thief, stop that boy; he's a thief!" He started toward Cyle.

Cyle was out the door and running down the street. The man ran out into the street bellowing his accusation so that everyone could hear. Some of the bystanders joined in the chase. Cyle ducked into a narrow alleyway and ran as fast as he could, heart pounding in his chest. He turned again down an adjoining alley pulling over a stack of barrels to block the path behind him. They rolled over causing a few of his pursuers to fall, and slowing the rest. He turned another corner and disappeared from their sight. Suddenly someone grabbed him from behind and pulled him through a door. Fighting against Cyle's panicked attempt to get free, the stranger forced him into a dark room and shut the door behind them. Cyle's arms were pinned to his side, so he lifted both of his legs and braced them against the wall to push backwards. Through the struggle and grunting of the two of them he heard a whisper through the darkness. "Cyle, it's me, Choppa, be quiet or they'll find us."

Bixby was tired. He had been traveling all day for two days and all last night. A sense of urgency was driving him onward, but his energy was spent and his body longed to find rest. It was late in the afternoon so he decided to get a room at the tavern he had stayed at the last time he passed this way. He was surprised to see that it was still in business, and for the most part it looked the same as when he last stayed here. It was a welcome sight for his weary legs. He was looking for a soft bed and a hot meal.

He was pleased to find that they had a room and the price was reasonable. The current owner was a thin elderly man, a bit sickly looking. He was kind enough to send his daughter to draw water for him so he could take a warm bath before his meal. She was young, sweet-natured and eager to please him. The peasant's gown she wore was tattered and worn. Her red hair dangled playfully upon her shoulders and bounced about as she walked. When Bixby entered his room she was already drawing water for his bath. "Sir," she spoke to him sheepishly, "are you a Knight?"

Responding with gentle laughter, he said, "Some would say that I am. Why do you ask?"

"I have heard rumors of war in the land of Talinor; I thought you might be headed there."

"You are quite perceptive for your age, so tell me, what is your name?"

"My name is Karina," she smiled and offered a slight curtsey. Then she poured another pail of hot water into his bath. "What king do you serve, good Knight?"

"Are you always so full of questions for strangers, Karina?" She blushed at the question, her face turning the color of her crimson red hair. "The King that I serve doesn't really have a name."

"A King without a name, how strange." she mused, "How can this be?"

"Some call him the 'Unseen King'. Others call him the 'King that Ever Was.'"

"And what, pray tell, do you call him, Sir Knight?" she asked curiously as she filled her pot with more warm water from the hearth.

"I call him the 'Ancient of Days', as do all who serve Him," he answered with a smile.

Just then there was a shuffle of feet at the door and her father appeared. "Come, Karina, stop bothering this man; let him take his bath. The inn is filling up and I need your help downstairs."

After she had filled the bath, he thanked her and gave her a few coins, and she seemed overwhelmed by his kindness.

He soaked in the water until it turned cold, then dressed himself, thinking a hot meal was just what he needed before he turned in for a good night's rest. The tavern was full of travelers and some local farmers drinking ale and harassing the women waiting on the tables.

The pork steak and potatoes he ordered were flavorful and tender to the cut; some of the best he had eaten in a while. Bixby was just about to head upstairs for bed when he noticed a man sitting in the corner slightly covered in shadow. A chill danced across his neck. He could tell by the way the man was dressed that he was a warlock. He wore a black cloak draped over his black clothes and a silver band around his head. A large silver amulet hung from a chain around his neck and his coal black hair was tied back in a tail, revealing his hawk-like features and pointed beard. He sensed the man was watching him, and wondered if he had followed him to this place. Bixby was sure that the warlock knew who he was, and that made him uncomfortable.

Warlocks were sworn enemies of anyone who served the Ancient of Days, and this one was probably on his way to Talinor. He held something in his hand, no doubt some kind of a talisman used to summon the powers of the dark magic that he served. The warlock waved to some of the men at the bar to join him where he was sitting, offering them a drink from the flask on his table. They were happy to oblige. After a time of conversation they finished toasting each other and walked back over to the bar and sat down.

A few minutes later a disturbance broke out up at the bar. "Come on, sweetie, let's take a little walk." One of the men that had shared a drink with the warlock was putting his paws all over Karina, the tavern owner's daughter. She looked terrified and appeared to be pleading to be released. He grabbed her by the arm and gave her a solid jerk in his direction. "Come on, girlie," he slobbered the words out as he dragged her toward the door. The girl shook like a rag doll. The warlock looked pleased with what was unfolding. No doubt he was behind it.

"Excuse me, sir," the tavern owner spoke with an uneasy tone. "Could you please let her go and I will pour you another cup of ale on the house?"

"It's not ale I'm wanting now, old man; it's your daughter." Some of his friends laughed at his remark, and then urged him onward. The rest of the crowd in the room watched with dulled interest.

"Please sir, kindly show respect to my establishment and my daughter." The old man pleaded one more time. The lumbering oaf turned a deaf ear to his pleas and headed for the door. The girl struggled helplessly to free herself from his grasp. She looked back at her father with pleading eyes; he hung his head in shame, feeling powerless to help her. The big man kicked the door open and stopped dead in his tracks. Bixby stood in his path, blocking the man's way to the street.

"Sir, it would serve you well to let the girl go," he spoke in a calm and deliberate voice. The half-drunken man sized him up and down with his eyes, carefully weighing his options. Bixby was not as big as the other man, but he was muscular, lean, and stood at a medium height.

"And who might you be to interfere in my evening plans?" The man bellowed the words out in a rage. Bixby was close enough to smell the ale on his breath and the stink of his sweat.

"Sir, I implore you to let the girl go, and this can be over."

"As you wish," he said in disdain and gave the girl a cruel push that landed her on the ground. Then without warning he lunged at Bixby with both hands groping for his throat. Stepping to the side, Bixby blocked the man's arms and spun him around. He grabbed him with one hand by the back of his collar, and with the other hand he grabbed the back of his pants, and slammed him against the doorpost. With bloodied face the big man fell like a wounded ox back into the inn and lay moaning on the floor. Some of the crowd cheered while his three friends scowled and started toward their friend's attacker.

The crowd in the tavern was up on their feet yelling and cheering for Bixby. The warlock sat in silence watching the whole thing unfold. One of the men pulled a long knife from under his cloak and charged, thrusting the weapon forward. In a fluid motion Bixby reached over his shoulder and withdrew the sword strapped to his back. It came down in one smooth arc nearly severing the man's hand as the knife fell to the floor. He screamed in rage as he grabbed his wrist, writhing in pain. His friend was already moving to attack when he was met with the hilt of Bixby's sword square in the face. The force of the blow sent him to the floor in a crumpled heap. The third man held up his hands as if to surrender and moved to help his friends up from the floor. They grunted and strained their way out the front of the tavern into the street, all the while cursing and yelling idle threats.

The tavern patrons offered up a cheer and one of them yelled, "Ale for the nobleman." Then Bixby felt something touching his hand. It was the girl, Karina. She looked at him with admiring eyes and said, "Thank you, Good Knight of the Invisible Kingdom." Then she embraced him around his waist. Bixby glanced over in the corner to see if the warlock was still there. He was gone.

CHAPTER 9

Running into Choppa was both a shock and a welcome surprise for Cyle. After fleeing the village they headed for a place in the woods where Choppa had stashed some supplies. They hurried to gather them up. Cyle was happy to see that there was plenty of food to eat, as well as some outdoor blankets and a coat for him. Cyle noticed that Choppa had brought his own crossbow. It reminded him of their hunting trips for small game in the forest near the castle.

The two of them ran far and hard to create as much distance between them and the villagers as they could. As far as they could tell no one was following them. At first they had to travel up steep terrain covered with fallen logs and thick scrub oak that scratched and tore at their clothes.

After moving at a slow run for two hours Cyle finally had a chance to speak. "How did you find me? I didn't think I would ever see you again, at least not for a long time."

"It wasn't that difficult," Choppa responded as he gasped to catch his breath. "After I gathered supplies and talked to your grandmother I headed toward the mill. I soon discovered that the King's trackers were just a step ahead of me. So I held back and followed them at a safe distance. Of course, when they gave up on you after that swamp snake attacked the dogs. I wasn't sure what to do. I didn't know if you were dead or alive."

"After the King's men left I just sat there at the edge of the marsh, feeling stuck. I decided to go back to Talinor, believing the worst had probably happened to you." Choppa hesitated for a moment as if to ponder his words. "I mean, I thought for sure you had been taken by the swamp serpent, so going back was my only option. Then I saw someone or something moving in the shadows. I got real scared and ran in the only direction I could run. The way to the castle was blocked, so I ran toward the north end of the marshlands. Whatever it was, it kept following me, but strangely it seemed to keep its distance, as if it was stalking me. I'm sure it could have caught up to me if it wanted to."

"I know what you mean," interrupted Cyle excitedly. "I saw something too. That's why I headed into the marsh instead of keeping to the dry land."

"I wasn't going to take any chances," continued Choppa, "so I decided to run through the night until early morning the next day." Then I finally took some time to sleep and when I woke up I heard noises, so I followed them to the village. That's when I saw you getting run off by that shop owner."

"What about my grandmother? How is she?"

"She's all right, I guess." Choppa hesitated a little. "She is worried about you and she sends you her love. Most of the supplies that I brought with me were from your grandmother's own cupboard. She wanted me to tell you that she believes in you."

Cyle stared off into the distance. "How is the King?" His words echoed concern.

"I don't know. I had to leave before I heard any more news of his health."

"So where do we go now?" asked Choppa.

"We head for Kenna. I have cousins there." Cyle turned to walk.

"Kenna!" Choppa exclaimed. "What about the Gap Warriors? Aren't you going to look for them?"

"How did you know about that?"

"Your grandmother told me what happened with Graybeard and the vision. She thinks you went after the Gap Warriors."

"Does she still think they are real, or...or that they still exist?" Cyle stumbled over the question.

"All she said was that she would be praying for you and that she believes in you."

"She's been praying and walking those streets for years and look where it's gotten her. The people of Talinor have betrayed their God, the only hope they have against the dark magic and Ashkron's hordes. What can I do?"

"You can find the Gap Warriors and bring them back to Talinor."

"I can't go back to Talinor," exclaimed Cyle ruefully. "I am a wanted man. All we can do now is head for Kenna and wait until this thing is over. Maybe the Priests of Zarish will be able to help Talinor; besides, I wouldn't know where to begin looking for a Gap Warrior even if they did exist." He was very aware of the anger that was stirring in him, but he didn't know where it was coming from. For some reason he felt angry every time he thought about looking for the Gap Warriors. Maybe it had something to do with being forced to leave Talinor against his will. Or maybe it was because he wanted to be back at Talinor fighting alongside the rest of the men, instead of running away from the battle that lay ahead.

Choppa wanted to persuade his friend to take up the quest. After all, what would it hurt to try to find them? It was better than hiding out in a seaport city doing nothing; besides, he had always wanted to know if the Gap Warriors were for real. Cyle had made a decision. Trying to convince him to change his mind was a waste of time, and Choppa knew it.

They continued down the trail that led them into a part of the forest that grew darker as the trees became larger. Eventually the path took them down into a valley where they came upon a road headed in the direction they wanted to go, so they took it.

Cyle spent the afternoon telling Choppa how he had survived the marshes. He told him how Gruber had helped him. Choppa was completely taken by the story and wanted to go back and find the moss man, if the opportunity would ever present itself again. Cyle could tell that his friend was disappointed that the two of them would not be going in search of the Gap Warriors. Choppa had brought it up twice during the day, but Cyle cut him off each time he mentioned it. Nonetheless, Cyle was grateful for his company, and Choppa was excited for whatever adventure lay ahead.

After walking for a few hours with little spoken between them, they met some other travelers who informed them that the King's military was patrolling this section of the road. So they decided it would be safer to travel in the woods and shadow the road.

They came to a small brook and decided to stop and fill their water flasks. The water was just what they needed. Cyle and Choppa both dipped their heads, letting the cool liquid roll over the back of their necks. Cyle was getting hungry, and he began to wonder what they would have in the food bag for their evening meal. He thought of his grandmother's cooking, wondering what she would be eating tonight. The young cupbearer missed coming home to a home-cooked meal and a warm bed. He realized how much he had taken it for granted

Cyle looked up from the water and noticed that Choppa was nowhere to be seen. A familiar frustration set in. "He's always taking off," thought Cyle. Choppa reappeared from the bushes frantically signaling to follow him. "What is it?" Cyle asked.

"Quiet," Choppa warned, waving him over in his direction. Cyle grabbed his supplies and followed him. Choppa led him through some scrub oak and up an incline to a ridge where they could look down on the clearing below them. A group of men wearing unfamiliar battle garb had gathered together in the clearing. Both Cyle and Choppa watched from a concealed place behind some bushes. At first it was difficult to see what was going on. Muffled voices could be heard, but they were talking too softly to make out what they were saying.

A noise came from the edge of the clearing as a new group of men entered the clearing, joining the others. Cyle was not prepared for what he saw next. To his horror it was Micah and Cree along with two other Tal warriors under the guard of five soldiers, probably Boogaran. They were shoved into the middle of the clearing, falling over one another with hands bound behind their backs. Cyle had no idea that Ashkron's men were this close to Talinor.

The soldiers surrounded their captives, holding them at sword's length. "Hold them here," commanded one of the men. The soldiers obeyed while Micah and the other Tal warriors stood, bound and powerless to defend themselves.

Then something appeared in ghost-like form out of the shadowed woods, cloaked in a black robe and hood that covered its face. Cyle's blood ran cold at the sight of him.

"Shadow Wraith," whispered Choppa.

Fear threatened to choke off Cyle's breathing. He had never seen a demon before, but he had heard the stories late at night around the fires of the soldiers, when tales are told that a young man should never have to hear - tales of the dark creatures that stalk children in their dreams at night, leaving them in a cold sweat.

The others in the clearing quickly parted to allow room for the demon's approach. The clearing was covered in shadows now and devoid of the creature sounds that usually fill the air.

The cloaked figure stood silently staring at Micah and the others until it finally broke the silence. "What have we here?" Its voice was deep and sinister, like none Cyle had ever heard before.

"They were returning to their captain to report our presence here when we captured them," said the leader.

The wraith moved toward Cree and stood facing him. "Are there any others that know of our presence here?" The words hissed, snake-like as they cleared the demon's throat.

Cree stuttered in fear, fighting to find the words and mustering as much defiance in his voice as he could. "I will not betray my kingdom to a demon. You will have to kill me first."

"That can be arranged." The Shadow Wraith grabbed a sword from one of the guards and plunged the blade into Cree's midsection. The young warrior stood motionless at first with a look of horror in his eyes, gasping for air, then falling to the ground, blood pouring from his wound. Micah reached for him through his restraints but was held back.

A torrent of thoughts raced through Cyle as he desperately searched for something to hold onto, a thought or an idea that would propel him into action. Everything his mind attempted to grasp was swept away by an all-consuming terror of death. It was so vast and overwhelming that he felt as though he was being sucked into a dark and bottomless void. Then he remembered Choppa. He glanced over at his friend hoping to find strength in his presence, but he was gone.

Cyle's heart pounded fiercely. He turned and ran as fast as his legs would move, fear choking the life from him. Tree limbs lashed out at his face and legs. He didn't notice, because he was numb to the world around him as he fell, crashing into the forest underbrush and rolling down an embankment. He was back up in an instant, running in a panic-driven flight.

"What was that?" hissed the Shadow Wraith from beneath

his cowl.

"I hear and see nothing," replied the soldier in command.

The demon stepped away from the others in the clearing, quickly scanning the trees and hills around him as if he were looking into another realm. "Someone was here," he raged, his voice echoing off the trees. Then he held both of his hands in front of him and began to move them in a circular motion. Micah watched in disbelief as sparks appeared at the demon's fingertips. The howling coming from it was low at first, and then it began to build until it reached a primal scream that rent the air. Through the bushes and into the clearing charged three hideous looking beasts, wolf-like in appearance, only twisted and distorted in form. Primal groans filled the clearing, red eyes glaring, drool oozing from their gaping jaws.

The Shadow Wraith motioned one hand in the direction of the three beasts that stood strangely silent, as if in a trance, waiting for the Shadow Wraith's command. Without saying a word, the demon pointed a crooked finger in the direction the two had run. They turned, snarling, and then ran into the woods, howling after their prey.

Cyle had stopped running, his chest heaving as he gulped in air to catch his breath. The trees had cleared some and he was able to see the beasts just moments after he heard their insidious howls. He bounded over the rocks and fallen logs as the twisted creatures of darkness emerged from the twilight mist that covered the ground. Hissing and howling, they pursued in a lust for blood, summoned to this realm by the dark magic. Somehow the demon had detected his presence back at the meadow and sent these beasts after him.

He was off again, running as fast as he could. Arms flailing and heart racing, he could feel desperation rising in him with every step. Louder and louder the howls and screams grew. He imagined their hot breath upon the back of his neck. He was beginning to falter. Two days of travel and all the running was taking its toll. They were almost upon him now; he dared not look back as he reached deep within himself to find what reserves of energy he might have left to push onward. The growl exploded in his ears as hot breath wafted over his neck. The beast slammed into him from behind as lights flashed in his head and all went black.

The streets of Talinor were more crowded now that the surrounding villagers had come to take refuge within its walls. They were quickly organized and put to work on reinforcing the gates and building the battlements upon the ramparts. Food stores were almost filled to capacity. Even the restoration of the main temple was nearing its completion.

The Priests had begun their daily rituals and once again there was life in the old temple. Some of the local critics on the streets doubted that their magic was as powerful as they had been led to believe, but most were willing to stand behind them. What other choice did they have? The common man or woman of Talinor had little interest in the supernatural. Those matters had been long forgotten with the passing of time and were better left to the priests who knew how to handle them.

Darius was in a state of high anxiety, pacing back and forth in the King's war chamber, spilling his concerns to the head Priest, Orom. "How can we know for sure that your magic is stronger than the dark magic that the Shadow Wraiths command?" Darius played nervously with the tassels on his robe, while waiting impatiently for a reply.

The Priest responded in a very calm and priestly manner. "My dear Darius, all magic comes from the same source. It is up to those who wield it to choose its purpose. Some choose to use it for evil, some for good." Orom walked over to the window and fixed his gaze over the city. "There are no guarantees when it comes to the use of magic. Those who practice it must perfect their ability to wield it. The magic is neither good nor evil. You must stop referring to it as good or bad. There is not one form of magic that is more powerful than another form of magic. The one who uses it must master his abilities to wield it and not allow it to rule over him. The

Priests of Zarish have worked for generations to perfect the magic arts and keep our hearts pure; you must trust us."

"But what about the Shadow Wraiths? Are they not human and spirit combined, if not all spirit?"

"The Shadow Wraiths were created long ago by an evil warlock named Gizshra who was a master in the black arts. There are many who believe the Wraiths were created by what many call the dark magic, but there is no such thing as dark magic. Gizshra himself was dark. The Shadow Wraiths were created by Gizshra to serve his lust for power. He gave his own name to the leader of the Shadow Wraiths so that his memory would live on forever."

Darius knew the time of battle was drawing near, and with that reality a growing restlessness haunted him. He remembered the last great battle and the lethal power of the Shadow Wraiths. The Gap Warriors had defended Talinor using their powerful weapons against the Wraiths. Without them, Talinor would have fallen.

"Talinor has put her trust in you, Orom, and in the Priests who serve you. We know that you are good at heart, but only time will tell if you have the power to overcome the evil that waits to consume us."

The first thing Cyle noticed was the pain of pine needles pressing into his face and the brightness of the sunshine around him. He struggled to overcome the throbbing in his head. After a few deep breaths he steadied himself and the world around him came into focus.

He couldn't believe what he saw. The beasts that had attacked him were strewn about him on the ground lying dead, reeking of a sulfurous stench. Cyle could barely stomach the smell. He stood up slowly and stumbled backward, staring in disbelief at what had happened around him. Had Choppa come back and saved his life? That couldn't be. There were no arrows, and besides, he didn't think his friend had it in him.

A soft voice from behind him said, "Cyle, are you all right?"

Choppa ran up to him out of breath. "What happened here?"

"I don't know," Cyle mumbled, still staring at the whole scene in a half daze.

"Come on, Cyle, let's get out of here before someone else shows up." Choppa took him by the arm and led him away. They walked for a long time without speaking a word to each other. The shame of running away the night before had silenced them. Cyle was the first to break that silence.

"I almost died last night," said Cyle softly.

"Yeah, well I —."

"Where were you?" Cyle interrupted him.

"I, uh," Choppa stuttered.

"Never mind," Cyle interrupted him a second time. He didn't want to know. After all, who was he to criticize after his own cowardly act the night before, leaving his cousin there in the clearing with Ashkron's men and the Shadow Wraith? Choppa may have run from the scene, but so had he, leaving his own cousin behind. Shame flooded his heart every time he recalled the incident. He tried to push it back with little success. It was his first encounter with evil of this magnitude. He had been overwhelmed at its intensity. The stories he had heard about the Shadow Wraiths paled in comparison to what he saw firsthand. Words could not adequately describe such an evil presence. Cyle hoped that he would never have to see one again.

They walked on together in silence for most of the morning until Cyle suggested they stop for a break. They were careful not to sit in the open. Now that Ashkron's men had been spotted, they knew they could not take any chances. Cyle was exhausted from his ordeal and his head would not stop throbbing. He had dreamt about the stranger in the woods after he was knocked unconscious. It was the same dream only with some minor variations. The stranger with the staff was there again teaching him how to fight with a staff, only this time the training was even more intense than before. The dreams were starting to concern him. He had never had a dream repeat itself over and over like this one. He thought it was strange the way it seemed to pick up where it left off each time.

Choppa had been affected by last night's events as well. He had been terrified by the experience. He, too, had never seen a Shadow Wraith and had never felt that kind of terror before in his life. He hadn't been strong in the old religion of Talinor. Like most of the rest of the kingdom he was too busy enjoying life. Religion was far too serious a business for him. It wasn't that he didn't have respect for the teachings of the faith because he had always believed there must be a god or some higher power. After seeing the Shadow Wraith the night before, he thought he might give it some more thought. It was enough to scare him into thinking more seriously about the God he had given so little attention to in the past. His grandmother had raised him in her faith and tried diligently to instill its principles in his life, but he had feigned interest out of respect for her.

"They're here," Choppa finally spoke to break the silence.

"Who's here?"

"Ashkron's army and the Shadow Wraiths," responded Choppa. "I never really thought it would actually happen. We have lived for so long in the safety of Talinor with so little to fear from the outside world. That's all gone now."

"I may never be able to go back home," said Cyle sadly. "They believe that I poisoned the King." The weight of his world was crashing down upon him. He hadn't had much time to think about it until now. He missed his grandmother, and he missed the company of the King as well. He even missed Darius.

And then there was Micah. He would be haunted forever by his betrayal of his cousin. If only he had found a way to help him, he might still be alive.

CHAPTER 10

Shame and remorse bore down upon Cyle with every step he took. It was as if some invisible anchor was slowing him down. The more Cyle thought about what had happened back in the clearing with Micah and the Shadow Wraith, the deeper the shame twisted into his soul, like a thorn relentlessly driving its poison deeper into an infected wound. No matter how hard he tried to think about other things, the same haunting thoughts kept coming back to him. "You are a failure, a coward. How could you have left your cousin there alone to die?" At times other thoughts tried to enter in and comfort him. They tried to tell him that there was nothing he could have done; that it wasn't his fault. Those thoughts were quickly crowded out by the thoughts of self-condemnation and loathing. He and Choppa had not talked about it any further. They were both battling with their own demons of failure.

Choppa had never had to take care of anyone but himself. That was not a difficult task because he was well taken care of by the palace officials. He never had been in want of the essentials that life required of him to survive. It wasn't that he was pampered. He was just allowed to do as he pleased, and that was what he had grown accustomed to.

When he left Talinor this time to find Cyle, his desire was to be a true friend to him. He wanted to help him. Until now he had never wanted to commit to that kind of relationship. It seemed that life was much simpler without attachments to others. Taking care of him self was much easier and freed him from the worries that came with committed relationships. He and Cyle had been friends for a long time, but their relationship was mostly based on having a good time. That was how Choppa had wanted it.

He struggled with the fact that he had let Cyle down when he ran from the Shadow Wraith. In the past he had let others down in much smaller ways, but it never seemed to bother him until now. He, too, felt a deep shame for having abandoned his friend when he needed him. This was the first real commitment he had made to someone in a long time and he had failed. Hoping to quiet his own shame, he vowed in his heart that he would make it up to him.

The wind blew through the trees as the last of the fall leaves floated gently to the forest floor. The air grew ever cooler with each passing day. Early in the mornings and late in the afternoons a misty fog would hug the ground in a chilling embrace, giving the forest a haunted appearance. Fortunately the days were still warm enough to make them comfortable for travel.

After walking for most of the morning they came to a road heading in their direction and decided to follow it. They would have to be careful to avoid any contact with the enemy forces. Cyle wondered how far he was from Kenna.

Choppa was the first to spot the smoke rising above the trees in the distance ahead. They moved quickly back near the trees beside the road.

"I smell something cooking!" said Choppa excitedly. Cyle sniffed the air and smelled nothing. "Leave it to Choppa," he thought, "to smell food."

"It's some kind of settlement," Cyle said as he shielded his eyes to get a better look at things.

"Let's get a closer look and then decide." Choppa was famous for getting closer looks, Cyle thought. They moved through the trees until they could see the place clearly. There were a few small huts set mostly in a circle. In the middle was a huge fire pit where a short stocky woman was cooking a large piece of meat on a spit. Choppa had been right about smelling something. Gathered around the cooking pit sitting on logs and stumps was a group of hunters visiting as they drank ale and waited for the meat to finish cooking. The crowd grew steadily as others came to join them.

"I say we join the party," Choppa broke the silence.

Cyle agreed. "If anyone asks us, we are headed to Kenna to

join a fishing fleet."

As they approached the fire a few of the men stared at the two boys while the others continued their conversations. An old Dwarf with a patch over one eye was doing most of the talking. "They're everywhere, I tell you. I've seen them on the roads and out in some of the fields. They don't think we know why they are here, but I know. They are spies sent from the other side. They're trying to look like us. It don't fool me." The Dwarf was very animated, and he spoke loudly with a scratchy voice. "The sooner we get to Easthold the better. I expect the fighting will start there any day now." Most of those who were gathered around the fire pit seemed to agree with the one-eyed Dwarf.

"Talinor needs every available man to fight this battle," said the Dwarf looking at Cyle and Choppa. "How about you two? Are you going with us to Easthold to defend Talinor?" At first there was an awkward silence as all eyes shifted toward the two of them.

"Yes," Choppa blurted out, "that's where we were headed, to Easthold to fight." Cyle glared at Choppa trying to conceal his shock.

"Well then, the two of you can share this elk with us and join us on the trail to Easthold, the more the better." The two of them nodded compliantly.

"By the way my name is Ginzer and the rest of this motley crew will remain nameless until you care to gather their names." The Dwarf pointed to the others around the fire who were waiting patiently for their meal to finish on the spit. There were at least ten others in the party, all of them armed, and with the exception of a few younger ones, they looked like men who may have had experience in battle.

"How about the two of you, what be your names and where do you come from?" asked a tall bearded man standing among them.

"I am Choppa and this is Cyle. We are from Gelshir."

"Gelshir, that's not far from here. How are things there?"

asked the man as he stroked his beard.

"Everyone prepares for the battle. Many are headed for Easthold just as we are," responded Choppa.

"Hmm, mostly farmers that bunch, but every hand will be needed," said the man thoughtfully. "My name is Telfir. Good to have you with us." Telfir offered his hand in greeting. Cyle wanted to ask him where he was from but he thought the better of it, not wanting to draw any more attention to himself than necessary.

"Come get your meat before it spoils," announced the rotund little lady turning the elk over the fire. She waddled around the meat slicing off pieces to taste her work. The others moved in and started cutting chunks off the spit and eating it with their bare hands.

Cyle pulled Choppa aside and whispered in a low and irritated tone. "Why did you tell them we were going to Easthold?"

"What did you expect me to say, that we're two cowards headed for Kenna to escape the war?" He had a point, thought Cyle.

"You two better grab some meat while you can; we will be leaving for Easthold within the hour." said Telfir.

The meat was sweet and tender with just the right amount of spices. Both Cyle and Choppa were hungry and each of them ate their share almost too fast to enjoy it. After the meal, all of them gathered their belongings and started for Easthold.

The small company of men traveled at a brisk pace. Cyle and Choppa had little trouble keeping up with them. Even though they had not planned to go to Easthold, Cyle felt that things had turned out for the best. It would give him a chance to fight for Talinor, and he was unknown there so he wouldn't have to worry about the trouble back at the palace.

Several times during the rest of the afternoon Ginzer the Dwarf spotted suspicious looking travelers and the group would take cover until they had passed. Everyone felt that the best thing they could do was get to Easthold without any trouble to slow them down. They would be most helpful to the cause of Talinor fighting in Easthold alongside the others there.

Easthold would play a small but vital role in the war. The best the fortified city could hope for was to slow down Ashkron's army and give Talinor a little more time to prepare for battle. Easthold was originally a military outpost designed to protect Talinor from any potential invasion from the east. Since the time of its beginnings, it had grown into a smaller version of Talinor. Built against steep cliffs on the north side of the pass, Easthold had access to a tunnel system built by the Dwarves to allow them an escape route if they were to be taken siege by their enemies in battle. Talinor's plan was to send troops to reinforce the effort against the first wave of attack, and then flee through the tunnels when the inevitable happened.

The company of men stopped at a stream to replenish their water supplies and take a short break. Cyle had met all of the men during the day's walk, but there was one man who had left a strong impression on him. Of all the men in their group this one looked the most like a warrior. He had long sandy-colored hair and stood at a medium height. His arms were muscular and when he spoke, Cyle was touched by his gentle kindness. A sword hung over his back wrapped in a leather sheath and at his side he wore a long knife.

Cyle was bending over the stream splashing water over his face the first time the man approached him. "Where did you get the eagle?" Cyle froze inside not sure how to respond. He saw the reflection of the pendant in the water as it dangled from his neck. He sat up and tucked the eagle back into his tunic before answering the warrior.

"It was a gift from my grandmother." Not wanting to say anymore about it, Cyle quickly changed the subject. "And what is your name? I haven't met you yet."

"My name is Bixby—and what do they call you?"

"I am Cyle, and that is my friend, Choppa," he motioned to him across the stream."

"It is my pleasure to meet you, Cyle. Tell me, have you ever fought in a battle before?"

"No, sir, I have not." Cyle felt a little embarrassed at his answer.

"Well, I guess that war reaches everyone eventually," said Bixby. "We will just have to look out for each other, won't we?" Cyle felt that his words were sincere, but he barely knew the man. Why would he care what happens to him?

Bixby stood to leave and as he turned to walk away he looked back over his shoulder to where Cyle was standing and said, "By the way Cyle, I have an eagle too." Then as he turned away without looking back the warrior reached up over his shoulder and pulled the sword that was strapped to his back just far enough out of its sheath to expose a beautifully carved eagle on the blade near its hilt. An unexpected wave of energy washed over Cyle. With legs trembling, he stumbled toward the ground, falling to one knee. He found himself breathing deeply and shaking all over. What's happening to me, he wondered? A small tear formed in the corner of his eye.

The small band of warriors had traveled together for two days without incident except for a few close encounters with enemy scouting parities.

"I smell smoke," said Ginzer.

"Could be a campfire?" offered Telfir as he jumped up from the rock he was sitting on.

"Could be," Ginzer sniffed the air again. "We're not far from Easthold. Let's get going and see if we can get there before dark." The Dwarf grabbed his battle-axe and headed down the trail as the rest followed.

The terrain started to level out and the trees grew thicker in density. Cyle thought they might be getting closer to the Eastern Pass, also known as Shandel's Pass. He and Choppa walked with Bixby at the end of the line. To pass the time Choppa had been talking about his dreams of eating sweet bread and honey when they got to Easthold. He was craving the stuff and it had been too long since he had eaten anything sweet.

Cyle looked ahead and could see that Ginzer and Telfir had stopped, and the two of them were staring at something. Cyle could tell by the way they were moving that something was wrong. He and Choppa ran to see what was happening, and when they cleared the trees they were taken back by what they saw.

Easthold had fallen. Smoke billowed from what was left of the city. The main gate was destroyed with fire and most of the front wall lay in rubble. The last of the Boogaran soldiers were leaving the city. In the distance they could see a massive army marching toward the Valley of Talinor. Now that Easthold had fallen, there was nothing between them and the great city. It was only a matter of days and the Boogaran army would be standing at their doorstep.

"I'm going in," Bixby was the first to break the silence.

"What? Why would you do that?" Ginzer peered at him with his one eye and walked over to face Bixby.

"Easthold is gone; there is nothing here," offered Ginzer forcefully. "We should head for Talinor where we can do some good."

"Ginzer, you are a good man with a good heart that is filled with passion. If Talinor is where you should go, then go. First I must go to Easthold to see what it holds for me; besides, there may be prisoners there that need setting free. If we are not too late, we can free them."

"We would like to go with you." This time Cyle spoke for himself and Choppa. Choppa looked at him wide-eyed. Cyle wasn't sure why, but he knew that it was what he was supposed to do.

"Very well, we can look out for each other." Bixby looked at Cyle and gave him a wink.

"Then I will go with you as well," said Telfir. "You will need someone who knows Easthold to show you the way. The others looked at Ginzer to see what the Dwarf would do. He had become their leader and they would follow him wherever he led them.

Ginzer had an anxious look on his face as he rolled his battle-axe in his hand. He looked toward Easthold and then to the great valley beyond. "We will stay together then. After Easthold we will go on to Talinor."

Telfir led the group to an escape cave that was supposed to lead them into the back of Easthold through the cliffs. Ginzer agreed that this would be their best route to take, drawing the least amount of attention to them. The caves were dark and damp so they had to assemble torches, using cloth and pork grease, to help light the way. At times Telfir would hesitate, appearing to be lost. The cave would come to a dead-end, and then they would have to backtrack to go another way.

Ginzer kept questioning Telfir's knowledge of the caves. It is a well-known fact that Dwarves are master cave builders. Still, as far as Ginzer was concerned, they couldn't get out of there soon enough. Cyle couldn't agree with Ginzer more. He hated dark and cramped places and chose to walk next to Bixby where he felt safe. Bixby seemed to be taking the whole thing in stride while Choppa appeared nervous and on edge.

"This is it. This is where the opening should be," exclaimed Telfir. "It looks like it's been blocked on purpose."

"The Boogarans must have known about the caves and blocked them to prevent escape," said Bixby. "We will have to dig through."

It took half the day with all of them working together to clear the landslide. When they removed the last of the rubble they got their first look at the inside of Easthold. Most of the buildings were burning and sections of Easthold's walls lay toppled in heaps of charred rubble. The smell of death and smoke threatened to gag everyone. In every direction there were dead bodies strewn about the landscape. Cyle averted his gaze to avoid the horror. He had never seen such devastation and destruction in all his life. If this was war, he wanted nothing to do with it. All of his fantasies about being a warrior were being stripped away by this cruel reality. How could he have fantasized about something so horrible?

"Hold steady, Cyle," said Bixby, as he placed a reassuring

hand upon his shoulder. "Are you all right, Choppa?" asked Bixby. Choppa gave a faint nod. Cyle wasn't used to seeing his friend at a loss for words.

"What now, Bixby?" asked Ginzer.

Just then there was an inhuman scream from somewhere far away. Everyone looked to see where it had come from. Then there was another gut-wrenching scream. This time it sounded human.

"What was that?" asked Jalob, one of Ginzer's men.

"That was a scavenger, also known as a scav." Bixby looked around studying the area carefully.

"What are they doing here?" pressed Jalob with eyes wide.

"Scavengers are melded from the ancient magic of sorcery, created in times past to serve the Shadow Wraiths in battle. A kind of hunting hound, if you will, only they feed off the life force of human souls when they are the most helpless."

"That's what came after me in the forest," said Cyle.

Bixby continued, "The Shadow Wraiths release them into the cities after the conquering army has left to consume the souls of the fallen and to make sure there is no living person left after a battle."

Another howl pierced the night followed by a tortured scream, only this time it sounded closer than before. Weapons were drawn for protection. "If we stay together we should be all right. Scavs feed on fear and helplessness; together we are strong."

"I say we get out of here now," offered Jalob nervously. "These things want to eat us for their dinner."

"We can't do that," stated Bixby firmly. "There's a good chance that there are still soldiers within the city that have been imprisoned and left behind for the scavs to feed on, a common practice of the Wraiths. If we move quickly, we may be able to find them before it is too late."

"I say we get on with it," growled Ginzer, rolling his battle-axe in his hand and spitting on the ground. "I've never left a man behind, and I'm not about to start now."

"I don't know about this," said Jalob nervously. "This place is haunted, and I don't like it one bit."

"You do what you have to do. If anyone else wants to go, now is the time to leave while you can," said the Dwarf as he surveyed the group with his one eye. A few moments passed and no one moved. "Okay then," Ginzer growled, "let's find those warriors."

"Somewhere in the city there has to be a prison or some kind of holding cell," offered Bixby. "My guess is that's where we will find them. Does anyone have any ideas where we should look to find such a place?"

"I think I know," responded Choppa sheepishly. "This city is similar to Talinor in design. The prison would be somewhere near the center of the city, behind the main palace."

"How does that sound to you Telfir?" Ginzer looked at him with his one eye. Telfir nodded. "I have been here before. Let me lead the way." He turned and started into the rubble as the others followed with weapons in hand.

The smell of death grew stronger as they walked. They had to pass by many of the bodies that littered the streets. Cyle tried to avoid looking at them, but he couldn't help noticing that even in death many of their faces were stricken with terror. Something evil had stolen their last breath and wrenched them from this world.

The ghostly howls of the scavengers continued to grow louder as the small band made their way through the rubble. There were moments when Cyle and the others thought they had seen something move between buildings. It was difficult to tell if what they were seeing was a scav or fearful imaginings. The haze from the smoke and the night's darkness made it difficult to see clearly. If it were not for the light from the fires, travel would be almost impossible.

Bixby made sure that Cyle and Choppa remained close to him. Cyle thought it odd that the swordsman would take an interest in protecting the two of them. He found some comfort in the fact that the man had an eagle etched on his sword blade, and he was thankful for the stranger's kindness.

The road they had been traveling on was wide enough for them to see anyone or anything that might approach them until Telfir decided to turn up a narrow street. The howls and cries of the scavengers grew louder still. Jalob suddenly stopped in their midst, body shaking and sweat pouring from his forehead. He appeared to be on the edge of panic as he slowly backed away from the group. "I can't do this any longer," Jalob screamed.

"Jalob!" Ginzer yelled at him as he grabbed him by his tunic with both hands and pulled him close until he was staring face to face with him through his one eye. "Hold on man, you can't lose it now. You've got to hold steady!" Ginzer was not getting through to him. Jalob pushed himself away, breaking free from Ginzer's grasp.

"No, I have to get out of here." Jalob looked about nervously and then ran back toward the street they had just left behind them. No sooner had he cleared the side street than they heard a terrifying growl. Before anyone of them could move, a massive blur swept over him. Jalob struggled to defend himself, but it was no use. Teeth and claws lashed out with lightning speed. The twisted form stripped away at Jalob's life as his arms flailed in defense. Cyle stared in silence remembering Bixby's admonition to stay together, because they would be stronger traveling in a group. He had been nervously watching the creatures stalking their group, hanging back at the edges of the darkness, waiting for the right moment to attack. Their patience had paid off. Jalob had lost his senses. By fleeing, he put himself in a weak and defenseless position, and the demons were there to take advantage of his panic.

Ginzer and the others moved to save him, but it was too late. Jalob screamed again as the scavenger clamped on to him with its jaws, and then there was silence. The creature hovered over him, feeding off what life was left in its fallen prey. It was over as quickly as it had begun, and then the scav disappeared back into the darkness.

"Come, there is nothing we can do now," growled Ginzer. His frustration was obvious.

"Listen everyone, you must control your fear," warned Bixby, "The scavs are drawn to it, and when they smell it they come running like a pack of hungry dogs. As long as we stay together we have a chance."

The street they turned onto was more like a narrow alleyway. On both sides there were burned out homes that had been torn and ravaged by the war. Many of the smaller buildings were still standing, but most of the larger ones had been set on fire. Screams cried out through the smoke-filled darkness as the scavs rummaged through the city looking for any survivors they might feast upon to satisfy their insatiable hunger.

Bixby was determined to find out if any of the Tal warriors were still living, or anyone else for that matter. So far they had seen no one. He pressed forward, driving the small group of warriors through the maze of rubble. Ginzer had taken up the same calling and was equally committed to the task. The one-eyed Dwarf was the oldest of the small band of warriors and had fought and survived in many wars. He was not about to leave a fellow soldier behind in a time of need. The scavs would be looking for the captured warriors as well. Hopefully, they hadn't already found them.

Choppa told Cyle that he was growing uneasy about the direction that Telfir was leading them. Easthold's streets were laid out in the same design as Talinor's, and if anyone knew the streets of Talinor, Choppa did. He knew the city's streets and back alleys as well as anyone who lived there. He was surprised at how similar Easthold's design was to Talinor and in a haunting way felt as though he was back in Talinor. Finally he spoke up. "This doesn't seem like the right direction to me. I'm almost positive that the palace is in that direction." Choppa pointed back in another direction where they had passed earlier.

"Nonsense, this way will save us time," said Telfir in an irritated tone. Just then the narrow alleyway opened up into a larger area still surrounded by buildings.

"No, this can't be right. We are walking away from the palace. How can this be a shortcut?" Before Telfir could answer there was movement in the shadows, first in one direction and then another. Bixby noticed the movement and motioned the small band of warriors to move to the middle of the small square. Through the smoke and flickering firelight the shadows shifted and slithered between the buildings. Waiting and watching, their eyes could be seen glowing from the shadows.

"They've come for us," Ginzer snarled, raising his axe to a fighting position. "I'll not be anyone's lunch without a fight." The old Dwarf set his stance and peered back at the loathsome creatures through his one eye. For the first time since they had entered the city, Bixby drew his sword from the sheath on his back and gripped it with both hands near the hilt. Cyle thought he saw something flicker at the base of the blade near where the eagle emblem was etched.

"What's happening here, Telfir?" asked Bixby suspiciously. Something was wrong and he knew it. It seemed as if everyone in the company came to that realization at the same time. The scavs appeared ghost-like as they moved into the opening from their places of concealment.

Telfir turned and set his gaze upon them; a wicked smile crossed his face. When he spoke the tone of his voice began to change. "It's dinner time. My friends are hungry." Then he laughed, and as he did so his form began to change. It was almost undetectable at first until the changes became more visibly obvious. Telfir's body was bulging and twisting, his face grimacing with pain until the transformation was complete. Standing before them was a hideous-looking creature twice its original height, gaping jaws oozing slime, and claws razor sharp. From deep within its throat a feral scream was released, piercing the ears of the warriors.

Bixby squared to face it, sword drawn and ready for the attack. Ginzer was quick to join him at his side. "It's okay, old friend," said the swordsman. "I'll take care of this one. You help the others with the scavs." Then there was a rush of movement as the dark creatures rushed in upon them from every direction. Telfir in his new form growled and charged Bixby, claws lashing out at the knight. Warriors and demonic creatures merged as they slammed together in battle. Blades flashed and arrows flew. Cyle fumbled for his knife. The small blade seemed a hopeless weapon against such odds. The deafening sounds of growls surrounded him, and for a moment he had lost sight of Choppa. Then something pounded against his side sending him reeling through the air and he landed on his chest, gasping for air. He quickly found his feet just in time to see a scavenger running toward him. Instinctively he turned and ran toward the nearest alley. Choppa saw what was happening and fired an arrow from his crossbow. It found its mark in the scav's hip causing the beast to let out a scream and stagger briefly, then it seemed to regain its strength, but not before it gave Cyle a chance to put some distance between the two of them.

He gripped the knife in his hand, feeling the desperation closing in on him. If at all possible, he did not want to have to make a stand against the thing. His fear was giving him the strength to run, and it was the same fear driving Cyle that was stirring the passions of the creature that stalked him.

Running into a building, Cyle closed the door behind him. As he fumbled for the handle, he latched it shut. The scavenger slammed against it in a fury and tore its claws into the wooden frame. Squinting through the darkness, the terrified cupbearer scanned desperately for another way out of the room. Barely discerning what looked like a window, he lunged at its shutters ripping them from their hinges, and he was out the back and onto another street, running for his life. The door he had latched shattered, and then the creature was clawing its way through the window.

As Cyle ran he came to an open area where the building opened into a square. Across the square he saw more buildings and another door. If he could make it to the building before the creature reached him, maybe he could get inside safely. Suddenly, out of the corner of his eye, he saw something move causing him to look in that direction. A fresh wave of fear swept over him as one of the beasts materialized out of the smoke, growling and hissing. Cyle stumbled, and then he was up again running for the building. Just as he reached the steps he saw a third scav, and maybe a fourth joining the chase. Grabbing for the door latch he twisted it with both hands. It wouldn't open. He tried to force it by kicking at it and slamming his shoulder into it, but it wouldn't budge. He pounded on the door and screamed, "Let me in! Someone let me in!" But it was no use. There was no one there.

Bixby hurled himself toward the monster that once was Telfir, his sword held in an iron grip as it flared to life. A small flicker of light danced upon the blade near the hilt. Then it shot out, slowly at first, toward the tip of the blade until it picked up speed and exploded into shards of light.

Telfir screamed at the sight of it and lunged at the Knight, his claws slashing out in deadly intent. Bixby swung his sword around in a wide arc until the glistening blade found contact with Telfir's arm. Sparks erupted from the metal shaft as the monster bellowed out a searing scream of pain that could be heard above the noise of battle. Then Telfir in his demonic form struck out again, knocking Bixby backward, but he fell into a roll and was up on his feet again. Just then one of the scavengers leapt through the air and with two hands on his sword Bixby brought it over his head and caught the beast in midair. The blade sliced through the scavs midsection bringing a small explosion of sparks when the blade passed through its body. The creature fell in two pieces on the ground smoking as its fetid smell filled the air. Telfir's beastly form seized the advantage of Bixby's momentary distraction and was upon him before he could turn around. Then Ginzer appeared from out of the tangled battle. He moved quickly for his age and size and was upon the demon before it knew what was happening. His axe sliced through the air and lodged near the creature's hip. The thing stumbled briefly, but it was enough time for Bixby to respond. Spinning around with cat-like reflexes, he planted his sword in the creature's chest with a deadly force. There was a bolt of light and an explosion as the demon screamed in agony. It shuddered violently and then fell to the earth with smoke billowing from its dead carcass.

"By Shadazar, that thing stinks!" cried Ginzer, as he waved his hand in front of his face trying to fan away the smell. As soon as Telfir had fallen, the scavengers that were still alive scattered into the darkness.

"What was that thing?" asked Ginzer, still gasping for breath.

"It was a changeling," answered Bixby gasping for breath. "The dark magic is growing stronger in the land now that the Shadow Wraiths are moving in. Changelings have the ability to take over and inhabit an animal or a human form. As you can see, they make excellent spies."

"That's a first for me," said Ginzer. "It would suit me just fine if I never see one again. Tell me about your sword," Ginzer stepped close to Bixby and spoke softly under his breath. "Looks like you have a bit of magic working on your side." Bixby smiled, ignored the question and turned away to survey the small company for causalities.

Two of their company had fallen during the battle with the scavs. Four dead scavs lay dead along with two of their own. Choppa was untouched and Folger, one the archers, had suffered minor scrapes and a bruised shoulder.

"Where is Cyle?" Bixby was the first to notice he was gone as he spun around surveying the area for any sign of him.

"I saw him run that way," Choppa pointed. "One of those things was after him. I think I slowed it down a bit with an arrow, but that was all I could do at the time."

"We have to find him," said Bixby as he motioned the others to follow him.

Lena shivered against the chill of a cold easterly wind as she walked the streets beneath the rays of a full moon; her timid form cast a faint shadow upon the cobbled path she had become so familiar with. The weather was turning colder with the passing of one season into another. It was fall and most of the leaves had turned a bright crimson mixed with different shades of yellow and orange. The air was crisp and fresh during the early mornings and throughout most of the day. But once the sun slipped behind the horizon, the temperature would drop to a cold chill.

Once again the intercessor had come there to pray on the streets, always faithful and never yielding to fatigue or discouragement. Tonight the streets were noisier than usual. They were growing more crowded as the days drew nearer to the time of battle. Guards stood sentry upon the ramparts, watching over the land beyond the city walls. They stood silhouetted against the moonlight reminding everyone of the impending threat that was soon to come. Their presence brought little comfort to the frightened souls of the city dwellers.

An unexpected rush of fear came over her. Something was wrong, terribly wrong. The thought came to her in a rush, "Pray for Cyle." Tears filled her eyes as she prayed for the Ancient of Days to protect him. Her stomach churned as she bent over in pain; her palms started to sweat in agony as she cried out to her God. "What is it?" She spoke the words out loud to herself. "What could it be?"

Cyle held the knife in front of him. It looked puny in his hand compared to the bloodthirsty scavs that were closing in on him. The three twisted forms moved in a cat-like motion, stalking and preparing to pounce on him. The look in their eyes reflected a deep and primal lust for death. Cyle glanced desperately about him looking for something, anything that would give him a fighting chance. He could feel his breath shortening and his vision growing dim. The beast in the middle crept forward with fangs gleaming, guttural growls coming forth, and drool falling from its gaping jaws. Then it leapt at him shrieking as it went airborne.

What happened next was almost too fast to comprehend. Out of the corner of his eye a blur of blackness shot out. Then there was a flash like lightning that pierced through the darkness and briefly lit up the street. The airborne scav screamed in pain as it fell lifeless to the ground. Sparks sizzled and danced upon its hide as smoke lifted and rose into the air. The other two turned and disappeared into the shadows. Whatever it was that destroyed the beast was gone as quickly as it had appeared.

Cyle stood there in awe at what he had just witnessed. Twice in a very short period of time this had happened. Someone was out there watching over him and protecting him. Why would anyone do that? His thoughts were interrupted when he heard Choppa's voice cut through and call out to him, "Cyle, where are you?"

"Over here," Cyle waved his arms. Choppa and the others appeared from around the corner as they ran across the street to join him. Choppa was the first to see the scavenger lying on the ground; smoke rising from its severed body. He looked at the beast and then he looked at Cyle.

"What happened? Did you do that?" asked Choppa in amazement, staring at the knife in Cyle's hand.

Bixby interrupted before Cyle could speak. "We need to move. Everyone stay close. I don't think we have a lot of time left. Choppa, you need to show us the way to the prison."

CHAPTER 11

Choppa appeared sure of himself as he led the way. They traveled down dark alleys and cluttered streets where the smoke grew thicker from the burning buildings, making it difficult to breathe. The cries of those who had fallen to the demon-sent scavengers could be heard through the darkness. Each time they cried out in the night they took a piece of hope with them. All the while scavengers could still be seen lurking about at the edges of the darkness.

For a brief moment Choppa seemed confused about his direction, but after further calculation he seemed to find his way again. They came to an open courtyard when Choppa stopped to motion, "Over there is where we want to go." He gestured again across the courtyard pointing at a large structure with massive columns across the front. There were scavengers scratching and clawing at the doors trying desperately to find a way in.

"This has to be it. The scavs are a good sign we're not too late," Bixby said as he pointed at the creatures.

"How do we get past those things?" asked Ginzer. "They're everywhere."

"Choppa," asked the swordsman, "is there another way in?"

"There should be; it depends on how closely this place is fashioned after Talinor. They followed Choppa as he led them through another series of alleys that brought them to a door far away from where they had seen the scavs. After prying it open, they stepped inside to an empty room. At the center of the room was a square brick enclosure with a wooden door. "Yes." Choppa exclaimed, "This is just what I was looking for. Below this door is the water canal that should lead to the palace. Help me lift it." With little effort the door pulled open. "The water is low enough for us to use this as a way through," explained Choppa.

The tunnel was dark and the water was only up to their knees. Ginzer had fashioned a crude torch that provided enough light for them to see their way. Before long they came to a wooden ladder leading upward. Choppa made his way up the ladder and the others followed. He pushed open a wooden hatch and climbed through. Inside the room they found a wall of empty prison cells. At first there was concern that they had come to the wrong place, but Choppa moved on toward another door on the far side of the room. It amazed Cyle how reliable Choppa could be at times like this, but then at other times he could be so fickle. He could tell his friend was enjoying the attention that came with this opportunity to be in the lead.

The door was jammed, so Ginzer hammered it with his battle-axe until it finally shattered with the force of several blows. They entered into a room, and then passed through several other doors until entering into a larger room where through the darkness, with the aid of Ginzer's fading torch, they could see soldiers lashed to poles with ropes and chains. It was difficult at first glance to tell how many were still alive. Some of the prisoners stared back at them through hollow eyes.

One man lay dead at the door; somehow he had been able to free himself from his chains and close the door to protect the others from the scavengers outside. His efforts had cost him his life. He had torn his flesh and severed his hand on the shackles, then bled to death saving the life of his comrades in the process.

"You two get some water," Ginzer barked the orders to his men. "The rest of you help me free these soldiers." Choppa found the keys to open the shackles and those that were lashed with ropes were cut down. There were close to two hundred men lashed to the walls and poles. Some of them had already died, and others were close to death.

Cyle worked his way from man to man cutting the ropes with his knife. Some would fall to the ground lifeless while others would slowly crumble to their knees, exhausted from being lashed to the poles in a standing position. One man was bent forward, hanging limp from his ropes. Cyle could tell by the labored movement of his stomach that he was still breathing. He cut his ropes and helped him gently to the ground, and then he leaned him back against the wall. A surge of excitement rushed through Cyle as the man's appearance grew suddenly familiar. "Micah, is that you?" The man looked at him and smiled a faint smile. It was his cousin. Cyle was all at once filled with both shame and relief. "Water, bring water," Cyle yelled across the room. Choppa came running with a gourd splashing water onto the ground.

"Is that Micah?" Choppa asked with the sound of disbelief in his voice.

"Yes, and I think he's going to be all right." Cyle held him in his lap, tears forming in his eyes.

"Who are these that defiantly enter the city of Easthold after we have brought it to destruction?" bellowed Gizshra in anger at one of his commanders as he paced the floor.

"Master, one of them carries a sword with the mark of the eagle upon it."

"What?" The Wraith lord screamed in a rage. "How can this be? There hasn't been a Gap Warrior in these parts for years, and now one just appears out of nowhere."

"Master, he wields great power with his sword. He killed one of our changelings in battle."

"And who are these that travel with him?"

"There is an old Dwarf and a few younger men, mostly a scattered lot from different colonies. Most of them seem to be under the charge of the Dwarf."

"A single Gap Warrior standing alone is little to worry about, but where there is one, there may be others." Gizshra paced nervously with his robes flapping behind him. "Send the warlock, Drok Relnik. I believe he is already traveling in the area. Tell him I need him to either stop the warrior or create some kind of a distraction to keep him from finding any others of his kind. I fear that where there is one there may be more, and they will be looking for each other. We can't let that happen."

Choppa had found some food in the palace kitchen. There wasn't a lot, but there was enough for everyone to have a little. It would go a long way toward bringing back some of the men's strength. Ginzer and his men were busy bringing the soldiers weapons from the armory. They would need them to get clear of the city and make their way back to Talinor. Micah was feeling better after drinking some water and eating some food. Cyle didn't have the courage to tell him that he had been there when his cousin was captured. Maybe some day he would tell him; then again, maybe not.

Bixby, Ginzer, and some of the higher-ranking soldiers gathered in the corner to discuss their next move.

Cyle and Choppa sat with Micah sharing their stories with each other. Micah had already heard about the accusation that Cyle had tried to poison the King. Cyle told him about how they had tried to arrest him and his flight from Talinor. As far as Cyle knew, he was still a wanted man. Fortunately his secret was safe with Micah. Most of these soldiers were from Easthold so they would not recognize him. The few that were from Talinor were still recovering and had not noticed the fugitive in their midst. Cyle knew it would only be a matter of time and one of them would recognize who he was.

Ginzer shuffled over to where they were sitting and spoke softly to them. "It is time for us to leave. The soldiers will be staying here for a little while longer to gather their strength. They have weapons and they will soon be returning to Talinor. We need to be going; we have other business to attend to." Cyle looked at Micah with fear and apprehension in his eyes.

"It's all right, Cyle," Micah put his hand on his shoulder, "We will be heading back to Talinor soon. There are plenty of us to make our way out of the city past the scavengers."

"Bixby says we have to get going," Ginzer cut in sounding a little impatient.

The two cousins said their brief farewells and as Cyle was walking away Micah asked, "What will you do? You can't go back to Talinor?" Cyle looked at him and shrugged his shoulders, and then he turned to join the others.

He wasn't really sure what he would do. He felt that making plans at this point was a waste of time; it seemed that every time he made them something happened to change them.

The small company of men walked back through the water canal and made their way up to the streets. Ginzer left three of his men behind to help the soldiers. That left them with a total of seven in their party. Ginzer and Bixby led the way while three of Ginzer's men, Brok, Nelf, and Folger followed behind them. Cyle and Choppa took up the rear and for the first time since they had entered the city the two of them had time to talk.

He felt that in some strange way he had become a part of the small band of men he was traveling with. In the short time they had been together they had been bonded by the adversity they had faced together. There was Ginzer the Dwarf with his one eye and rugged ways. Cyle knew he could trust the old Dwarf who had proven his loyalty to the cause. Then there was Bixby. Choppa told him about the battle with Telfir. He shuddered at the thought of how close he had been to Telfir, and yet he had no idea he was a demon. When Choppa told him about the power in Bixby's sword, for the first time he began to see things a little more clearly.

He asked Choppa if he thought Bixby was a Gap Warrior. "I don't know," said Choppa. "There are so many strange things going on around here that I am unfamiliar with, I don't know what to think." Cyle felt that he knew the answer to his own question. Bixby was surely a Gap Warrior; there was little doubt left in his mind about the matter.

Graybeard was right after all. There are still Gap Warriors among us. Now he had to decide what he was going to do about it. Believing that Gap Warriors still existed was one thing, believing that he was suppose to find them and bring them back to Talinor where he was a wanted man, was a different matter altogether.

Bixby and Ginzer led them to a tower overlooking the

city where the view was stunning. Fires burned all over Easthold. Smoke rose upward in haunting billows of black and white plumes, disappearing into the midnight sky. Subtle movements could still be seen among the shadowy ruins. Scavs continued their search as they moved in and out of buildings seeking to satisfy their unquenchable thirst for blood and human souls.

"We need to rest," said Bixby as they reached the last of the stairs at the top of the tower. "None of us have slept for hours. We should be safe here if we take turns standing guard." No one argued. They were exhausted, and they had all been through a lot in the last few days.

"I'll take first watch," offered Bixby. "The rest of you get some sleep." It wasn't long before everyone was asleep except for Cyle. For some reason he was wide-awake; his body ached, but his mind was racing.

He found himself studying the Gap Warrior who stood sentry looking out over the city. He had shoulder-length hair that was a sandy brown color and his body was strong and well-defined. Cyle couldn't help noticing the kindness in his eyes and the gentleness in his words when he spoke to him. He gathered the courage to talk to the swordsman. Rising slowly from where he sat, he made his way over to where Bixby stood.

"Cyle, you should be asleep," said Bixby. "You're going to need your strength tomorrow." Cyle just stared at him and offered no response. "What is it, Cyle, are you all right?"

"Are you a Gap Warrior?" Cyle felt a little embarrassed after he had posed the question.

"That is the name that has been given to me and those who serve the same cause that I do."

"So there are others?"

"There are always others," said Bixby with a smile crossing his face. "And what about you, Cyle, are you the little eagle in my dream?"

"What dream?" Cyle felt uneasy with Bixby's question. Without realizing it, he reached for the eagle pendant tied to the chain around his neck and felt its warmth in his palm. When he realized what he was doing he let go of the pendant.

"I had a dream about a little eagle that would lead a group of larger eagles into battle. Are you that eagle, Cyle?" Bixby looked right through him as he asked the question.

Cyle was surprised that his heart pounded inside him as his breathing grew heavy and his palms started to sweat. Before he could respond to the question, Bixby spoke again. "What are you afraid of, Cyle?"

"I don't know for sure. It's all a little overwhelming to me; this whole week has been unbelievable. Nothing like this has ever happened to me before." Cyle paused, glancing out over the burning city to gather his thoughts. "How can I go back to Talinor with the Gap Warriors? I am a wanted man there, besides I don't know the first thing about finding Gap Warriors."

Bixby smiled. "You found me, didn't you?" Cyle hadn't thought of that.

"But I wasn't even looking for you," he protested.

"See how good you are at it? You weren't even looking for me and you found me. Just think how good you would be at it if you put your heart into it."

A flood of memories rushed through Cyle's head as he thought of the events that had led up to this point in time -- the Priests of Zarish, the message Graybeard had given to his grandmother, and the first War Council meeting. It was clearly stated in that meeting that the Gap Warriors were the key to giving Talinor a fighting chance against the Boogarans and the Shadow Wraiths.

Before now the Shadow Wraiths had only existed in his mind from the scattered stories he had heard, part of a distant myth. Now they were all too real to him. He had seen their malevolent power and evil at work before his very eyes. Their dark magic combined with the Boogaran forces seemed to him to be unstoppable. The destruction of Easthold was a powerful reminder of that.

"I don't know what to do," Cyle said sheepishly.

"What are you afraid of, Cyle?" Bixby's question was warm and full of concern, drawing him out of his shell.

"Most of my life I have wanted to be a warrior. I guess I never realized what that meant. I didn't know that the face of death was so dark," said Cyle, feeling foolish for having glorified such an ugly reality.

"Everyone dreams of being a hero, Cyle; for most of us those dreams are sincere, and for some they are a foolish fantasy that provides a means of escaping life as it is."

"I guess I'm not sure what they meant for me. I didn't appreciate the life I had before I left Talinor. I did spend a lot of time daydreaming about wanting to be something more than I was. I thought that being a warrior would somehow make my life more meaningful."

"Maybe it will. I'm a warrior, and even though it can be ugly at times I can't imagine doing anything else. Everyone has to fight for something sooner or later. I guess it all depends on what you are fighting for."

"And what do you fight for, Bixby?"

"I fight for the freedom of those enslaved and for the One who has called me to fight."

"What do you mean, 'called'?" asked Cyle.

"Some fight for their property; others fight for their King. I fight for the One who is the author of freedom, the Ancient of Days. And He is the one who called me to this life, and gifted me with the passion and skill to live it."

"How did you know you were called to this?"

"It happens in different ways for everyone, but one thing is the same for all of us who are called to this purpose. We all have a passion to see people set free, and it cannot be denied. If we deny the call, it is like a fire shut up in our bones. If we surrender to it, we will follow its path to the end. Anything less will mean losing our own freedom."

"How can you lose your own freedom?" asked Cyle.

"How can anyone be free if he chooses to be anything less than what he was meant to be?"

"I'm ashamed to admit it, but I'm afraid of them, the Shadow Wraiths, I mean. Now that I have seen what they can do, I don't know if I can face them again," said Cyle restlessly.

"Evil personified is usually an overwhelming first impression. Remember the first time you encountered it and how afraid you were of it. The second time around, you probably handled it with a greater measure of courage."

Cyle thought about what Bixby was saying. When he had faced the scavs he was afraid, but he wasn't terrified. But how could he compare that to his first encounter with the Shadow Wraith in the meadow. The one he saw had a much greater depth of power, and its evil was more terrifying. As far as he was concerned, he never wanted to see one of those again.

"Is that the way it was for you?" asked Cyle. "Were you afraid at first?

"I was terrified, and the last thing I wanted to do was deal with the fear I was feeling. Fortunately, someone helped me to face my fears. It's all right to ask for help; few of us make it alone."

"How do you do that? I mean how do you face the fear that evil brings?"

"It starts with faith. You know about faith don't you?"

"Yeah, I know about it. My grandmother has taught me about it for as long as I can remember. I have just never had to use it before now."

Bixby shifted his position and looked Cyle straight in the eyes, and then he placed his hands on his shoulders and said, "Cyle, you have to believe that the One you serve is greater than the one who seeks to destroy you."

The Gap Warrior's words were both penetrating and unsettling. Cyle had watched his grandmother put her faith in a God that she couldn't see. For all those years she had remained faithful to her beliefs. Where had that left her? Walking the streets of Talinor, alone and rejected by those she prays for each night.

As if Bixby had read his mind he said, "Cyle, I want you to remember that evil does not give up without a terrible fight. Sometimes people die ugly deaths, and sometimes battles are lost. When all signs point to defeat it doesn't mean that it's over. Some victories will be costly. It is the nature of war."

Cyle sighed, his bones aching from all he had been through in the past few days.

"Enough talking for now, you need to get some sleep."

It wasn't long before Cyle fell into a deep sleep and the dreaming started almost immediately. The man from his past dreams stood before him in a meadow surrounded with trees. He was holding the staff that he had been using before to train Cyle. When he spoke to Cyle his voice was deep and powerful, resonating with conviction. "It is time for you to decide, Cyle. The Ancient of Days is waiting for your decision." Then the man did something that surprised Cyle. He threw the staff on the ground between the two of them. "You have been summoned by the Ancient of Days to find the Gap Warriors and return to Talinor with them. If you accept this calling, then pick up the staff."

A myriad of emotions flooded over him as he considered the stranger's words. He stared at the staff as if it was a snake that wanted to strike out at him. Somehow he knew deep within his heart that if he picked it up his life would never again be the same. In his mind he could see the Shadow Wraith that had terrified him just a few days ago. There was a clear understanding in his heart that if he picked up the staff he would have to face that kind of evil again. He could feel the weight of the world falling down upon his shoulders, driving his spirit downward.

"I can't do it; I'm not ready." He stepped back from the staff hoping it would disappear, but it seemed to grow larger in his eyes.

"You have been chosen for this by the One you claim to serve. His wisdom in choosing you for this task is not to be questioned by you or anyone else."

"Chosen!" that word blasted into Cyle's conscience. It

seized his heart and gripped his mind. He thought of all the times that he had wanted his life to count for something important, recalling the frustration he had so often felt that his lot in life had left him stuck in a position doing work he had no desire to do. The fact that someone was choosing him for something noble, something important, was awakening a primal part of him he had never felt before. The staff lay there before him, calling out to his spirit. Cyle stepped forward slowly, his hands trembling and mouth dry, taking a deep breath he reached for the staff and picked it up.

CHAPTER 12

When Cyle woke up he could feel the soreness in his shoulders from sleeping on the hard ground. The sun was just coming up, and the sky was a hazy brown from the smoke that still filled the sky. The city was deathly quiet, and there was no sign of scavs or any other form of life. He heard a shuffling sound behind him. Glancing back he noticed that Ginzer was standing at the watch while the others still slept. As Cyle moved to get up he felt something brush against his leg; looking down he was startled to find a staff lying next to him leaning against the wall.

At first he just stared at it in disbelief thinking he might still be dreaming, but his senses told him he wasn't asleep. The staff was made of a light colored wood, possibly ash. At the top of it was a carving of an eagle's head. Just below the carving, there were leather bindings wrapped around it. Farther down there was a series of designs. Cyle wondered if they were for decoration or if they carried some kind of a hidden message.

After staring at it for a while, he reached out for it. Grasping it in both his hands he felt a tingling sensation in his fingers. He held it tighter as a warm sensation danced along his skin, and a wave of emotion flowed through him. He almost fell over from the wash of power that surged through him.

Something about this seemed right. He squeezed the staff in his hands; it felt sure and powerful. A thought began to form in his mind, distant at first, whispering from out of the darkness. "What have you done? Then more came with greater intensity. "Are you crazy? What do you think you are doing? You betrayed your own cousin; what makes you think you can fight this fight?" Doubt began to overshadow his decision.

"Don't listen to them." Looking up he saw Bixby standing there. "You have made your decision; it is expected that doubts will follow. Now you must learn to recognize the difference between the voice of doubt and the voice of your calling. It will take some time, but you will learn."

"What now?" asked Cyle, staring at the staff in his hands.

"It's time for us to move on, but first we will go to the market place to see if we can gather supplies, and then we have some Gap Warriors to find. Now that it's daylight, the scavs will be in hiding to avoid the light. We should have more freedom to move about the city."

The others were beginning to stir from their sleep. Choppa was the first to speak through his stretching. "I'm starving. What's for breakfast?"

"We're going to head toward the Market Square," said Bixby. "Maybe we will get lucky and find some food to restock our supplies." Choppa's eyes lit up at the prospect of something to fill his stomach.

The city looked different during the day as the smoke covered the sun giving it a brownish hue, but the place still reeked of death. The scavs were nowhere to be seen. They had crawled back into another dimension to wait for the darkness to return, and then they would be back scavenging for souls once again.

The seven that were left in the small band moved quickly through the carts and shops in the market place to do some scavenging of their own. In less than an hour they had collected enough supplies to last them for at least two days. When they finished eating and packing their gatherings, they headed for the outskirts of Easthold.

Once they had made their way clear of the city they decided to leave the main road and head for the forest trails to avoid an encounter with the Boogaran military. Ginzer and Choppa spent most of the morning talking about the Dwarf culture and the old wars against the Elves. They had long since become allies, but the stories fascinated Choppa. Ginzer had noticed that Choppa was part Dwarf and part Elf. It was that realization that opened the door to their conversations.

Cyle wondered how they were going to find any Gap Warriors in the forestlands that bordered the eastern valleys. There were settlements in these forests that were mostly made up of hunters and trappers. They were a rugged culture that preferred to stay to them selves and avoid outsiders, unless, of course, you had an interest in buying some of their furs.

The band of travelers had been walking for three hours since leaving Easthold. The trail they were on was steep and narrow. It wound its way up the side of a steep cliff. On one side there was solid rock, and to the other side was a sudden drop-off to a river several feet below. From where they were on the trail they could look out over a rugged alpine valley with majestic granite peaks. The valley below was covered with the rich green colors of the high mountain trees and the blues of the lakes and streams that fed them.

As they approached the top of the summit where the trail suddenly cut back over the saddle, the land and trees spread out before them into a meadow. At the end of the meadow there stood a building that appeared to be a supply station, or possibly a tavern. Muffled voices could be heard coming from the building. Bixby motioned them on, urging them to be careful. The group moved cautiously forward until Bixby stopped them about fifty paces from the front door.

"Ginzer," Bixby pulled him aside from the rest of them and said, "can you and your men wait out here for us? If there is any sign of trouble, let us know." Ginzer nodded in agreement; he would wait outside with the others. The old Dwarf and the Gap Warrior had a bond of trust that had been forged out of the adversity they had faced together.

"I'm going to take Cyle with me." Ginzer directed his men to hold back while Bixby motioned Cyle to follow him.

Bixby cautiously pushed open the tavern door to peer inside. He was surprised at what he saw. The tavern was busy with about a dozen men and a few women drinking and eating. As they entered the door, a tall man in the middle of the room called out, "Friend or foe?"

"We are friends of Talinor," Bixby answered him. With that response everyone turned back to what they had been doing.

A short portly man behind the bar yelled across the crowd, "Ale for the thirsty travelers? Get it while it's wet." Bixby waved the man off and moved toward the center of the room to take a look around.

Sprawled out over a bench next to the stairs was a man who appeared to be passed out or sleeping. The Gap Warrior walked over to him while those in the tavern ignored his approach to the sleeping patron. Cyle wondered what Bixby was up to as he leaned over the man and grabbed his bushy black hair to pull his head back. Bixby peered at the man's face as he furled his brow, trying not to smell his fetid breath. The drunken man groaned, and Bixby let go of his hair as his head flopped back onto the bench.

"Well, Cyle, it looks like we have found one of our Gap Warriors," said Bixby with disgust in his voice.

"How do you know he's a Gap Warrior?" asked Cyle with a confused look on his face.

"I know him," answered Bixby, sighing with a deep breath of frustration before letting it out. "His name is Gafney, and as far as I'm concerned his Gap fighting days are long over. Come on, let's go." Bixby turned to leave the room, walked right past Cyle, and headed for the door.

"Wait, we can't leave here without him. We have to take him with us," pleaded Cyle.

"Look at him; he's in no condition to fight or walk for that matter. The only thing he's willing to fight for is another bottle of ale, and from the looks of things, he would lose," said Bixby angrily. It was the first time Cyle had seen that side of the Gap Warrior.

"He is the reason we are here, you said so yourself. We have to take him with us," countered Cyle with conviction in his voice.

Bixby glanced over at Gafney who was lying drunk and sprawled out over the bench; then he looked back at Cyle. "It's your call, but I think we're going to regret it later," he said looking disgruntled. "Why don't you go outside and get the others. We're going to need help getting him out of here."

Carrying the man was no easy task. He had massive arms and legs that hung from his stocky frame. His body lay limply, adding to the burden of picking him up and carrying him. All seven of them took turns dragging him by his feet until they came to a pond behind the tavern. Ginzer had questioned the task initially, but Bixby had assured him that it was what they needed to do.

When Bixby noticed that his old friend was beginning to stir from his slumber, he motioned for help, and with the aid of Brok and Folger, they dumped him into the pond. Gafney staggered to get up, all the while slipping on the muddy bottom, spitting water from his mouth, cursing and yelling threats. The grin on Bixby's face revealed how much he was enjoying Gafney's misfortune.

Gaffney looked around in a rage, his eyes glaring, trying desperately to make sense of where he was. Murky water dripped in ringlets from his long dark hair and thickly matted beard. He was about to lunge out at Folger who was standing nearby when Bixby stepped in to cut short the charge. "Gafney," said Bixby with a grin, "welcome back among the living." Gafney wiped the water from his eyes, and then a look of surprise came over his face as he recognized who was speaking to him.

"Bix!" Gafney seemed genuinely happy to see him. "Where did you come from?" Gafney stumbled out of the water and wrapped his wet arms around Bixby in a bear-like embrace, picking him up off the ground. Bixby resisted the wet hug, but it was no use. Gafney was upon him before he knew what was happening. "It's good to see you, old friend," Gafney said as he released his embrace and stepped back to size up his friend. "Who are these fools?" the tone in his voice hinting sarcasm as he surveyed the group?

"These are your rescuers," said Bixby sarcastically. Gafney looked around at the men standing nearby.

"Rescuers? I didn't need rescuing. I was doing just fine." Gafney laughed as he spat the words out. "So, why did you haul me out of there? There was still a good amount of ale left in the tavern barrels that I was planning lowering the levels of."

"This is Cyle," Bixby took Cyle by the arm and moved him between the two of them. "I think he should tell you why; it was his idea."

Gafney looked perplexed and stood there with his hands on his hips waiting for an answer. Cyle just stared at Gafney, lost for words. "Well boy, speak up. I don't have all day," demanded Gafney gruffly.

"I, uh, well," Cyle stammered. "Are you a Gap Warrior?"

Gafney smiled and snickered softly. He shook his head dismissively and turned away from Cyle as if he were going to walk away from him. Pausing for a moment, he turned back around to face him. All the while Cyle was anxiously awaiting his answer as the others looked on. "Why do you care about that, kid?" Gafney grunted out the answer as he rubbed his shaggy head, no doubt suffering from all the drinking he had been doing.

"Talinor needs you, sir," Cyle responded politely.

"Oh, I don't think Talinor needs me, boy."

"Gafney, listen to the boy," said Bixby firmly.

"Okay, all right. Why do you want me to go to Talinor?"

"Because you are a Gap Warrior and Talinor needs you to fight the Shadow Wraiths." Cyle was beginning to sound a little more confident.

"I haven't fought in a Gap war in years, kid. I don't think I am your man for the job."

"So what are you going to do, Gafney?" Bixby interjected. "Look for the nearest tavern and drink yourself unconscious while the world around you goes down in flames?"

"Maybe I will." A stubborn look crossed Gafney's face. With his hands on his hips he glared at Bixby and Cyle as if to challenge them to talk him into it.

"Come on, Cyle, he's not going to budge. Obviously he has more important things to do." Bixby turned to walk away as a look of disgust played across his face. "Gafney's fighting days are obviously over."

"Hang on a minute, Bixby. I said I wouldn't fight in a Gap war, I didn't say I wouldn't fight at all. I'll go with you to Talinor, and I will fight the Boogarans, the filthy beasts, but my Gap fighting days are over."

Cyle started to speak, but Bixby spoke sooner. "Then let's get on with it." Bixby moved to gather up some of the supplies and handed Gafney his sword. "We need to get moving; we've wasted enough time already."

Cyle was beginning to wonder if they had made a mistake pulling Gafney out of the tavern like they did. He wasn't at all what he had expected in a Gap Warrior. Not that he had had a lot of experience with them. The only Gap Warrior Cyle had ever met was Bixby, and he was very different from Gafney. Sure of himself and committed to the task before him, Bixby fit Cyle's image of a warrior, while Gafney was intimidating, big and obnoxious. Maybe Bixby was right; maybe they would regret bringing him along. Besides, they needed Gap Warriors and Gafney was unwilling to fight as one.

King Shandon stood in his war tower gazing out of the huge arched window toward the area that would soon become a killing ground. Darius studied him from a distance, watching his King, deep in thought. He stood statue-like and unmoving with his back toward the others in the room. The Priests of Zarish were there, led by Orom their leader. Somuel, the Captain of the Guard, and various other advisors stood quietly with them.

"Your Majesty." Somuel was the first to break the silence. "We have positioned our first line of defense on the valley floor. Bernard and Gerrid will command the lines together from there. Bernard and his Dwarves will form the middle of the line at the front. The border guards along with volunteers from outlying villages will join them."

"Thank you, Somuel," the King turned toward his Captain, "you have done well in assembling the troops. Is there anything else we need to do to prepare for this battle?" Before Somuel could answer, Orom stepped forward,

"Your Majesty." Orom bowed his head slightly forward to show reverence and humility.

"Yes, Orom, what is it?"

"Your Majesty, I would suggest that we cleanse our hearts of all fear and doubt."

"A difficult thing to do in times of war, good priest," said Darius with a hint of sarcasm in his voice.

"We shall do our best," said the King. "Thank you for your advice; it is well taken."

"Your Majesty, what of the Elves?" asked Darius.

The King turned again to look out the window, his mood turning more solemn. "The Elves have not changed their minds, so they will not be joining us as it seems they disagree with the alliance we have made with the Priests of Zarish. They are slow to change from the old ways of thinking."

Darius turned as white as a ghost. "But, Your Majesty, how can we stand without their help?"

"You are an anxious one, Darius. Perhaps that is your job,

to worry. Whatever the outcome, we will make a strong stand for Talinor. The Elves have been our friends for years; they are only doing what they believe is right."

"We are growing in numbers every day. I am confident we will find a way," stated Somuel, in the calm manner that he was accustomed to speak.

Just then a trumpet sounded from the main tower gate at the entrance of the city. As the inhabitants of the King's war tower turned their gaze upon the north they saw a massive cavalcade of soldiers descending upon the fields of Talinor, dressed mostly in black with Boogaran banners flying high against the wind. Upon the banners was the symbol of the kingdom of Boogara, a yellow dragon upon a field of black.

From a distance Drashkar, son of Ashkron, watched his men slowly file into the valley as they marched in formation onto the killing field toward the Talinor formation. The two armies met at the center until both stood face to face with a small stretch of land separating them. Wisely, Talinor had always chosen to fight their battles on the valley floor where they would hold their ground for as long as they could before retreating behind the walls of the city to make a final stand.

Drashkar's couriers prepared to deliver a message to the Talinor field commander, Bernard. The Boogaran army would demand the surrender of Talinor's forces. Bernard in turn would send a courier with a notice of refusal to surrender. Then there would be a day of praying and sacrificing to whatever gods the Boogarans served. The following day the battle would begin.

"They appear frightened and unsure of themselves, commander," said Kazar, Drashkar's first in command.

"Appearances in times of war mean very little, Kazar. When the first blade is lifted to draw blood they will fight like true heroes."

"They will also die like heroes," hissed Kazar. Drashkar smiled as he surveyed the battlefield.

"We outnumber them four to one, Kazar," Drashkar's grin

114

grew larger. "How long do you think it will take us to reach the city walls?"

Kazar studied the troops for a moment before answering, "Two, maybe three days."

"Excellent. Some of the Shadow Wraiths have already entered the city. They will use their magic from the inside. That will give us the leverage we need when we begin our assault on the city gates."

Drashkar could feel the excitement rising within him. He craved this victory more than anything he had ever wanted before. All his life he had heard the stories of how the Boogarans had fallen in battle to the army of Talinor. He was sick of those stories, and he hated them with a vengeance. His father lay near death, and he had vowed that he would conquer Talinor in his father's lifetime.

"Tomorrow morning, at dawn's first light, we attack," ordered Drashkar.

"At dawn's first light," Kazar responded to the order and turned to pass on the order to the Boogaran troops.

CHAPTER 13

Gafney strolled into camp with an elk draped over his shoulders and dropped it on the ground near the fire. He knelt down and drew the long knife from his belt. The blade reflected a golden color from the firelight. As he prepared to gut the creature, Ginzer asked, "How did you bag the elk without a bow and arrow?" Gafney was carrying a long knife, but he had no other weapons except a sword.

"I hit him with a rock," Gafney grunted the words as he peeled back the animal's hide, exposing the red meat.

"A rock," exclaimed Ginzer. "You will have to show me that trick some day." Gafney ignored him. "Don't I know you from somewhere?" Ginzer asked with a perplexed look on his face.

"I doubt it. I haven't been in these parts for over fifteen years."

"I'm sure I know you from somewhere, I just can't place it."

"Forget about it," Gafney's muscles bulged as he ripped back some more of the hide, "you don't know me." Gafney stood up for a moment and looked over at Cyle. "Hey kid, we need some water." Cyle nodded, jumped up and headed for the creek. He thought Gafney seemed uneasy with Ginzer's questions. He must be hiding something. Cyle was sure of it.

The creek wasn't far from camp and Cyle was glad for a chance to splash some water on his neck. The water was cool and refreshing. When he had finished filling all of the water flasks, he noticed a reflection in the pool near the water's edge. Startled, he jumped backward and fell on his backside. Looking up he saw a tall bearded man standing on the other side of the creek holding a staff.

"You," Cyle forced the words to come out, "you are the one in my dreams."

"Sometimes dreams are the best place to meet," said the man in a deep voice and with a slight smile on his face.

"How did you do that? I mean, how did you come to my dreams like that?"

"Didn't your grandmother ever teach you about the Guardians?" Cyle paused for a moment, attempting to recall the possibility. He was having a hard time remembering anything about Guardians.

"Hey, wait a minute, how did you know about my grandmother?"

"She's an intercessor. All Guardians know of the intercessors," said the stranger.

"Sure, I guess so," Cyle said suspiciously. "But who are you, and how did you get into my dreams?"

"Come with me," ordered the stranger and turned to walk

in the other direction away from the river. Cyle just stared at first, and then he grabbed his staff, crossed the creek and followed after him. Soon they came to a clearing and the stranger turned to face him. "There will be time for more questions later. For now, all you need to know is that I am your Guardian. I can only maintain the form of flesh and blood for a short period of time. Soon I will have to return to my natural form."

"You mean you are not a person?"

"Of course I am a person, but I am a supernatural person."

"You mean like a Shadow Wraith?" Cyle wished he hadn't said it, but he had, and it was too late to retract the statement.

"Yes, in some ways I am like a Shadow Wraith. I exist in the same realm as the Shadow Wraiths, but I do not serve the dark magic. The dark magic and the Shadow Wraiths are my enemies."

"How do I know that you are not a Shadow Wraith, one of those shape-changers or whatever you call them?"

"That is a good question, Cyle; the kind of question that should be asked at times like these. There is much deception in the world and things are not always as they appear. So I ask you. How do you judge something to be good or evil?"

"My grandmother always taught me to judge a person by their deeds. She says if a person is evil their deeds will be evil."

The big man smiled. "That sounds like good advice to me."

"But I don't know you, so how can I judge you by your deeds?" asked Cyle.

"Oh, but you do know me, Cyle, and you have seen my deeds; who do you think it was that saved your life from the scavengers?"

"That was you!" Cyle exclaimed. "I can't believe it! It was you!" This time his words came with conviction.

"Yes, it was I. Like I said, I am your Guardian. Now hold out your staff." The Guardian lunged at him with his own staff outstretched. Cyle deflected the blow automatically. Surprised at how his instincts took over, he moved in a fluid motion as he blocked the Guardian's assaults. "Very good, Cyle, for once your dreams have done you some good," the Guardian smiled. "My time is running short; soon I will have to return to my spirit form. There are two more Gap Warriors that will be joining you. One will be joining you in the next few days, and the other will join you back at Talinor. You must leave tonight for the Caverns of Lorus. Bixby can show you the way."

"But why and for what purpose?"

"For the strength you will need to complete this journey. I must go now. Bixby can tell you what you need to know." The Guardian turned to walk away.

"Wait, do you have a name?"

"My name is Melidar," said the Guardian. Then he turned and disappeared into the darkness of the forest; a faint flash of light appeared briefly, and then it was gone.

Cyle stood there in a daze. His memory was coming back to him piece by piece. The more he thought about it he was able to recall something his grandmother had told him at a very young age. She would put him to bed at night; later he would call her back into his room after he had been awakened from a nightmare. She would say to him, "Do not be afraid, little man. Your Guardian will protect you. He watches over you to keep you from harm." It had been so long since he had heard that, and he was so very young at the time. He had forgotten about it until now.

Cyle gathered his water flasks and headed back to camp, pondering what had just happened. When he arrived, the meat was finished cooking and Gafney was growing impatient for his water.

"What took you, boy? I was beginning to fear a wild animal had eaten you for dinner," Gafney scowled and grabbed a water flask from Cyle's hand as he took a bite out of the piece of meat he was eating. Then he took his long knife and carved off a piece of meat and handed it to Cyle. "Here, eat this. You look like you could stand to put on a little more muscle."

Choppa was passing out some of the fruit they had

gathered when they were in Easthold. When he was through he sat down next to Cyle. "I think this Gafney guy is crazy," he whispered under his breath to Cyle. While you were gone he and Bixby started arguing, and it almost went to blows. I feared for Bixby. That Gafney looks as strong as an ox."

"What were they arguing about?"

"Gafney wanted to go to a tavern just west of here. I think he was yearning for a drink. Bixby wouldn't stand for it. He told him to go ahead, but that we would be moving on with out him."

"Then what happened," Cyle pressed.

"Gafney called him a few choice names, and then he grabbed Bixby by his tunic and the rest of us were on our feet with our weapons drawn. Ginzer was the first to warn him. "Let him go," he said, "or I'll cut your arms off." Bixby was smiling the whole time. Bixby said, "It's okay, Ginzer, he gets this way when he's hungry." Then Gafney walked away mumbling something under his breath, and it was over. I can't tell whether the two of them like each other or hate each other," said Choppa looking confused.

"Something haunts him," said Cyle as he looked at Gafney standing by the fire. "I'm sure of it."

"You're right, young Cyle." Cyle and Choppa jumped as they turned to see Bixby standing behind them. "Gafney has not always been as you see him now. There was a time when Gafney and I fought side by side and he could be counted on to the end. Now he is as unpredictable as the wind. Something did happen to him that caused him to grow bitter; he's not the man I once knew. But don't worry he won't hurt me. He knows he's stronger than me and he likes to remind me of it from time to time"

"Why is he with us if he won't fight the Shadow Wraiths?" asked Choppa.

"He doesn't have anything else to do," said Bixby. " I know it doesn't make a lot of sense, but that is just the way Gafney is. He is here today, but he could be gone tomorrow. Like the wind, he comes and goes as he pleases; that's the way he likes it."

"Do you know what happened to him?" asked Cyle.

"Yes, I know what happened to him. Gafney has been a Gap Warrior for as long as I have known him. He was one of the greatest of all Gap Warriors before his falling away. Years ago, Gafney and I, along with some other Gap Warriors fought in a battle for the kingdom of Azzakon against the Felnerin. He not only fought valiantly against the Shadow Wraiths, he helped turn the tide of battle against the Felnerin. The battle was nearing an end with Azzakon's victory in sight. In one last desperate attempt, the Felnerin created a breach in one of the smaller gates of the Azzakon fortress. Gafney along with a small group of warriors turned back the intruders. He defeated their chief commander in one final showdown, and his leadership brought victory and a final end to that war."

"Overnight, he became a hero. The people adored him and the king asked him to stay in Azzakon, offering him the position of the Captain of the Palace Guard. He stayed in Azzakon for the following four seasons and fell in love with the king's daughter. They made plans to be married and the king of Azzakon blessed their desire to be wed. Just ten days before the wedding was to be held, the princess wanted to travel to a nearby market to purchase supplies for her wedding. Due to unrest in the region, Gafney tried to talk her out of her decision, but she insisted on going. Gafney and a group of palace guards rode as escorts to protect the princess and her entourage. While returning from the trip, a group of rebels attacked the caravan and most of the guards were killed, along with the princess."

"The king blamed Gafney for the death of his daughter and Gafney blamed himself. He left Azzakon in shame, and has lived the life of a restless wanderer ever since. His life changed that day forever, and with the passing of time he grew bitter against his faith, and eventually forsook his call as a Gap Warrior."

Cyle looked over at Gafney who was talking with Folger as the two of them finished the last of their meal. He felt pity for him. Bixby interrupted Cyle's thoughts. "Don't pity Gafney; he has chosen the road he walks. Yes, life has dealt him a difficult hand, but we all fight our own personal battles. Sometimes we win them, and sometimes we lose them. Gafney is a survivor and a loner. He rarely accepts help from anyone. The last thing he wants is your pity."

CHAPTER 14

Drashkar stood motionless in the middle of the clearing, anticipating the arrival of the Shadow Wraith. He loathed the idea of having to depend on demons. He did it because his father wanted him to, and because he knew their power would be a great help to him. Being in the presence of the demon was unsettling to say the least. The night air grew cold and a haunting mist settled in around the Boogaran warlord. From the edge of the clearing a ghost-like apparition slowly emerged out of smoke, shapeless at first. Drashkar could feel its oppressive presence beginning to envelop him. He wondered if the demon enjoyed intimidating him with its insidious power.

At first its form was misty and undefined, then slowly it swirled into shape as a loathsome creature took form. When the demon spoke its voice was deep and full of vibration. "Greetings, young prince, it seems the time of battle draws near. Are your men ready to win a victory?" The demon's eyes glowed yellow as they penetrated the mist.

"My men will fight to the death."

"I care little whether they die or live. Victory is all that matters to me," the words came out in a slow whisper.

"Why did you call me here?" asked Drashkar, "I have much to do to prepare for tomorrow's battle; we must be ready to strike at first light."

"I sense a lack of gratitude on your part for the service we are offering you, young prince."

"And what of the service we offer you, demon?" Drashkar's words were filled with anger and impatience. He was growing tired of being questioned by this creature of the dark magic.

The demon appeared to smile beneath the hood that covered its formless face. "It seems you have little respect for the power we possess."

"I have seen little to convince me of respect," offered Drashkar boldly. "If your power is so great, then why did we lose the last war against Talinor?"

The demon just stood there, staring back at him through the darkness. Drashkar was growing uneasy with the silence. Finally the Shadow Wraith spoke in a low hiss. "So, it is as I suspected; you do not respect the power of the dark magic." Slowly it raised its clawed hand with its palm extended outward, a dark, invisible force slammed against Drashkar, bringing him to his knees. Pain and fear coursed through his body as he hunched over in agony. Darkness surrounded him and squeezed the air out of his lungs. He could hear the demon's wicked laughter echoing as if it came from a distance. He struggled to remain conscious, as the world around him was spinning out of control.

Then, as suddenly as it had started, it stopped. Gasping for breath, he rose slowly to his feet. Fighting to keep his balance, Drashkar looked across the clearing. The demon was gone.

Talinor's forces appeared as statues in the early morning mist as they stood in formation upon the valley floor. Bernard, captain of the Dwarves, and Gerrid, Chief Commander of the soldiers of Talinor, stood together at the front of the fighting lines. The Dwarves had always been known for their might in battle. Smaller in stature than the sons of men, yet they were powerful in strength and stealth. Most of them fought with the traditional battle-axe, while some preferred broad swords.

Sunlight softly brightened the morning mist as dawn's first

rays of light fought to penetrate the canopy of fog that covered the valley. The two armies stood facing each other on the field of battle, each awaiting the command to charge. "And now it begins." Gerrid spoke in hushed tones to his friend, Bernard.

"We shall give them the fight of their lives," said Bernard as he stepped forward to give the command to his troops. "Warriors," Bernard's voice broke the silence of the morning quiet, "draw your weapons." The shrill sound of metal banging on metal could be heard as soldiers joined swords and axes with fellow soldiers in a show of unity. Banners were raised with the sign of the shooting star as the army of Talinor lifted a cheer that thundered throughout the valley, and echoed off the surrounding hills in the distance.

As the cheers died away, once again there was silence in the valley and then came the response, softly at first, rising from the ranks of the enemy. Like a distant storm, cries erupted. The beginning of it was barely a whisper that grew steadily to a deafening roar, piercing the air and shaking the ground. The Boogarans raised their weapons, waving them overhead. They were the first to charge as the sound of their footsteps thundered across the valley floor, rising as a giant wave to crush the life from their enemies. Talinor responded with equal force, and when the two armies collided the clash of metal upon metal was deafening.

The Priests of Zarish prayed fervently in the temple, burning incense and chanting their mantras. Women and children joined them in their religious meditations, desperately clinging to the hope that their loved ones would survive this battle.

King Shandon stood high in the King's War Tower with his Captain of the Guard, Somuel, and his advisor, Darius. From their position they could easily see the field of battle in the distance. The sounds of the men's cries could be heard as their voices traveled across the fields and over the city to the War Tower.

The King stared transfixed upon the battle scene that unfolded before him, thinking, surely he had done the right thing calling upon the Priests of Zarish to help them fight this battle. After all, his kingdom was at great risk. Deep within himself, he wondered if he was betraying something sacred, something powerful, but his desperation to save his people was the stronger force that drove his decisions. It had been years since he had seen any of the dark magic. Maybe it had died away and the Boogarans would have to fight this battle without it. His hopes were vain imaginations, and deep in his heart he knew it. He also knew that they had no solid evidence that the Priests of Zarish possessed any real power. It was too late to do anything about it. Now all they could do was wait to find what kind of power the Priests commanded. They would find out soon enough when the time came for them to make a stand against the dark magic.

So much had changed since the last war. Before the last Boogaran attack against his kingdom, he had a wife whom he dearly loved. She served by his side faithfully, and the people loved her for her beauty and her wisdom. She was the one the people really respected, and he had always known that to be true. She died shortly after the last war, and a part of him died with her, as did part of the kingdom. She was strong in the faith, and she had inspired the people to stay strong in their faith. After she passed away, things began to change.

The King had realized long ago that she was the strength of his own faith. He had never really developed a strong and abiding faith of his own. After she was gone, he felt hopeless and devoid of purpose or vision for himself or his kingdom. Without a son to inherit the throne he would some day leave behind, he felt very alone in this world. The one person he had felt closest to was gone. He missed his talks with his cupbearer, Cyle. Sitting by the hearth on cold winter nights, the two of them would drink cider and talk things out. He wondered where he was now, if he was even still alive. The guards had told the king the story of how Cyle had escaped into the marsh and of the serpent's attack. His heart sank with heaviness at the thought of never seeing him again.

Now that the king had lost Cyle, the aching loneliness he carried within him grew even deeper. A part of him was dying and he didn't know how to get it back. But he could not afford to think about that because all that mattered now was saving his kingdom.

CHAPTER 15

"A bog beast is a far greater adversary to defeat than a troll. Trolls are slow and stupid." huffed Ginzer as he stared at Gafney through his one good eye. "Besides, trolls tire quickly and that gives you the advantage."

"You've lost your gelnods old Dwarf," said Gafney sarcastically. "Trolls can fight with weapons, and they are as cunning as a dragon. A bog beast is a stupid animal that's driven by its untamed hunger."

Cyle was growing weary of the arguing between the two men. They had been going at it for hours now. He tried to block out their conversation so he could focus on what Bixby had said to him about the Caverns of Lorus. Not that he had told him very much at all. He did know that he was going to meet someone called the "Princess" in the caverns. Bixby seemed to be withholding something from him, but Cyle was unable to get him to say much at all about the Princess or the caverns. He just told him that it was necessary for him to go and meet the Princess, and that it was part of his training.

Cyle had never heard of this Princess before. He had heard of the Caverns of Lorus high in the Raggletooth peaks. "Monsters live there, and evil spirits go there when they are being punished," Choppa had told him that once a long time ago when they were spending the night in the War Tower. It was something they used to do from time to time during the summer months when the nights were warm. At night, high in the War Tower, the soft breezes would blow through the huge open windows offering a cool refuge from the warm summer evenings. Cyle remembered those times fondly. Late at night Choppa would tell tales of monsters and other ghost stories. Cyle was pretty confident that they were only stories; although Choppa displayed a look of concern when he found out they were headed for the caverns.

They had walked through the rest of the afternoon before they had reached the peaks of Raggletooth. Raggletooth was the name of a dragon that had lived in these rocks many years ago. The creature had ruled over this region for many years until a small band of bounty hunters captured it and sold it to the highest bidder.

"This is far enough," said Bixby. "The caverns are just a little higher up from here. I'll take Cyle with me and the rest of you can wait here until we return."

Gafney motioned Bixby over to speak to him in private. "Do you have to take the boy up there? He seems a little young for this kind of thing."

"You know how this thing works. I don't have any choice in the matter," said Bixby under his breath.

"There's always a choice," Gafney huffed.

"Yeah, you've obviously made yours, haven't you?"

"Don't start on me. I'm here, aren't I?"

"Yeah, you're here," Bixby paused for a moment, "today anyway." Then he turned and walked away to join Cyle.

It was colder on the peaks than in the lower regions making the air fresh and crisp. Cyle liked how it felt on his skin. Most of the trees were below them with the exception of a few smaller ones that had managed to survive in the thin air. Huge rocks jutted up all around them, and little creatures scurried about in and out of their holes looking for food. Bixby was completely silent as they made their way over the rocks to the caverns. Suddenly they came to a rock wall that had a huge crack that ran from the base reaching all the way to the top. It was just wide enough for a person to squeeze into.

Bixby stopped and stared at the opening in the rock wall. He stood there for a while deep in thought, and then he turned to Cyle. "You will have to go on from here alone, Cyle." His voice was calm and reassuring. Fear captured the look on Cyle's face. He hadn't planned on this happening. Going in there alone was not something he had bargained for.

Bixby squared off in front of Cyle and once again put his hand on the boy's shoulder. "You have been through a lot, Cyle. Every step of the way you have not been alone. Even though there have been times that it seemed so, you have always had someone watching over you. Entering the Caverns of Lorus is an important part of the journey you are on. I would tell you more, but words cannot explain what you are about to experience."

"Hey, wait a minute." Cyle started, shaking his head and backing away from the Gap Warrior. "What's going to happen in there?"

"Cyle, the task you have been given is a difficult one, especially for a young man of your age." Cyle recoiled at the idea of being too young. He wanted to be a man not a little boy. "If you are going to serve the Ancient of Days, you must learn that faith does not always give you the whole picture before it asks you to respond to its leading. Right now, all that you know is that you are to go into the caverns. More will be revealed to you after you have taken that step of faith."

"But why can't I know ahead of time?" Cyle pleaded.

"It is the nature of faith. Faith will always require that we risk something. It is in the risking that we learn to depend on the Ancient One, and it is in risking that we learn that He is real."

Cyle's head was reeling as he tried to take it all in. He had seen his grandmother live by faith. She prayed all the time, but where had it gotten her. People mocked her and called her the "crazy old woman that wandered the streets at night." Even her own kingdom was now turning away from the faith that she held dear. Until now Cyle had never had to make any personal decisions based on faith. His grandmother had always taken care of that. He wasn't sure he knew how to use his own faith.

"It doesn't feel right," said Cyle. He didn't want to admit that fear was getting the better of him.

"Does it have to feel right to know that it is right?" asked the Gap Warrior.

Suddenly a picture flashed in Cyle's mind of the time Darius had made him climb the rock and fall backwards at his command. It didn't feel right then, but he did it anyway, and Darius had caught him. Looking down at the staff in his hand he was reminded of the commitment he had made to fulfill his calling.

"All right, I'll do it." He took a deep breath and tried to blow the tension out of his stomach.

"There's one more thing," said Bixby. "There will be a voice to guide you through the caverns. It is the voice of the Princess. It is a voice as sweet as the evening lark. When you hear it you will feel a peace and a calm come over you. It is time; you must go now."

Cyle nodded and slowly turned toward the opening in the wall. Stepping inside, a sudden chill swept over his body. He rubbed his arms to fight it. After a few more steps, the light from the entrance began to fade in the distance behind him. Soon it was completely black and he had to fight the urge to panic. What had he gotten himself into? What could he possibly gain from this exercise?

Using his staff to feel his way through the darkness, he managed to move on without running into the walls. The sound of dripping water could be heard all around, as the dampness in the air grew thicker on his skin. The ground was surprisingly free of rocks and holes, allowing his steps to be sure and free of stumbling. After walking for quite some time and not really knowing where his steps were taking him, the narrow passage came to a sudden end. He began feeling around with his staff but could find no other openings. Frustration grew inside him as he felt he was losing control. Standing there in the blackness not knowing what to do next, with his anger growing, he grasped his staff firmly and raised it to strike the rock wall in front of him.

"No, Cyle." The voice that spoke the words was soft and sweet. It was the voice of a woman. "Do not use your staff in anger against the rock," said the voice again in a calm tone. Cyle remembered Bixby's admonishment about the voice.

"Who are you? What is your name?" There was no answer. "Tell me who you are, please," Cyle pleaded. The voice was silent as if it did not hear him. After a few more moments Cyle realized the voice was not going to answer, so he stood in silence and waited for a reply.

"Touch the staff on the rock." Cyle felt relief this time when he heard her voice. There was a tingling sensation in his palms as he raised his staff before him. Softly he touched the wall with the staff, and then he heard grinding noise as it moved to the side. Stepping cautiously through the entrance the stone had left, he found himself in a giant cavern filled with outcroppings of rock and a lake that covered most of the floor. Rays of light beamed from the ceiling in splintering shards, falling upon the lake below, causing the waters to sparkle like diamonds. If not for the light shining on the lake, it would have been a dark and cheerless place. To his right was a trail that followed along the side of a cliff; somehow he knew it was the path to take.

The lights reflecting on the surface of the lake provided little help in seeing the trail, but the staff provided secure footing enabling Cyle to move along at a good pace. He had no thoughts of hunger or thirst. This surprised him because he hadn't eaten for hours. Ahead he saw something glowing softly against the cavern walls. The trail was headed in the direction of the light, and the closer he walked toward the light, the brighter it grew, making it easier for him to see his surroundings.

Just when it was getting easier to see, he stumbled over a rock and tumbled to the ground. As he landed he dropped his staff, and it clanged against the stone and rolled down the path in front of him. After regaining his feet a strong sense of apprehension flowed over him as he sensed a presence. It must be my imagination, he thought, but he couldn't be certain. Moving toward his staff to pick it up, he stopped in his tracks as a dark shadow passed over the ground. Cyle looked about in every direction and saw nothing, and then he heard a noise that sounded like a fluttering of wings. The light in the cavern shifted overhead. Stumbling backward, he looked up and saw the shadow of a large winged creature flying toward him.

Swooping down it passed within inches, wind swirling about his head. Through the light and shadows Cyle could make out its leathery wings and pincer-like claws as they lashed out at him. Instinctively he ducked and rolled across the path toward his staff. Grabbing it with both hands he twirled it twice above his head and brought it to the attack position. A sudden surge of warmth flowed through his hands along with that familiar tingling sensation in his body, only this time it was stronger than before. The creature sent out a high-pitched screech as it circled above him. The lights from the ceiling of the cave flickered upon its wings; red eyes peered down at him, stalking him.

"Do not move when it attacks," said the lady's voice as it echoed through his mind. The monster circled two more times and then it dove straight at him, screeching and clawing at the air. Reacting to the fear within, Cyle instinctively rolled left into a summersault across the path and came up ready to attack. A stabbing pain lanced through his left shoulder. The thing must have caught him before he made the roll, he thought. His grip on his staff was weaker now, warm blood rolled down his back. Fighting the sensation of dizziness, Cyle steadied himself for the second attack.

Again he heard the voice. "Do not retreat from this creature. Stand your ground and be still. It can only find you if you are moving. That's how it knows where you are." This time Cyle vowed to obey the voice. The creature circled above waiting for its prey to move. Then it screamed again and dove in his direction. "Hold your ground," Cyle spoke to himself in a whisper. "Do not move this time." With his heart pounding

DEFENDERS OF THE BREACH

wildly within him he watched as the creature dove toward him. It was inches away from striking when it suddenly changed course and flew upward toward the roof of the cavern. After circling two or three more times and screeching in vain it changed its direction, turned and flew away.

Gafney and Choppa were getting hungry. The two of them had been climbing over the rocks for hours looking for game. Gafney was in a rare, but welcome, cheerful mood and he kept Choppa amused with stories of his adventures while traveling in the southern forest of Telza. Although entertaining, Choppa found some of the stories a little hard to believe-- Like the time he did battle with a two-headed dragon in the Valley of Skulls. Apparently, it had kidnapped the daughter of a rich land baron. The man was so grieved over the loss of his daughter that he offered Gafney the rights to all of his estate if he returned the girl to him unharmed.

He tracked the beast for days, following it deep into the Valley of Skulls. The place was named that because the dragon would drag its victims into its den and consume the bodies. Then leave the bones from the neck down in its lair, while the skulls were tossed out into the valley to warn others that the beast ruled in that place.

After finding the Dragon's lair, he waited for three days, hiding high up in a tree until the beast went off looking for something to eat. The girl was still alive when he found her, but the dragon returned before they could make a safe escape. Gafney claimed he fought the beast for four days until he finally cut off one of its heads. After returning the girl to her father he decided to turn down the offer of the estate, settling instead for a keg of mulled wine and a new horse. Later he traded the horse for some more wine, claiming that he wasn't fond of riding horses.

When Choppa looked at Gafney he saw a man who was built like a bull and very confident in his own strength, maybe a little too confident, thought Choppa. At times he was warm and friendly and could bring a laugh when he was in the mood for it, but at other times he was cold and insensitive. In spite of his moodiness and abrupt ways, Choppa found himself being drawn to the big man. He had never met anyone quite like Gafney before, and the man's wild and unpredictable ways were appealing to him.

"Something moves," said Gafney in a whisper as he came to a sudden halt. Choppa looked in the same direction as Gafney, who was peering at a sparse stand of scrub oak. He could see nothing unusual.

"What do you see?" asked Choppa under his breath.

"I don't know. It's like the air that ripples above a fire, but I am not sure; maybe I'm just seeing things. Come on. Let's move this way, toward the rocks, and see what happens."

Choppa was sure Gafney was seeing things, but he decided to go along with him anyway. He had already learned that when Gafney wanted something a certain way it was no use arguing the point.

As they walked over the rocks the big man nervously looked back over his shoulder as if he was afraid they were being followed. The sun was nearing the horizon and the air was growing colder. If they were going to find food, they would need to find it soon before it grew any darker.

"Wait," said Gafney as he held out his arm suddenly to motion a halt. When Choppa walked into it he almost fell down. It was like walking into a tree stump. "Look, over there, a stag drinks from the water. Do you think you can hit it from here with your crossbow?"

"No problem," said Choppa confidently. He set the arrow and drew back the string. Pausing for a moment to read the wind, he took aim. The arrow flew toward its mark but sailed over the animal, hitting the rocks behind it. The creature jumped, startled by the noise, and looked up. Choppa hurried to restring, but it was too late. The stag turned to run for the brush but, before it could reach cover, something grabbed it and slammed it to the ground. There was a growling noise as the deer kicked against the air.

"It's there, I tell you. Whatever I saw earlier, it's there," exclaimed Gafney.

Choppa squinted to see through the shadows of the darkening twilight. This time he did see the rippling that Gafney had described, something was distorting the true appearance of things. "What do you think it is?" asked Choppa.

"Some kind of ghost that hunts deer," Gafney looked at Choppa and shrugged. Gafney reached for his broad sword. "I've heard of such creatures that can become invisible at will. They are very rare, but I've never seen one before. I guess that's the point; we aren't supposed to see them."

"Shouldn't we leave?" asked Choppa cautiously.

"It's busy eating. "Let's see if we can get a closer look at it."

"Do what?" exclaimed Choppa. "Are you crazy?"

"Some people will tell you that about me. Are you coming or staying here?" Choppa had to think about this before answering. He didn't know if he could trust Gafney well enough to follow him any further. "While you're thinking about your options, I'm going." The big man started walking in the direction where the deer had been slain. Choppa reluctantly followed with crossbow in hand. He thought if he stayed far enough behind Gafney he might have a chance to run for safety if anything went wrong. Maybe the thing would take Gafney first and he could get out of harms' way. Choppa didn't like to think of himself as a coward. He preferred to think of it as doing the wise thing by playing it safe.

The wind suddenly kicked up, causing a sudden drop in temperature as the last of the day's light was slowly fading away. It was unnaturally quiet as they approached the edge of the brush. Suddenly there came a growl and a parting of the bushes as a giant wolf leapt out at Gafney. Before he could draw his sword to make a defense against it, he was pinned to the ground beneath its massive paws.

Choppa had already turned to run in the other direction. He bounded up some boulders, almost tripping along the way.

He dropped down behind one of them for cover. Out of breath and in a panic, he realized he had lost his crossbow in all the excitement. Curiosity overcame fear; he wanted to see what was happening with Gafney. He crawled until he could get a look back. From where he was, he could see a giant silver wolf; the biggest he had ever seen in his life, was standing over Gafney, snarling with teeth bared, holding him pinned to the ground. Gafney lay frozen staring the beast in the eyes just inches from its snarling fangs.

Then a strange thing happened, the sound of music floated across the meadow. It sounded like a flute, but Choppa couldn't be sure from where he stood. The music seemed to calm the wolf. It stopped growling and slowly backed off Gafney. At first Gafney was stunned by what he saw, and then he regained his wits and reached for his sword. The music stopped and voice cried out. "Don't move." And in a flicker of time a young Elfin girl stood next to the wolf, holding a flute in her hand. "Keesha will not harm you, and Keesha will not be harmed," said the girl. She reached out and stroked the silver fur of the great wolf.

Gafney's eyes widened and his jaw dropped open. It was the first time Choppa had seen him at a loss for words. Fascinated by what he was seeing and no longer fearing the threat of danger, Choppa moved out from behind the rocks and made his way to where he could get a better look at what was happening.

After the girl called the wolf off Gafney, he slowly stood to his feet. "Is this the creature that stole our dinner right out from under us?" He sounded slightly annoyed. The girl started laughing as she crossed her arms.

"I guess there are times when the race goes to the swiftest," she responded with a hint of pride in her voice.

"What manner of creature is this that it can take on the appearance of its surroundings?" asked Gafney.

"She's a blender; her name is Keesha. I rescued her from a band of pirates."

Choppa was now standing next to Gafney where he could

see things better. The Elf girl was slight in stature like most elves and had short brown hair strung with black yarn and decorated with small wild flowers. The silver wolf stood next to her with its eyes watching suspiciously, noting every move Gafney and Choppa made.

"And what is your name?" asked Gafney.

"I am Tryska," replied the girl.

"I am Gafney and this is Choppa. We were hunting for some game when we saw your wolf drag the stag into the brush. Is there any chance we could have some of the meat?" asked Gafney, sounding uncharacteristically polite. The girl crossed her arms and wrinkled her nose as she paused before responding to the request. "I might be able to help you out," she said. "Maybe you can help me out. I am looking for someone; perhaps you have seen him."

"This is a big wilderness," said Choppa. "What chance do we have of seeing someone out here that you are looking for?"

"I have reason to believe he travels in these very mountains; his name is Bixby. Have you seen him?"

"Whoa!" exclaimed Choppa. "I don't believe it-- Bixby the swordsman! He travels with us." A look of delight crossed the Elf girl's face.

"Is he as handsome as he always was?" Gafney ruffled at the question.

"I don't know," said Choppa, "you will have to ask Gafney that one. He's known him longer than I have."

"What do you want with Bixby?" asked Gafney suspiciously.

"He goes to fight the dark magic; I intend to join him."

Gafney glanced at Choppa with a look of confusion on his face. Choppa shrugged his shoulders and Gafney responded, sarcastically, "Battling the dark ones is no small task especially for a little girl. Perhaps you are confused. This high mountain air does that to people." Tryska smiled, her eyes brightened, and then she started laughing while looking right past them.

"She is not confused." The two men jumped with a start at

the voice that came from behind them. It was Bixby. "I see you have met Tryska, a mighty Warrior of the Gap," declared Bixby with a grin on his face. The girl screeched as she ran to Bixby and embraced him. The great wolf howled and danced about before it trotted over to where the two of them were hugging each other, attempting to nuzzle its nose between them. "Keesha, you haven't changed a bit," said Bixby as he reached out to her, playfully rubbing her neck. "You still can't stand to miss out on any chance at affection."

"Keesha almost ate your friend Gafney," said Tryska with a smile on her face, glancing over at Gafney playfully. Gafney frowned.

"It's a good thing she didn't," said Bixby. "She might have taken ill." Choppa laughed and Gafney shot him a glance that silenced him instantly.

"Enough time wasted," mumbled Gafney under his breath. "I'm getting hungry and that meat is spoiling. It's time to get back to camp where we can cook some of it to fill our bellies."

CHAPTER 16

The muffled sounds of battle could be heard within the safety of the walled city. Beyond those walls Talinor's soldiers fought desperately to hold back the Boogaran horde. It would not be long before they would be pushed back into the city with the barbarians pressing at their front gates. Men stood on the ramparts watching their comrades in the fields below fighting to hold back the oncoming wave. It was like trying to sweep back the ocean with a broom. If not for the fierce fighting of the Dwarf Warriors and the skill and courage of the Tal soldiers, the line of defense would have collapsed by now.

The iron gates swung open as new troops prepared to depart to the front line. At the same time the wounded were being carried in on stretchers. Wives and children waited and watched in horror next to the gate to see if any of the wounded belonged to them. Heart wrenching wails of remorse for those that did not make it were a constant reminder that after almost twenty years of peace, war had returned to Talinor.

In the military courtyard soldiers prepared for battle by practicing their skills. The new ones had a lot to learn in a short amount of time. A heavyset commander yelled at the fresh recruits, mostly farmers and traders from the outlying provinces, pressing them to gain command of the new military skills they would so desperately need to survive. Some of the men fell under the weight of exhaustion; others nearby would pick them up just in time to save them from the commander's wrath.

Suddenly a wind swept into the courtyard as the dust on the ground swirled and howled into a raging torrent. The soldiers ceased their training and backed away from the center of the force. A dark mist fell upon the courtyard, and the soldiers scrambled like rats for cover. A sound similar to thunder emanated from the center of the swirling winds. A demonic apparition appreared dressed in black robes with skull-like features partially covered by its hood. In its skinless hand was a reaper's blade. The demon laughed with insidious glee reaching out its empty hand, pointing a skeletal finger at the cowering crowd of soldiers. The finger moved in a circular motion. A voice could be heard above the gushing of wind. "I will have you," the demon taunted. "I will have you all."

Just then there was a commotion at the corner of the courtyard. Three men stepped boldly into the square; the one in the middle held a talisman of gold and silver in the form of a staff. On the end of the staff was a ruby red globe pulsating with light. Their robes carried the emblem of a falling star.

"Now we shall see what power the Priests of Zarish have to defend us," cried one man to his friend. The Priests moved slowly toward the apparition and then stopped a hundred feet away. The one in the middle, Orom, raised the talisman and chanted some words in an unknown tongue. The orb on the end of the golden staff began to glow with a brilliant cascade of colors as jagged shafts of light shot forth out from the talisman at the demon, enveloping it in a swirl of gossamer light. It howled and screamed in terror, fighting to free itself from the invading power of the Priests, and then it was gone almost as quickly as it had appeared. Orom, the High Priest, fell to the ground, exhausted by his efforts as the other Priests rushed to minister to him.

Cheers rang out through the streets as the wind died down and the mist lifted from the courtyard. News spread quickly of the Priests' victory over the demon. The King and the citizens of Talinor, empowered with confidence, had found a champion against the dark magic.

Cyle had lost all sense of time as he walked along the stone-cut path that jutted out from the cliff. The air had grown warmer and dryer as he moved closer toward the glowing lights. He was surprisingly calm considering his situation. He found that his mind would start to wander back to Talinor and earlier days there, but he knew it was important to stay focused on what was going on around him. The bat creature might come back and he needed to be ready.

After squeezing through a stand of boulders, he found himself standing in a flat open area looking up at a rock wall that was carved in the shape of a castle. There was a large open doorway with six massive columns on each side. Just beyond in the distance, circular spires jutted into the dark sky of the cavern. A faint glow could be seen emanating from the doorway; it began to brighten until its color was a brilliant white, filling the whole doorway. Cyle had to cover his eyes because of the intensity of the brightness. The silhouette of a figure in flowing robes appeared in the doorway. Fear threatened to overwhelm the cupbearer until he heard the familiar sound of the lady's voice.

"Fear not, Cyle," said the voice. "It is I, Shariana, leader of the Guardians and servant of the Ancient of Days." An invisible force washed over Cyle, knocking him backward to the ground; his body vibrated all over as tears flooded his eyes. A great peace invaded every corner of his being, drawing him out of himself, and yet he remained still and silent. The light from the doorway slowly faded. Once again Cyle had lost all sense of time while lying on the rocky ground. When the tears faded and the emotions softened, he raised himself on trembling knees and found himself looking into the face of a beautiful angelic creature with glowing features. Her robes were purple and gold and in her right hand she held a staff. On top of the staff sat an eagle that appeared to be engulfed in flames, yet untouched by them. In her left hand she held a book.

"Rise and listen to me, Cyle," commanded the lady with words that were gentle yet firm. "I have words of great importance to speak to you." Cyle rose shakily to his feet. The staff in his hand was vibrating, and he could feel a slight tingling in his palms.

"Wh...why...am I, I...here, My Lady?" asked Cyle, stuttering on his words.

"You are here because you must know the truth of heartache," said the Lady softly. "Your heart is young and innocent; that is one reason you have been chosen for this quest. You are also naïve about some things that could hurt you, but we shall put an end to that soon." Cyle looked confused. He knew he lacked knowledge because he had grown up inside a fortress and had seen very little of the outside world. In the last few weeks he had seen enough to last him a lifetime, at least he thought he had. He wasn't sure that he wanted any more reality at this point in his life.

"What must I do?" he asked reluctantly as he gazed up at the Lady.

"You must enter the Cavern of Lost Souls."

"The cavern of what?" Cyle responded in confusion.

"It is a place where all of the souls that have been taken

captive by the dark magic are held. It is time for you to go there if you are to continue this quest."

"I don't understand."

"Exactly, it is important that you understand the full scope of your quest. If you are going to fight against the dark magic, then you must understand the depth of bondage that it brings into a life. The only way to do that is to see what lies within the Valley of Lost Souls." Cyle stumbled backwards. "Don't worry Cyle, I will be with you."

"I… I agreed to go on this quest to bring the Gap Warriors back to Talinor to fight the Shadow Wraiths and their dark magic. No one said anything about my fighting them too."

"It has been the plan from the beginning. Why do you think you have been in training with the staff?" said the Princess. "Things are rarely revealed in whole from the start. It is the way of the training of the Guardians."

"The training." Cyle's mind raced back to the training the mysterious Guardian had been giving him, teaching him the use of the staff and the maneuvers that go along with it. "You mean I was being trained to fight the Shadow Wraiths? I don't believe it. How did I miss that?"

"The path you have been on is unfamiliar to you. Your confusion is understandable."

Feeling the rich texture on the wood of the staff in his hands, he stared down at it as if it would give him the answers he was looking for. "Does this…" he hesitated for a moment. "Does this mean I am being trained to be a Gap Warrior?" He knew the answer even before it came, and he felt overwhelmed with the prospect. His whole life he had dreamed of being a warrior and finally he was getting the chance to have that dream come true. But was that what he really wanted? He thought of the night when he had seen the Shadow Wraith in the meadow. The fear of that moment was still strong within him and the shame he had felt for letting Micah down. How could he ever stand against a creature with such immense power like a Shadow Wraith? He looked blankly at the staff again, wondering what good would it do him, especially against a creature of dark magic.

"Cyle!" The Lady's voice shook him from his thoughts and brought him back to the present. "This is not the first Warrior we have trained to fight the dark magic. The weapon you have been given was especially formed and shaped for you. It will serve you well, but you must have faith and complete your training."

'Faith,' there was that word again, taunting him. It was becoming more of a threat every time he heard it. Looking down at the staff in his hands, Cyle felt a tinge of disappointment. It was just a staff with the carving of an eagle. It was nothing compared to a sword or an axe.

"The key to using your weapon will always be your faith, Cyle-- not just the faith that calls you to trust when you can find no answers, but the kind of faith that you have been raised with. This is the faith of your grandmother and your parents as well. It is faith in the Unseen One who has led you here today. You must always remember that."

Cyle knew that he had a long way to go before he had the kind of faith she was talking about. He was still nagged by the reality that his grandmother had prayed for years, and yet she was still wandering the streets alone, praying for what seemed like a lost cause.

"I know you have many questions that have yet to be answered," said the Lady as she smiled at him. Cyle's stomach churned.

"It is time," she declared in a stately manner holding up her scepter and pointing it at the rock behind her. The eagle upon it took flight and burst into flames smashing into the wall of stone until a door formed in the midst of a shower of sparks. "Enter in and see the destruction of the dark magic. Remember, my presence will be with you."

Cyle walked tentatively toward the door as it slowly opened before him. Screams of desperation and agony came from within, echoing off the cavern walls; they sounded like the wails of thousands of souls. He stopped and looked at the Princess. "It's all right. You will not be harmed."

Upon entering the room, a swirl of bright lights appeared before him and the screams grew louder. Cries of agony lifted from the floor of the valley, a jumble of twisted phrases, "Stop, no, please, no." The lights continued to intensify but finally they softened and dissipated into a dark cloud that slowly dissolved into a mist. When the mist had fallen to the floor of the cavern, Cyle was able to see more clearly. Nothing could have prepared him for what he was seeing, thousands of beings crying in agony.

An orange glow emanated from the floor of the valley reflecting off the surrounding stone walls. The beings were the sons and daughters of man. Cyle could tell by their basic appearance and the sounds of their voices. As he drew near, one of the figures looked up, reached out to him and cried, "Help me. Please, help me." His wretched body was withered down to mere skin and bones with hollow sockets where the eyes should have been. There was a black chain connected to a post in the rock floor. The chain ran from the post to his chest, where it entered through an opening and wrapped around his heart. Cyle was taken aback by the fact that he could see inside the chest area where the chain was connected by jagged prongs to a black beating heart. When the man held in bondage tried to move away from the post, the chain would grow taught and he would let out an agonizing scream of horrific pain.

Each captive stood before a great pool of water that filled the valley. Cyle noticed that most of them were chained and staring into the pool at their feet as they cried out in deep remorse. He kept hearing the word "Why?" over and over again. Their voices filled the cavern and echoed in a haunting harmony off the massive rock walls.

Something in the pool was causing them great sorrow and Cyle wanted to know what it was. Cautiously he made his way over rocks down to the edge of the water where he was able to look into the pond. He was surprised to see his own reflection, but he saw something in his appearance that he had never seen before. He was amazed to see that his mirror image appeared to have a royal aspect. He found himself in awe of the reflection. Then he heard her voice floating softly across the water, "This is the path you are destined to travel, Cyle; this is what you were created to be."

Cyle's heart raced with fear and excitement. He could never have imagined himself in this way. He appeared noble and strong, full of confidence. He studied the reflection in disbelief, but it was his reflection all right, only different from his natural earthly appearance, more powerful and mature.

A scream from nearby interrupted his thoughts. Close to where he stood was one of the captives chained to a post, staring grief-stricken into the pond. He walked over to see what the man was looking at in the water. It was the man's own reflection, and yet it looked nothing like the man who was gazing into the water. It was an image of what the haggard and pathetic man could have been. Reflected there in the crystal clear waters was the image of a noble and powerful figure staring back into the hollow eyes of a lost and tortured soul. Cyle grieved as he looked upon the image of the captive man. He knew that everything the man was meant to be had been lost to the ages, never to be realized, held captive by a chain of regrets and the haunting reality of what he could have been. The horror of living with his unfulfilled destiny minute-by-minute, day-by-day, for all time would torture him throughout eternity. The captive's words of unquenchable sorrow echoed in Cyle's mind long after he heard the man speak them, "If only it could have been different," he cried remorsefully. "If only I had followed the chosen path." Over and over again, he sobbed the words as if in a never-ending trance.

Then there was a swirl of mist and light that manifested before Cyle engulfing his vision. As the mist settled and the lights dimmed he found himself standing in the courtyard where he had first entered. The Lady Shariana stood before him looking more regal than before, her eyes sparkling like the sun. She was strikingly beautiful and yet there was an awesome power emanating from her. "Are you all right?" she asked with concern in her voice.

Cyle was still reeling from the experience. He wasn't sure how to answer the question. "I'm all right, I guess," he said tentatively.

"It was important for you to see what happens to someone who is taken captive by the dark magic. You must never forget what you saw in the Valley of Lost Souls; it is what you will fight to prevent as a Gap Warrior, freedom from the darkness and freedom to become what one is meant to be. Once a heart is captured by the power of the dark magic, it is almost impossible to bring it back to the place it was intended to be."

Cyle pondered her words deeply before asking the question that was on his heart. "What about me? I mean, could that happen to me?"

"Yes, it could happen to you. It could happen to anyone, especially a Gap Warrior." The Lady spoke in somber tones.

"But I don't understand. I thought Gap Warriors were supposed to defeat the dark magic."

"The evil that you seek to destroy will seek to destroy you. Make no mistake; it will do everything in its power to destroy you. Your weaknesses, your doubts and your fears will become a target. As a Gap Warrior you are one of the greatest threats to the Shadow Wraiths and their cause. They will do whatever they can to keep you from fulfilling your mission as a Gap Warrior."

Cyle had to think about her statement for a moment. He wasn't comfortable yet with the idea of being a Gap Warrior and Shariana's words were not making it any easier. Suddenly he was aware of the staff in his hands. Rolling it in his sweaty palms, he wondered if it was a blessing or a curse. Then he remembered Gafney. Cyle wanted to ask the Lady if the burly Gap Warrior had lost his way in the battle with evil, but for some reason he was afraid to ask the question. Maybe he didn't want to think about it, or maybe he wanted to believe that there was still a way to bring him back to the path he once followed. Either way, he realized it was important to him.

"Cyle," the Lady said softly, "the road ahead of you is a difficult one, and the quest you have been called to will not be accomplished without great sacrifice on your part, as well as the others who fight with you. The road you travel is perilous. Be careful whom you choose to trust. Just remember there is one you will always be able to trust, your Guardian." The Lady smiled. "He is there to train you and to guide you on your journey. Trust him. He will not let you down."

"Do the others have Guardians?" asked Cyle.

"Of course, and some day you will meet them." As she walked over to the young Gap Warrior and stood before him, a glow appeared around her. "Are you ready to continue on your quest?"

"Yes, My Lady." Cyle knelt before her, bowing his head. Somehow he knew it was the thing to do as he felt a deep sense of respect and awe for the princess. She opened the book in her right hand and began reading a passage from it. "Darkness stands against the light. Warriors are called to fight the fight. Let those who hear it heed the call, and life will come to one and all."

Reaching forth with scepter in hand, the Princess touched the flame to his lips, but there was no burning and there was no fear. The heat from the flame surged through his body deep into his spirit, and the staff in his hand vibrated with life. Tears filled his eyes.

"By the Ancient of Days I anoint you, Warrior of the Gap." Light filled the room so intensely that Cyle closed his eyes for just a brief moment, and when he opened them he was outside in the bright sunlight under a blue sky. In the distance he could hear the voices of his friends.

CHAPTER 17

Rain fell in torrents upon the blood-soaked battlefield; small rivers of crimson red water flowed into puddles. The sound of war cries and clashing blades filled the air all day long, finally giving way as the sun shed its last rays upon the valley. At the end of a seemingly endless day of battling, Talinor was still holding its first line of defense. There was a great loss of life for both sides that were now busy gathering their dead and wounded.

The Dwarves had held the middle of the line valiantly; on three different occasions during the day the Boogaran army had mounted a charge at the center of the Talinor defense. Each time they hammered away with their spearmen and cavalry, and each time as they were about to breach the center, the Dwarves mounted a resistance to push them back again.

"We fared better than I had hoped for," said Bernard, captain of the Dwarves.

"Thanks to the stalwart effort of your men we made a good showing today," replied Gerrid. "We're going to need reinforcements soon. We can't keep this pace up for much longer. There are still some that are coming from the surrounding villages and cities, but they are few in number. Without the Elves we are at a great disadvantage. It makes the way of victory a difficult one."

Bernard breathed in deeply and stroked his blood-soaked beard. "I have known Nephli of the Elves for many years," offered Bernard. "He is a good and brave man, but he and his people will not deny their faith to fight in a battle that does not recognize and respect their own beliefs. Perhaps we have made a mistake in denying the old faith."

"I have served my King for many years as Commander of this military. I will not deny my King and country," said Gerrid passionately. "At one time I had a strong faith in the old teachings. I went to the temples and prayed often. I'm not sure what happened," he stared thoughtfully at the twilight horizon.

"Time seems to change things. The temples have crumbled away and the prophets have died off. I guess I just changed with the times. And what of you Bernard, where is your faith?"

"My faith has not changed. It may not be as strong as it once was, but it is still alive in me. I considered resisting the decisions made by the King and his Council, but I chose to believe that joining in this campaign was the best way to protect my people. The Dwarves are a small race compared to some. Most of us are scattered throughout the mountain lands, and we depend on the commerce and the protection of Talinor. Regardless of the King's decisions, I will fight to defend Talinor. He has been good to us. My people cannot afford to allow Talinor to fall. It would mean certain destruction for the Dwarves."

"Come my friend let us rest," said Gerrid. "Tomorrow promises to be a long and difficult day. It will be here soon enough, bringing with it all of its challenges."

"She has a wolf and it's huge," said Choppa excitedly. "It has the ability to blend with its surroundings until it disappears. I've never seen anything like it before." Choppa continued telling Cyle the story about how they had met Tryska and the giant wolf. He was surprised to hear that she was a Gap Warrior. When he first saw her he didn't think she looked like a Warrior. She was just a skinny Elf girl with a flute. Now the wolf, that was something else. It was the biggest creature of its kind he had ever seen.

When they met, she had introduced herself to Cyle first. "Hi, my name is Tryska; I'm a Gap Warrior." That unnerved Cyle. He was still getting used to being a Gap Warrior, and she seemed quite confident of her status. Bixby seemed genuinely pleased to have her along.

"A girl with a flute," said Cyle to Choppa with a note of sarcasm in his voice. "What kind of Warrior is that?"

"Don't ask me, you're the Gap Warrior. Don't you know about these things?"

"I guess I shouldn't be so negative. I am coming to realize

that things are not always as they seem."

The journey back to Talinor had begun once again. Their small party had grown by two more, one wolf and an Elf girl. Folger had gone ahead with Tryska and Bixby to scout out the safest way to descend the mountain.

Cyle had spoken little about his experience in the caverns, feeling it would be difficult to explain to his friend. Besides he was still sorting out what had happened to him there. He knew he would never forget the Valley of Lost Souls. The image he had seen of himself in the waters of the lake had left a powerful impression on him, and he was fearful of his own ability to live up to that image. His former imaginings of what it meant to be a man were very different from what he saw in the lake. His past self-images were filled with fantasies that served his own personal pride; however, the image in the lake was humble, yet powerful, and full of purpose beyond self.

The thoughts kept running over and over through Cyle's mind— I'm a Gap Warrior. I can't believe it. I'm a Gap Warrior. They only intensified one of his greatest fears, which had become a reality. Someday he may have to battle a Shadow Wraith face-to-face. The thought was still overwhelming. No matter how hard he tried, he couldn't seem to shake the horror of the memory of seeing one of the evil beings kill Cree that night in the meadow.

Once again the young Gap Warrior nervously studied the staff in his hands. Why was I given a stick? he thought resentfully. A sword or an axe seemed more fitting to him, not that it would ease his fear all that much. What kind of warrior fights with a stick? He recalled the Lady's words when she said, "Your faith is the key to your weapon." Thinking about it frustrated him even more. What was this mysterious force called 'faith'? It all seemed so difficult to grasp and he was reminded once again how little credence he had given to the faith he had been raised with.

"What do you mean the southern lands have the best wine?" Ginzer bellowed at Gafney, as his words erupted into Cyle's thoughts. "Everyone knows that the best wines come from the coastal valleys east of the Kernland River."

"Hog droppings," exclaimed Gafney, "I've tasted better swamp water in the bogs of Cavalera."

Ginzer looked at him through his one good eye. "It doesn't surprise me that you prefer the southern wines. Anyone who drinks swamp water is bound to ruin his tasting sensitivities as well as his mental capacities."

Gafney bristled at the comment. Bixby appeared at the rise, signaling for them to quietly come to him.

"Trackers are coming and they're armed for battle," whispered the swordsman.

"What now?" asked Ginzer.

"I say we take 'em now," said Gafney as he grabbed the hilt of his broad sword, muscles rippling on his massive arms. "No sense in playing cat and mouse with them from here to Talinor."

"It's too risky at this point," said Bixby. "There could be others in the area that we don't know about."

"How many are there in this group?" asked Cyle.

"Six, maybe more, I can't tell for sure. They don't look like military. They look like hired mercenaries."

"Is that it?" Gafney shot Bixby a suspicious glance as he pressed him.

"There were at least two trolls in the party," Bixby paused and then continued, "and a warlock high priest leads them."

"Well, that's going to make it a little difficult to avoid them now, isn't it?" Gafney hissed the words under his breath and appeared visibly anxious as he drummed his fingers on the hilt of his sword. Gafney knew that warlocks had certain powers available to them that enhanced their ability to track. "You know as well as I do that that warlock can find us."

"Tryska and her wolf will take care of that. She should be able to give us enough time to reach the base of the mountains. Then we can get some horses and make good time to Talinor, unless you want to stay and fight that warlock," said Bixby teasing Gafney. What Bixby knew was that Gafney wanted nothing to do with the warlock and his powers. He had resigned himself from that kind of business a long time ago.

"You have already made your plan," answered Gafney. "If we are going to do it, then let's get on with it."

"Come on then, Folger is waiting for us," said Bixby as he motioned the way for the others. Without question they moved to follow close behind the Gap Warrior.

Two hours later they had reached the bottom of the cliffs and then they made their way into the forest. It would be dark soon and they had seen no sign of their pursuers. They came to the edge of a small lake and stopped to replenish their water.

"Hold steady," Gafney's voice was quick and urgent. The small company of warriors froze at the edge of the lake to listen to the forest around them. "It's too quiet. Something's wrong."

"Frogs... I can't hear any frogs or crickets," whispered Choppa. "What does it mean?"

"Trouble." Gafney had barely spoken the word when a rush of wind blew across the lake and through the surrounding trees. It died down for just a minute and then picked up again and started to swirl in a circular motion over the lake. Cyle's hands started to vibrate along with the staff that he was holding in his hands.

Bixby's command could barely be heard above the sound of the wind. "To arms. Everyone to arms." Each one immediately drew their weapons. Ginzer pulled his axe and the elves drew their bows. Choppa fumbled for his crossbow as it clattered to the ground. Cyle looked at his staff as he felt a power stirring within its dephs.

They all saw it at the same time. At the edge of the trees stood a tall dark figure dressed in black robes that flapped wildly in the wind. The metal band he was wearing about his head sparkled. The silver wolf bore her teeth as her fur shimmered with light. She moved next to the elf girl as if to protect her. Gafney was the first to say the word and when he did there was a slight tremble of fear in his voice, "Warlock."

In his hand he held a talisman of metal, the conduit for the power he was wielding. The warlock raised it high above his head and chanted an incantation that was indiscernible. The wind began to blow with a greater vengeance as the water in the lake erupted in a spraying mist that showered outward onto the land. Beneath the surface of its dark and churning waters something evil stirred. Breaking free from the depths, it screamed and hissed in a fevered pitch, piercing the night. A gnarled mass of clawed tentacles lashed out at them.

"Spread out!" someone yelled above the deafening noise. Arrows flew into the beast; it screamed in rage. One of its tentacles shot forth, snake-like, wrapping around Folger's waist, dragging him toward the lake. Ginzer and Bixby ran to free him. Before they could reach Folger another tentacle encircled Ginzer's leg and started dragging the old Dwarf into the lake. Choppa and Brok shot arrows into the arm that was holding Folger, but it wasn't enough. The creature held tight to the squirming Folger who was stabbing at the limb with his knife. Gafney and Bixby both reached Ginzer at the same time. Bixby's sword flared along the hilt until it reached a brilliant white color that covered the whole blade. Both of the men hacked at the limb that clung to Ginzer's leg until finally their blades severed its grip.

Another tentacle lanced toward Bixby, but he and his sword were too fast, slicing through it in midair. Sparks flew from the flaming blade as it entered the creature's hide. Tentacles continued to lash out in every direction, groping, searching, until one of them was able to find Bixby and latch onto him, causing him to drop his sword. Cyle had been standing there in a daze through the whole thing until he saw Bixby's sword hit the ground. Courage surged forth from deep within, wresting him out of his state of shock. He would not let another comrade fall. Sparks danced along the staff in his grip. As it came to life, shards of light traveled from his hands to both ends of the shaft. Cyle ran toward Bixby, all the while spinning the staff above his head, and as he closed ground, he swung it in a wide arc. Then he gripped it with both hands, and it exploded when it collided with the creature's hide. Bixby was free and moving to regain his sword. Ginzer and Gafney had freed Folger while the others sent another barrage of arrows into the monster's midsection.

"Back away from the water," cried Gafney. Brok and Nelf grabbed Folger to assist him in his weakened state.

"It grows!" yelled Choppa as he pointed at the monster. The creature was changing shape and growing larger. The tentacles withdrew into the body as the creature morphed into a giant bear-like form. It walked out of the water toward the warriors, growling and clawing at the air.

The company of warriors backed away from the beast as it lumbered toward them. They were tired from the battle and almost completely spent. Bixby yelled at Gafney. "We need a plan. Any ideas?"

"I say we draw it to the edge of the bluff back there and try to knock it over the side," yelled Gafney.

Bixby looked behind them toward the bluff. There was no sign of the warlock. "Let's do it." Bixby nodded at Gafney.

With the monster closing in on them, the warriors turned and ran toward the bluff. Suddenly two trolls burst into the opening between them and the bluff where they wanted to go. Gafney muttered under his breath, "Trolls, I hate trolls." He and Ginzer were on them in an instant, charging, broadsword and axe striking out against them. Behind the trolls appeared six to eight mercenaries armed with swords and bows.

Arrows flew in both directions as they found themselves lodged between the monster and their attackers. "Hold them here," one of the mercenaries yelled an order to his men. "Let the creature have them."

Sensing the desperation of their plight, Bixby ran to attack the mercenaries in the hope of clearing a way through. The fire in his sword faded to cold metal as it met the sword of the first mercenary. Their blades clashed twice before Bixby's speed put him down. Spinning around, he turned to take on two more who were bearing down on him. Cyle was heading to assist him when the creature moved between him and the others. He heard Choppa yell as he let fly an arrow from his crossbow. It cut through the air and lodged in the thing's shoulder. The creature hardly noticed it. Cyle instinctively knew it was after him as he sensed some combination of primal blood lust and dark magic driving it toward him. Each time he moved to escape it would intersect to cut him off from the others. The staff in his hand continued to surge with power, but he knew that the staff alone would not be enough to take down this monster. Choppa appeared again with his crossbow discarded and blade in hand. The monster surprised them both as it turned toward Choppa and in a violent rage lunged at him. Choppa would not survive this attack, and Cyle desperately realized he was too far away to help him. Choppa back stepped to avoid the claws lashing at him and tripped backward, just avoiding the death strike that caught air within inches of his head. Seeing that the situation was slipping away from him, Cyle ran recklessly toward Choppa to try to save him, fearing that he would not make it to him in time.

The giant monster gathered itself for its final assault. Then something unexpected happened; the sound of flute music filled the air. Cyle spun around just in time to see a giant silver wolf bounding in the direction of the creature. As its howl rent the air, its feet left the ground and it slammed into the monster, driving it backward and freeing Choppa from its deadly intent. The wolf would not survive against the power and size of the beast, and Cyle knew it. Pointing his staff at its midsection, it flared to life and sparked with power. He ran toward the monster driving the staff deep into the creature as fire and light erupted. The beast screamed in pain and its massive paw struck out at the giant wolf and sent it flying through the air.

Then something happened that Cyle wasn't prepared for. The Elf girl appeared in front of the creature from out of nowhere. It towered over her, dwarfing her in size. She turned to Cyle and yelled above the screams and cries of battle, "Again. Drive the staff again." Lifting the flute to her mouth she began to play. As the music filled the air, Cyle felt a new surge of power flow through him and his staff. He obeyed her command without hesitation, and with all his might he drove the staff into the beast, and when he did, it exploded in a shower of sparks and light. An unbearable stench filled the air as the creature fell back and disappeared over the cliff, its screams and howls fading as it fell into darkness.

The air around them grew quiet once again and the wolf trotted over to lick the Elf girl on the face as she embraced it around the neck. Choppa stumbled to his feet as Bixby and the others rushed back to meet them. "They have retreated," cried Bixby. "We need to keep moving and find a place to hide so we can tend to injuries."

They made their way into the forest traveling at a steady pace for about an hour before Folger led them to an old hunter's cabin that was well covered by vines and branches, making it difficult to see among the trees.

Choppa and Brok stood guard outside while the others went into the hut. Ginzer tended to Folger's bruised ribs. Each one of them had their share of cuts and bruises, but they would heal. After settling into the cabin, Gafney pulled supplies from the bags, offering food to everyone.

Cyle reflected back on the battle they had just fought. Gafney and Bixby had fought together well, in spite of the obvious tension between them…Bixby with great skill and unmatched speed; Gafney with the savage rage of a barbarian. If they had not done so, the small company would have fallen. Even the Elf girl and her wolf had been there, fighting right along side them. Cyle wondered what power the flute possessed that enabled his staff to explode with such great force and finally destroy the creature.

"They know we're coming," said Bixby thoughtfully. "They've sent a warlock to stop us."

"Horses would help," said Ginzer. "Not that I particularly enjoy riding them, but it would help us cover more ground."

Gafney stood to his feet and declared gruffly. "I'm no

horseman. I'd rather ride a hog as to ride on a horse's back."

"You don't have to worry about that just yet," offered the usually quiet Brok. "We don't have any."

"There's a small farming village just west of here. We can buy horses there," said Folger, "I can take Brok with me and the rest of you can stay here until we get back."

"I'm going with you," demanded Gafney.

"Whatever suits you," responded Folger. "We should be back by morning if all goes well." Both Bixby and Ginzer nodded their approval.

As they exited the door, Choppa made a request, "Bring back something good to eat." Cyle smiled to himself. His chubby friend was losing weight on this quest and he seemed determined to slow the process as much as possible. He had also done well during the fight with the lake monster and Cyle had told him so.

The cabin was a little crowded, but it provided the warmth and cover that they needed. Tryska and the wolf took the first watch while the others had an evening meal of stale bread and jerky.

That night, before they went to sleep, they talked about the battle. "That was a first for me. I have never seen a warlock before or a monster created by the dark magic," said Choppa.

"He was sent by one of the Wraith lords, Gizshra, to test us." said Bixby.

"What do you mean he was testing us?" asked Cyle.

"He wanted to see how we would fare against the monster. It was Gizshra that called it up from the void."

"I hope we passed; I don't want any more tests." offered Choppa.

"We did the very thing that it hoped we would not do," Bixby paused.

"We killed it," exclaimed Choppa with the sound of pride swelling in his voice.

"Yes, we killed it, but we did something far more threatening to them than that. We fought as one. Now it knows that we are dangerous. The next time they will try to tear us apart before they try to kill us."

That night when Cyle slept, his Guardian visited him in his dreams. "Never forget tonight," admonished the Guardian. "Some battles are meant to be fought alone and others can only be won when Warriors of the Gap fight together. You will learn to know the difference between the two."

"But how?" asked Cyle with frustration rising in his voice. "I didn't think we were going to make it back there."

"You made it because you fought together as one," said Melidar in his familiar stoic tone. "There will be times when the demons will try to separate you from the others; beware of their strategy to do so. Together you have greater power and combined wisdom. Alone you can be more easily deceived and the power of your weapons is diminished. Shadow Wraiths are masters of deception. If you are not careful they will lead you into believing things that will open you to fear and doubt. Not all of your battles will be fought with a staff; some will be fought with your mind. Your ability to see truth is one of your greatest weapons-- truth to see yourself as you are and your enemies as they are. Rest now," commanded Melidar, as he faded from sight.

CHAPTER 18

Gafney and the others returned early the next morning with the horses. It was decided that Tryska and Bixby would share a mount, while the others rode alone. The horses were of average quality and a little underfed, but they would do. Gafney's was an older sway back mare. He said that he had picked it out especially for himself. Ginzer told him it was the closest thing to a pig he could find.

The travelers rode for four days toward Talinor without any trouble. On one occasion they encountered some of the Boogaran troops, but were able to elude them quickly without being spotted. On the fourth day, with less than a days ride to Talinor, they encountered a gray mist that fell upon them without warning and with it a sense of hopelessness.

"What is it?" asked Cyle, as the horses grew restless with the sudden change.

"The power of the dark magic grows in the land of Talinor," offered Bixby. "It decays the air and the land around us." Just then something moved in the shadows and Ginzer's horse reared.

"Easy," Brock grabbed the reigns on the old Dwarf's horse as he tried to steady the animal. Gafney looked about anxiously.

"It's the Scav's," said Bixby. "They're back, looking for any opportunity that might present itself. From here on we move with great caution and keep together. I'll take the lead." Bixby drew his sword to hold it ready.

"I'll take the backside," volunteered Gafney. "It will be a good place for this old mare. She can barely keep up as it is.

The mist grew thicker about them as they pressed forward, making it more difficult to navigate. The presence of evil intensified as the magic in the mist drained the life out of every living thing around it, including the travelers. A feeling of dread wrapped itself around their hearts, clawing and tearing at their spirits. Cyle was tormented by doubt for he knew that the challenges that lay ahead were bordering on impossible.

Bixby wrestled with his own thoughts. He could not be sure that the people of Talinor would even want the help of the Gap Warriors once they arrived in the city. They were planning to defend a kingdom from the very evil it had foolishly embraced and by embracing that evil, Talinor had given it greater power to destroy the Gap Warriors. Bixby would move on to Talinor regardless of the circumstances. He had learned a long time ago not to put too much weight on the appearance of things. There was never a guarantee of victory in these matters. He comforted himself with the fact that there was still at least one person in Talinor that held strongly to her faith in the Ancient of Days. Cyle had told him of his grandmother and how she would walk the streets at night and intercede for the kingdom. Bixby put great hope in the old lady and the work that she was doing there to prepare the way for the Gap Warriors. He wished there were more than one interceding in Talinor, but for now, one would have to do.

None of the small band of warriors would admit it, but each one of them was fighting their own personal battle of fear and doubt, especially Gafney. The memory of the battle that he had lost the day he failed to save the life of his love taunted him from the corners of his mind. When they had first met she had given his life new meaning. Her love had changed him and made him a better man. He had always been clear on what he wanted in life, but when he met her he was no longer sure. Like velvet and steel her love gripped his heart causing him to mellow some and feel more at peace with the world around him.

At first it was hard for him to get close to her. His stubbornness and hard exterior pushed her away. Until one day she approached him directly. "I know you are drawn to me," she said sweetly with a smile upon her lips. "Why do you try so hard to keep me at a distance?"

Her words had stunned him and left him speechless. When he finally found the words to speak, he took her hand in his and said, "Forgive me my lady. Sometimes it takes the heart a little longer to catch up with the foolish mind of a prideful warrior."

It was the first time he had been honest with her. She had a way of drawing his emotions out into the open and then gently accepting them with her warm embrace. He believed that she truly loved him for who he was and that he didn't have to pretend when he was with her.

The day she died he made a vow to himself that he would never love again. Not long after that he walked away from every thing that he once stood for as a Gap Warrior. He had spent so much of himself fighting for others and countless lives were spared because of his courage and skill. Why could he not save the one he loved the most? The more he thought about it the more he wanted to turn away from this current quest that he was on. Why was he here anyway? What could he possibly accomplish? The doubts kept coming. He knew Bixby was right. The closer they came to Talinor the greater the supernatural danger would be and he was not equipped to face that.

It had been years since he had seen his guardian or, for that matter, since he had used his chosen weapon. For a brief moment he thought of how it use be, how it felt when he would pull his saber axe from its holster. He remembered the power that coursed through his body when he would grip it. The axe would spark to life when he did battle against the dark magic. At the top end it had a doubled edged blade, similar to a traditional battle-axe, only it was a fine polished metal that shined brilliantly. At the bottom of the handle there was a smaller double-edged blade that was longer and more streamlined. Perfectly balanced in weight, it was an awesome weapon. A smile crossed his lips as he remembered some of the battles he had fought. But those good feelings were quickly interrupted with the memory of the loss of his love.

He missed being a Gap Warrior, but his anger at himself, at life, and at his God would not allow him to go back to the path of his calling. Like a cancer, his bitterness grew inside of him with each passing day, standing like an impenetrable barrier between himself and his revealed destiny as a Warrior of the Gap. The questions continued to haunt him. Why are you here? What can you possibly hope to accomplish? How can you help now that you have lost your anointing to fight in the gap? For the first time Gafney began to think about leaving the group.

The sounds of battle could be heard in the distance ahead of them. Cyle's stomach churned as the reality of how close they were to Talinor could not be denied. From the sound of things, the battle was still being fought on the valley floor and had not yet moved to the city walls. That meant that they would need to find a way to penetrate the Boogaran lines and then make their way to the city gates. Beyond that point there was no plan. They would offer their services as Gap Warriors in the hope that the people of Talinor could accept them. Whatever the outcome, Ginzer and his men would fight for Talinor and Gafney would probably do the same.

Bixby, Tryska, and Cyle had come for one single purpose, to fight the dark magic. Now that Cyle had accepted his call as a Gap Warrior things had changed dramatically. Instead of just leading the gap warriors to Talinor, he had become one himself. Until now he hadn't been too concerned about the details involved in fighting the dark magic. For the most part he didn't want to think about it. Now that they were on the doorstep of facing the demons he had to think about it.

Cyle was still unclear on exactly what a gap battle would look like. His guardian had explained things to him the best that he could. One day when they had finished a training session, Cyle had asked him to explain what happens in a battle against the dark magic. The Guardian Melidar had told him, "The Gap Warriors will do battle with the Shadow Wraiths and that means facing whatever form of dark magic the demons choose to wield against us. Most of that battle will happen in a place called the void, where a gap exists separating the worlds of flesh and spirit. It is the void that forms a barrier between the two worlds and for the most part prevents the two worlds from becoming one. As long as evil is resisted and held in check on this side of the void the Shadow Wraiths are limited in their power and influence. If the gap between the two worlds should ever be completely breached, the world of men would cease to exist, as we know it. The Shadow Wraiths would eventually gain dominion over this world and its inhabitants.

Even now as evil is gaining a foothold on this side of the

void the gap between the two worlds grows weaker allowing some lesser demons to cross through. The beast that you fought at the lake had crossed over through the void with the help of the warlock. If evil continues to increase, the breach in the void will open completely and there will be nothing to hold back the other demons from crossing over."

Melidar continued his explanation. "Remember that the dark magic grows in power as it subverts those over to its ways. If left unchallenged, anyone can be completely taken by its power." Remember what I said," the guardian warned, "when the evil on your side of the void increases its hold in the life of a person, especially a king or a ruler, the gap between the two worlds will grow weaker. Their greatest drive is to conquer your world so that they can inhabit it and control it."

"Why don't the Guardians do battle with the Shadow Wraiths instead of the Gap Warriors," asked Cyle.

"That is a very good question, Cyle. I was wondering when you would ask that," said the Guardian with a smile crossing his face. "Guardians are involved in the battle against the dark magic, although most of it is unseen to you. The main reason that we exist is to fight and defend the people of this land against the demons of the dark magic. We cannot do that with out the help of the Gap Warriors and Intercessors. Our powers and abilities are limited when we enter your world. The power that you are given through your weapons and the calling that is on your life allows you to fight against the darkness and enforce the rule of the Ancient of Days here in the world of flesh and blood. Because of that reality it has always been that Gap Warriors are trained to fight both in the void and in your world. Each one of us does our part. Gap Warriors, Guardians and Intercessors—we all play a part in the battle to defend the breach."

Cyle was amazed at what he was hearing. Once again his perceptions of the world he lived in were changing. There would be more than one battle going on at Talinor. The battle between two countries and the battle between two supernatural powers would be fought on different levels. He was finally seeing the picture more clearly. Until now he did not realized how important his grandmother's prayers were.

The more he thought about what was happening around him, the better he was able to understand things. Both Shadow Wraiths and Guardians are supernatural beings that exist outside of the realm of the physical. Even though they are able to take on a physical form, they can only maintain that form for a short period of time, unless they are able to gain complete dominion over a kingdom or a person. When that happens, they acquire the power they need to exist on this side of the void and maintain their physical form without losing the full force of the dark magic. What happened at Easthold was a glimpse of what could happen at Talinor."

Melidar continued, "So there you have it. If Talinor is conquered at the hands of the Boogarans, it will give the Shadow Wraiths a strategic stronghold that will enable them to move on and conquer all of the lands of men. That is why they must twist and subvert anyone or anything they can to serve them. It assures them the power they need to conquer and rule in the world of flesh and blood."

"The Boogarans lust to conquer and control is really born of the dark magic. There was a time long ago when Boogara was a nation very much like Talinor. Over time the Shadow Wraiths found ways to twist their magic into the hearts of those they desired to use for their own purposes. While promising power and control to the Boogarans, they are in reality exercising power and control over them. The Shadow Wraiths cannot succeed without the help of living creatures from this side of the void."

The mist that hung over the Valley of Talinor served as a constant reminder of the presence of evil. The small band of nine made there way along the edge of the marsh moving ever closer to the battle grounds. It was Gafney who had suggested that they try to break through near the end of the enemy's flank. Once it grew darker and the Boogaran warriors were bedding down for the night, they would make a run for it. If they were lucky they would make it through without facing a conflict.

The sounds of battle slowly died away as evening shadows melted over the forest floor until the mist that had clung to their clothes and their spirits began to dissipate into a crisp and cold night air. Rarely a word was spoken unless necessary and then, barely above a whisper.

Cyle noticed that everyone was on edge with the exception of the elf girl. She seemed to be taking it all in stride. The great wolf was nowhere to be seen. Tryska claimed it was looking for a way for us to pass through. She talked as if she could communicate with the wolf at will. As far as Cyle could tell, she could. The elf girl said little about her relationship with the creature, but he was sure she could communicate with the wolf through her flute. She seemed shy at times and then there were moments when she appeared to be in control and sure of her self, like the time they fought the lake monster. However, when he tried to talk to her, she kept her distance and avoided eye contact. She struggled to find the words to respond to his questions. Choppa had tried to warm up to her, but she found ways to avoid conversation with him. The only ones she was comfortable with were Bixby and the wolf.

Leaving the horses behind, they moved quietly along the edge of the marsh waters under the cover of the forest. Cyle caught his first glimpse of Talinor since he had left weeks before. The torches burned brightly upon the ramparts casting a faint glow on her towers that rose majestically into the night sky. He wondered how his grandmother was faring. Then his heart dropped as he caught sight of the banners that flew near the tower gates. The emblems on them were indiscernible from where he was, but he did not have to see them to know what the design was. He knew they carried the likeness of a shooting star, courtesy of the priests of Zarish.

"Hold here," Bixby whispered. There was a ripple of wind and out of the darkness the great wolf appeared, loping smoothly and soundlessly through the forest undergrowth. Tryska moved to her and gently stroked her fur. She appeared small and insignificant next to the giant creature.

"Keesha girl," she said affectionately as she wrapped her arms around the wolf's neck. "What do you have for me girl?" purred Tryska. Then the wolf turned and trotted away. Tryska motioned to follow her as she turned to pursue her giant friend.

Cyle wasn't sure how he felt about placing his safety in the hands of an animal. He looked at Choppa questioningly and he just shrugged and followed behind the rest of them. Minutes later the wolf came to a halt near the edge of the Boogaran camp where the troops had thinned out considerably near the edge of the trees. Tryska hugged it one more time and then it turned and slowly disappeared into the forest mist.

"This is it. This is where we make a run for it," said Tryska softly. Cyle's heart jumped as her words registered the gravity of the situation.

"Most of them are asleep, except for the sentries," said Bixby, then he nodded to Brok, Folger, and Nelf. They pulled out their bows and each of them nocked an arrow. Choppa followed their lead. "Cyle, wrap this around your head," Bixby handed him a long piece of cloth, "I don't want anyone to recognize you and haul you off to the dungeons when we get to the gates." Cyle took the piece of fabric and wound it around his head in the fashion of a shepherd boy, allowing part of it to hang around his eyes and his neck. He wondered if he was still a wanted man. It was best not to take any chances since they would be encountering soldiers soon.

"I'll take backside," said Gafney firmly. No one argued.

"We will need to move slowly for as far as we can," cautioned Bixby. "If the sentries see us and sound the alert before we can take them out with our arrows, then our first move is to run for the Talinor battle lines. Don't stop to fight unless it is absolutely necessary."

"How will our own know who we are once we reach

them?" asked Choppa.

"They won't," offered Bixby. "That's why we will need to yell, 'for Talinor' as loud as we can when we approach them."

"That's it? That's your plan?" growled Gafney under his breath. "You mean that's the best you can come up with?"

"If you've got a better idea, now is the time to put it out there." Gafney didn't respond at first. A wall of silence stood between. "Of course, no one's saying you have to go through with this. You're free to do as you please."

"Thanks for the reminder," grumbled Gafney. "Let's get on with it before I do change my mind." Bixby motioned Gafney over to him so they could speak in private.

"If your plan is to leave us, then do it now," warned Bixby under his breath. "I don't want to get into the middle of this and then suddenly find that you're not around to cover our rear." The words stung the big man's pride as he bristled against their bite.

"Have I ever let you down before?"

"Do you want me to answer that question?" asked Bixby, staring at him through the moonlight.

"What's that suppose to mean?"

"You're unpredictable, Gaf." Bixby hadn't called him that in a long time. "You're not the same man I used to know. You've lost your edge and besides, I can tell you've been thinking about leaving us."

"What do you mean I've lost my edge?" spat Gafney. "I held my own back there at the lake with that monster. What more do you want?"

"We're about to cross the line here Gaf. You know as well as I do that the evil that we have to face from this point on is ever increasing in power. Do you really think you are prepared to face that?" Gafney looked at the ground, his head hung in silence. Bixby waited uncomfortably for an answer. "Haven't you been running long enough? At some point you've got to move on."

Gafney grabbed Bixby forcefully by his leather tunic and pulled him close. "You don't know what I've been through. You don't know, so stay out of it." Rage filled the big man's eyes.

"It's too late for that," Bixby countered back at him with an equal amount of passion. "We are all here for a reason, including you. You were in my dream, you are supposed to stand with us and fight with us in the gap. Are you going to tell me you didn't have the same dream I did?"

Gafney let go of Bixby and sat back with shoulders slumped. "I haven't had a dream in years," he said with a touch of sadness in his voice. "And I haven't seen or heard from my Guardian in just as long. My time is past and you know it. It's too late for me now," said Gafney despondently.

Bixby did not respond. He didn't know what to say. Getting through to his old friend seemed like a lost cause. Once he was set in his way there was no changing his mind. He had always been as stubborn as a mountain troll.

The big man looked up at him through intense eyes and spoke softly, "I will get you to the Tal battle lines. It's the least I can do."

"Alright then," Bixby agreed, "have it your way. You take up the rear." The swordsman reached out his hand to his friend and Gafney received it. "Be careful back there Gaf."

Fires burned low and snoring could be heard throughout the camp. The nine of them moved slowly, crawling at first and then crouching. The bowmen stood ready to strike at the first sign of trouble. In the distance they could see the Tal troops and their fires burning and beyond that the citadel of Talinor.

At first the going was slow and tedious- better to move slowly than swiftly and get caught. Most of the sentries were watching in the direction of the enemy's camp, with their backs turned away from the nine figures crawling at the edge of the camp. They were almost ready to break free from the camp when one man sleeping near them sneezed. One of the sentries looked over in their direction where they lay still on the ground. He peered through the darkness as if he had seen something. After looking the area over he started to move toward them. Brok lay on his side with an arrow aimed right at the man's head. Then the guard saw him lying on the ground. For one brief moment their eyes locked on each other as terror registered on the guard's face. Brok let go the shaft, parting the air before it until it found its mark. As it entered the man's neck he managed a muffled scream that was just loud enough to alert the others.

One of the guards yelled, "Enemies among us," but those were his last words as an arrow lodged in his chest. Grabbing at it, he fell to the ground. "Time to move," Gafney's voice came from behind them.

Boogaran soldiers all around them were waking from their slumber. Confusion filled the air as more arrows flew. The small band of warriors was up and running toward the Talinor lines. They had surprise and the darkness on their side. One warrior stepped out in their path, half dressed and disoriented. Bixby raised his sword to cut him down but an arrow found him first. Another one came from the side wielding a sword. Cyle instinctively blocked it with his staff, and to his surprise it did not splinter. He held and blocked two more blows before Gafney slammed into the attacker and pummeled him with the butt of his sword. The man crumbled to the ground. "Run. Run for the Tal lines and don't look back," urged Gafney as he shoved Cyle in that direction. Men were up now looking for their weapons as shouting and cursing filled the air.

Bixby led them down into a ravine where the terrain would give them better cover. Behind them they could hear their enemies close in pursuit. Crossing the ravine, Bixby held his ground as he motioned the others past him up and the other side. When Gafney reached him he grabbed Bixby's arm. Out of breath and barely able to speak, he coughed out the words, "This is it. I'll stay here and hold them off while the rest of you make your way."

"No, we're okay," exhorted Bixby. "You come with us; we can all make it together."

"It's too late," said Gafney, as he turned pulling away from

Bixby's grip. He ran toward two oncoming warriors with his sword drawn; his blade slashing into them taking both of them down with fluid strokes. Bixby watched in horror as a flood of Boogaran warriors spilled over into the ravine. He knew he had no choice but to leave his friend. Gafney had made his choice and there was nothing he could do about it now. Bixby turned and disappeared over the hill.

As the small band drew closer to the Talinor camp, shouts of warning filled the air. "Who goes there?" shouted the guards as the company approached.

"We are for Talinor," cried Bixby as they ran into the midst of the camp.

CHAPTER 19

The Boogaran warriors had called off their pursuit, thanks to Gafney's efforts. A small group of Dwarves and Tal warriors came out to meet them with weapons drawn. "Name yourselves," one of them demanded.

"I am Bixby, and these are my men; we have come to stand with Talinor."

"How do we know you are not spies?" asked a burly Dwarf as he stepped out from the crowd. Cyle recognized him at once.

"Because, Captain Bernard," responded Ginzer in a course tone, "I have found little success when it comes to fighting against kinfolk." Bernard took a step forward to get a closer look at the one-eyed dwarf.

"Is that you, Cousin Ginzer?" Bernard asked suspiciously.

"It is I, Cousin Bernard; I have come to protect you from the Boogarans."

Bernard laughed as he approached Ginzer and hugged his

neck. Patting him on the back he said, "The last time I saw you, you had two eyes and you were a little taller."

The two men continued to exchange greetings, while Cyle noticed that Gafney was nowhere to be seen. He moved next to Bixby and whispered, "Where is Gafney? I don't see him."

Bixby hesitated before answering, not quite sure how he should put it. "He stayed behind to give us a chance. I don't think he made it," said Bixby sadly. Cyle's heart fell as feelings of despair flooded over him.

"How could this happen?" Cyle asked with a look of confusion on his face.

"I think he was looking for a way out," said Bixby, "and I think he found it."

Cyle knew Gafney's commitment was questionable, but he was sure that the burly warrior would have come around eventually. He looked back in the direction of the Boogaran camp as angst filled his heart. Somehow he felt less protected with the absence of the former Gap Warrior.

The next morning when the sun rose over the hills of Talinor, the outline of its towers was barely discernable through the mist that continued to shroud the land. Most of the warriors were positioned for the next attack while Bixby and Ginzer met with Gerrid and Bernard in the war tent to discuss the status of the troops and to see how they had fared so far. Cyle, Choppa and the others stayed outside and ate breakfast cakes and salted pork that had been prepared by the camp chef. The cakes reminded him of the ones his grandmother used to make for him, only not quite as sweet.

"There're only three of us now," Cyle said to Tryska, referring to the number of Gap Warriors. It was the first time he had spoken to her since early the day before. "How do you think we will do in battle with just the three of us?"

"I'm not sure; I've never fought a Gap war with just three Warriors before," the Elf girl seemed nervous and distant with her answer. "Besides, there should be another one here in

Talinor to join us."

"Here in Talinor!" said Cyle sarcastically. He had forgotten that his Guardian had told him that another Gap Warrior would meet them in Talinor. "I know what the Guardian said, but believe me, there are no Gap Warriors in Talinor, unless one has joined the effort recently."

"Have you no faith?" asked Tryska in an irritated tone.

"Well, I...uh,"

"That's what I thought." The Elf girl stood to her feet. "I know this is difficult for you, Cyle, this being your first time and all, but you have to remember that the battle we will fight is going to be fought on more than one level. We will only see a part of it; the Guardians will be doing their part, and the Intercessors will do theirs."

Cyle was taken back at her mention of Intercessors. He thought of his grandmother, the lone Intercessor. How could her prayers possibly help them now?

"There is only one Intercessor," said Cyle softly.

"What?" she snapped back at him. "There's only one Intercessor in all of Talinor?"

"Yes, it's my grandmother."

"Only one," said the Elf girl as she turned away with a look of dread.

"What...what is it?" Cyle pressed.

She looked at him, her eyes penetrating, "One is not enough; we will definitely need more than one." In a flurry of frustration she turned and walked away, leaving Cyle bewildered with her response.

Why was she so hard to talk to? He thought about their conversation and found himself swimming in a new pool of confusion and fear. Shadow Wraiths, dark magic and evil powers-- he wished he had never heard of them. Up until now his life had been a simple one. He had been taught most of his life that there were other world forces at work in this world, and yet, he had never really had to deal with them face to face. He wondered how things could have changed so quickly for him. One day he was living out his life behind the safety of Talinor's walls, now he was encountering those supernatural powers he had heard about at every turn.

The comment Tryska had made about his grandmother was only adding to the fear that was already resurfacing inside of him. What was so important about Intercessors anyway? The question haunted him. What did his praying grandmother have to do with all of this? He knew he would have to ask Bixby the first chance he got.

A sharp pain lanced through the former Gap Warrior's shoulder. Blood and dirt coated the edges of his mouth, and when he moved his jaw there was a searing pain. Gafney heard the voices of men talking in the distance in muffled tones. The ropes that bound his hands behind his back restricted his movement. His feet were tied behind him and connected to the rope that bound his hands. He could feel the numbness in his arms from the lack of circulation. Now he knew what a pig felt like on its way to the fire pit.

The position he was bound in was very uncomfortable, but he was alive, something Gafney really hadn't counted on. He remembered running back to face the Boogarans thinking it would be his last fight. The big man never expected to survive the skirmish, and didn't know whether to feel grateful or unfortunate with the way things had turned out. From what he had heard, death was a better option to being a prisoner of the barbarians that held him now.

The last thing he could recall before the thundering wall of blackness had caved in on him was charging into three men that he sent flying into six more. Then he turned and ran toward the river hoping to swim for freedom. Five more cut him off just before he reached the water's edge. After taking out two of them, something hit him from behind; light flashed in his head and he went down. The warriors surrounded him, cursing at him and all the while kicking him until he passed out. The next thing he remembered was waking up on the ground, tied and bound like a wild animal.

A pair of black boots appeared before his face; he struggled to look up to see who was wearing them. He stinks; Gafney thought to himself. He must be a Boogaran commander.

"Did you enjoy your rest, pig?" the man said laughing as the others standing around joined him in the laughter. Laughing with your commander at the right time was always a good thing, thought Gafney. "Tell me, who were those that you were traveling with?" Gafney remained silent and braced himself for a kick to the ribs, but it was never delivered; instead the man knelt down next to Gafney and moved his head close to the fallen Warrior's ear. "It seems as if the pig refuses to speak, what shall we do with him?"

"Nothing," said a voice in response to the question. Gafney strained to see who was speaking, but his view was blocked. Then there was some movement and a shuffling of feet, and when he saw who it was that had spoken the words, the hair on the back of his neck stood up. It was the Warlock they had seen back at the lake, standing with his hands behind his back with a ruinous look of joy upon his face.

"Come now, Drashkar, is that any way to treat our guest?" the warlock's words were smooth and full of malice. "I know who this man is and who he travels with; there's no sense in beating something out of him that we already know."

Drashkar stood to his feet to face the warlock, and then spoke in a firm tone. "Tell me then, Drok Relnik, who was it that this man was traveling with?"

"He was traveling with the Defenders."

"Then they have broken through," roared Drashkar, "I thought you were sent to stop them."

"You are mistaken," the warlock hissed back at Drashkar. "I was not sent to stop them, I was only sent to test them; besides it is too late for them now, our power has grown beyond their abilities. There is only one of them with any real experience and the other two are just children. The girl I know little of, and the boy is full of fear, and a novice in the ways of battle."

"What about this one?" Drashkar pointed at Gafney on the ground, "If he is a Defender, then he should be killed immediately."

Drok Relnik looked at the man lying tied up on the ground and a smile beaming with insidious pleasure crossed his face. "You don't have to worry about this one," he said smoothly. "He no longer defends the breach. He has forsaken his call. He is no real threat to us now."

Gafney hated hearing those words, but he knew they were true. He was no real threat to these people. Even if he were free from his captivity, he could offer no real help to Talinor.

"So…you are the fallen Gap Warrior, the one who has lost his faith." Gafney raged inside against Drashkar's cutting words. The Boogaran warlord stood over him with a look of loathing in his eyes that burned through like a torch.

A torrent of emotion flooded the fallen Gap Warrior as rage and bitterness, mixed with deep and unbearable regret, penetrated to the core of his being. Not only was he tied up like a pig, he was going to die like a pig. This world that he lived in was cruel, sometimes unbearable, and he had let it get to him. There was nothing he could do about it.

Until now, the forsaking of his calling had seemed mostly a personal decision. Whenever it was brought up in the past he had desperately clung to the idea that it was only he, himself, who would be affected by his decision. He was heartsick and full of shame with the realization of his foolishness.

"Oh yes, we know of your failures and your apostasy," said the warlock, with a touch of pride in his voice. "Were you not here twenty years ago when Ashkron, ruler of the Boogarans, led his warriors against Talinor?"

"Yes, I was here," said Gafney speaking for the first time. "As I remember, we sent you running back to your women and children." The comment cut deep into Drashkar's pride, but when he moved to kick at him, Drok Relnik held up his hand to stop him. Drashkar pushed the hand aside and kicked Gafney hard in the ribs. He started at him a second time, but the Warlock pressed him and was able to convince him to stop.

"It's a pity, you won't be joining them this time," said Drashkar, "at least not all of you. Maybe we can send your head to Talinor on the end of a spear just to let them know that things will be different this time."

"Tell me, who is the boy that travels with the Defenders?" asked the warlock. "I have not seen him before."

"I barely know the lad," answered Gafney, hoping to avoid any more kicks to the ribs.

"The boy seems unsure when he fights," said the Warlock. "What can you tell me of his heritage?"

"I told you, I know nothing of the lad. He is as much a mystery to me as he is to you."

"Enough of this jabbering, let's do away with this scum," said Drashkar. "We have other pressing matters to attend to."

"Wait," the warlock held up his hand, "I am not through with him yet; I may want to question him further." It was hard for Gafney to tell who was in command here. The Warlock appeared to hold the edge over Drashkar, but he couldn't be sure.

"So be it," said Drashkar, trying to project the sound of authority in his voice, "but tomorrow I want his head delivered to the front lines."

Bixby sat alone in the outlook tower near the main gate to the city watching the late morning sun fight to break through the veiling mist. There had been no signs of fighting all morning. Tryska entered the room and smiled at her friend. "You look like you are deep in thought. Would you like me to come back another time?"

"No, come in," said Bixby, as he stood to greet her. He reached out and ruffled the long brown hair that flowed over her shoulders in an unkempt manner; she liked it when he touched her with the innocent affection of a big brother.

"I was talking to Cyle," Tryska started, "Did you know that there was only one Intercessor here in Talinor?"

"Yes," Bixby smiled, "Cyle's grandmother."

"Why are you smiling?"

"Because I know what you're thinking? How can we possibly go on with only one intercessor against the increasing power of the dark magic?"

"You know me too well," said Tryska with a smile forming on her lips, and then it was gone as she continued. "It's obvious that the power of the dark magic is growing stronger in this place with each passing day. All you have to do is look around and you can see its effects-- the mist grows thicker and the scavs are everywhere. Have you seen the looks on everyone's faces, and did you know that there was a demon manifestation within the city walls about a week ago, and those Priests apparently defeated it?"

"Yes, I've already heard about it."

"Then how are we supposed to break loose a stronghold of this kind of power without more intercessors?"

"I don't know," said Bixby, his words growing solemn. "I have never entered a battle before where the dark magic was this deeply entrenched and there was only one intercessor to support us. But I will say this, she is a good one to have if there is only to be one."

"So you know of her then?"

"I know of her, and I hesitate to say too much more about it because I am not sure that we are out of the reach of evil's ear."

"When you speak of our situation you carry a strange balance of confidence and hesitancy. I am not sure what to think," said the Elf girl. "This is challenging my faith. Oh, listen to me, I'm going on and on dumping all of this on you, and you just lost your friend, Gafney. I'm sorry for not thinking about what you might be feeling."

Bixby glanced out the window; it was difficult for the Elf girl to tell what he was thinking as an awkward silence grew between them. "Would you like me to get you something to eat? I'm headed over to the tavern."

"Food. That sounds good," said Bixby. "I would like some…"

"Corn mush and eggs," Tryska cut in.

Bixby laughed, "So you do remember the night on the banks of the Rainbow River when that hermit served us corn mush and eggs."

"Yes, I remember how you threw up all night long, and when we woke up the next morning that poor hermit was nowhere to be found. I think he thought you were going to skin him alive."

Bixby laughed again. Then he walked over to the girl, put his arm around her shoulder and said, "Listen, you just make sure you play that flute when the time comes. We're going to need it."

She hugged him and then trotted for the door, "I'll bring you back something special, one of your favorites." And then she disappeared through the doorway, her garments flowing behind her.

The memory of Gafney's last stand ran through the Gap Warrior's mind; he hadn't had much time to think about it until now. They had fought together in a number of campaigns, mostly in the service of the Ancient of Days. Gafney had saved his life on more than one occasion. Even though he had struggled to trust his friend's stubborn ways, Bixby felt the loss deeply.

They had fought together, side by side in the battle of Talinor some twenty years ago when they were both much younger and stronger. Back then King Shandon was strong in his faith, and he had put his complete trust in the Gap Warriors. When the demons started to manifest in the streets of Talinor, the Gap Warriors cut them down swiftly and decisively. One huge demon had pinned Bixby up against the tower gate and was about to finish him when Gafney jumped from the tower with his axe spinning in his hand as he flew through the air. For a big man, he was as quick as Bixby had ever seen. He had named his weapon, Demon Slayer, and that is just what he did. He came down with the blade under the power of the full force of his body, and when it cut into the giant demon, it exploded in a shower of sparks and smoke. Cheers filled the air as that single act rallied the Warriors of Talinor together to make one final push against the Boogarans, leading to victory.

It wasn't long after that, when losing his beloved caused everything to change, that Bixby's friend became increasingly unreliable. There were battles that he failed to show up for, and when he did, his heart was not in it. Then came the time he fought in his very last battle. They were defending the elfin kingdom of Faldori on the island of Charell. Gafney and Bixby, along with some other Gap Warriors, had entered into the void and had just fought off the first wave of Shadow Wraiths when the mist surrounded them. Bixby had lost sight of his friend while he was busy fighting his own demons brought on by the mist. Then something happened that Bixby would never forget, the mist started to clear, and he saw Gafney leaving the void. He followed him to the edge of the portal and yelled at him, calling for him to come back. The big man turned at his friend and said gruffly, "That's it; I'm finished." As he spoke the words he dropped his axe, Demon Slayer, on the ground, and then he turned and walked away. Just like that, right in the middle of a Gap war. That was his last Gap battle. It was years before Bixby saw him again.

"He's alive." Bixby jumped when he heard the voice. Glancing over, he was surprised to see his Guardian Evan, standing before him, tall and powerful in appearance like a sentinel, dressed in full military garb, ready for battle.

"Who's alive?"

"Gafney," answered Evan.

"How can that be? He was out-numbered ten to one."

"They are holding him captive," answered the Guardian, "but they will kill him by morning."

"He made his choice last night," said Bixby as he stood to his feet to face his Guardian. "He will have to live with it, or die with it."

"Life is full of choices; we do not always make the right ones. Besides, he is one of us."

"He has not been one of us for a long time," said Bixby passionately. "Do you expect us to risk our lives for someone who would not do the same for us?" Even as he spoke the words he realized what he said was not true. Gafney had risked his life for them. If it hadn't been for him, they might not have made it last night. "I guess you're right," Bixby looked down at the ground as he spoke the words. "What would you have us do?"

"Tonight, under the cover of darkness, you and the girl will go in and bring him out. He is being held near the river. The wolf will lead you to him."

"Tonight then," said Bixby in a tone of conviction, "we will do our best." The Guardian turned to leave and hesitated, "You are glad for the news, are you not?"

Bixby smiled, "It is the best news I have heard today." The Guardian exited through the door, and as he disappeared around the corner there was a subtle flash of light.

CHAPTER 20

Talinor's soldiers stood their ground all day long waiting for the Boogaran forces to advance upon them, but nothing happened. The mist had lifted and the sun broke through at different times during the day, but still the Boogarans did not advance.

From the beginning of the battle the Dwarves had done a fine job of holding the middle of the line since. Since that time, the Tal army had only been pushed back a few hundred yards toward the city walls; there was still plenty of ground between them and the city. Gerrid's hopes were running high after a day of rest and no advance by their enemies. Even though the odds were greatly against it, he hoped to hold them here a few days longer and possibly turn them back. He was hoping against hope that they could prevent the battle from moving to the walls of the city.

Bernard, of course, was less optimistic, though both of them were greatly encouraged by the arrival of the Gap Warriors, and word of their arrival was spreading quickly throughout the city. They had been summoned to stand before the King and his Council on the morrow. Most of the excitement among the people was fueled by a curiosity to see the legendary Gap Warriors they had heard about only from the history of their kingdom.

At Cyle's request, Choppa had gone into the city to see if he could find his grandmother and to hear of news that might be of value. He was happy to be back in Talinor and thankful to be alive after all he had been through. Choppa had friends all over the city that could fill him in on what had been going on since they had been gone. Bull Dog was the most helpful; he told Choppa that the temple had been completely restored and that the crowds that worshiped there were growing steadily each day. The fear that war brings tends to increase the need for faith. The Priests of Zarish had established a strong following and the respect of the people had been established after the Priests' defeat of the demon in the streets of Talinor.

Choppa stopped at a fruit stand to eat some fresh apples. When he bit into one it snapped, spraying the sweet juice into his mouth. He hadn't eaten fresh fruit in almost three weeks, and he was savoring every bite. Digger, the fruit merchant, didn't charge him; he said to consider them a "welcome home" gift. In some ways the city hadn't changed at all, except that people seemed a little nicer and more considerate. Choppa thought it might be the pressures of war softening their hearts toward one another. Whatever the cause, it was a nice change.

It was getting dark so he headed for Cyle's grandmother's, hoping she would have some of her sweetbread baking in the oven. The closer he drew toward her house the quieter and less crowded the streets became. When he turned the corner, he could see her home through the afternoon shadows. Someone was standing outside near the front door. As he drew nearer he could see that it was a soldier.

"What is your purpose?" demanded the guard as he placed his hand on the pommel of his sword.

"I am here to see the Lady Lena," offered Choppa sheepishly.

"She is under house arrest by the order of the King, and there are no visitors allowed."

"How is it that the King would place such a gentle and meek woman like the Lady Lena under arrest? What grave threat could she possibly be to this kingdom?"

"She refuses to forsake the old faith. The king in his great mercy has spared her from the dungeons and allowed her to stay here at her home, under house arrest," said the guard as he stepped forward to get a closer look at the one who was speaking to him. "Who are you that you ask these questions?" asked the guard.

"I am but a simple messenger bringing news from family members," Choppa said, bowing in reverence. "Sir Knight, would it be possible to deliver the message to the Lady?"

"Give me the message, and I will make sure she receives it," said the guard as he held out his hand.

"I am afraid that won't do, for the message is held in my heart, and I was given strict orders to deliver it with my own words."

"I cannot allow it," said the guard in typical military fashion as he stood to attention.

"Very well then," said Choppa. "I guess she will have to live without the news of her beloved sister's passing and her last departing words."

Choppa turned in a dejected manner and started to walk away.

"Wait," the guard exclaimed as a hidden smile crossed Choppa's face. "I will give you three minutes, and no more."

His conversation with Cyle's grandmother had been brief, but meaningful. He was delighted with how pleased she was to see him. He told her of their return to Talinor and their plans to meet with the King's Council in the morning. She warned him to be careful; she didn't know if they would still blame Cyle for the King's sickness. It was difficult to judge the King's leadership. Lena believed that the Priests were making most of the decisions now, and she doubted that the King even knew of her arrest. Lena was concerned for Cyle's safety. Choppa told her that he was disguised as a shepherd boy with his head wrapped in shepherds' rags to protect his identity. Then the guard cut their conversation short, and he had to leave. Lena's last words to Cyle's friend were, "Tell them I am praying for them."

As darkness fell, it brought with it an absence of foot traffic upon the city streets. Choppa was happy to be back in his home and on familiar turf even though uneasiness tugged at the corners of his mind, causing him to feel that he should return to the tower gate where Cyle was waiting for him. He made his way through the back alleyways, following a route he had traveled many times before. The smell of evening cooking and fresh baked bread was driving his hunger.

Suddenly it grew darker all around him and Choppa noticed that something moved in the shadows. Without hesitation, he turned and ran in the other direction, his heart leaping. Then he heard footsteps pounding behind him. Too afraid to look back, he pressed on, squeezing through a small separation between two buildings. Once through, he broke free and ran down another street. Before turning the next corner, he glanced back to see if he was still being followed. Two dark figures broke into the street from between the buildings he had just passed through. Although he was afraid, he was also confident he could escape his pursuers. This was his city and he knew every crack and crevice in these streets. This wasn't the first time he had used his knowledge of the city to escape danger.

His heart jumped again as he caught the movement in front of him, but he couldn't see well enough to tell who it was. Maybe it would be someone who could help. Not wanting to take any chances, he made his way to a dark corner and backed into the darkness, disappearing from sight.

From where he stood, he could see out into the street, but he was sure no one could see him. Footsteps grew louder as three figures approached, stopping just a few feet away. The three of them surveyed the area before the tall thin one with the pockmarked face spoke. "We lost him. He got away."

"We can't lose him," said the man with the curved sword. "Relnik will cast a spell on us if we come back empty-handed."

"You idiot," said the short, bald headed man with the pointed beard, "Do you really believe that warlock can do anything to hurt you?" The words had just been spoken, when the man started gagging and gasping for breath. A robed figure stepped from the shadows, still partially cloaked in darkness.

"Drok Relnik," the man choked out the words in terror.

The Warlock waved his hand in front of him and the man stopped gagging, holding his throat and collapsing to the ground, as he strained to recapture the breath he had lost.

"You were saying?" taunted the warlock as he peered down at the bald-headed man on his knees. The man started to speak, but the warlock interrupted him, "Enough of these games. Where is the lad?"

The three of them fumbled hopelessly for explanations while Choppa stood frozen in the darkness of his hiding space; then the warlock looked straight at him and smiled, raising his bony finger in his direction.

"There," said the warlock.

Choppa bolted for freedom, but it was too late. They were on him instantly, pinning him to the ground, Choppa struggled to get free until the tall thin one produced a long knife and held it his throat.

"Move and I'll gut you like a pig," said the one with the knife as he wrenched his victim's arm in a vice like grip behind his back. Choppa winced at the pain lancing through his shoulder.

"So, you are the one who travels with the Defenders," said

the Warlock. "Maybe you can be of some help to us." Choppa did not respond.

"Where is the boy who was traveling with you?" asked the warlock calmly.

"What boy?" Choppa feigned ignorance.

"Do not play games with me," warned the warlock as he stepped closer to Choppa who could now recognize him from the battle at the lake. "I am in no mood for games. I want the boy and I am willing to make it worth your while to give him to me."

Choppa stared at the warlock for a brief moment, and then he glanced about at his three captors with thoughts spinning in his head, and fear ripping at his insides.

"What is your offer?" Choppa's words came out mousy and weak. He hated how he sounded.

Ginzer insisted on going along with Bixby and Tryska, and bringing Folger along as well. At first Bixby resisted it, but in the end Ginzer won out. Bixby didn't want to worry about Cyle's trying to follow them, so they slipped off into the darkness after the others had fallen asleep. Choppa had not returned yet, and no one seemed to notice except Cyle. His friend had been gone for a long time. He had worried about him until exhaustion won out, and then he finally fell into a deep sleep.

Moments after Bixby and the others had left for Gafney, Choppa slipped quietly into the room to join Cyle where he lay sleeping. The rescuers had only walked a few hundred paces from the city when Keesha, the silver wolf, appeared before them, massive and feral in appearance, yet as playful as a puppy when she greeted the Elf girl.

Tryska embraced her furry friend around the neck and whispered under her breath, "How are you, my friend?"

The four of them, Bixby, Tryska, Folger and Ginzer followed the wolf as it headed for the trees that edged the valley floor. When they reached the river's edge, they turned away from Talinor and headed toward the Boogaran camp.

The night was dark due to the mist that blanketed the stars overhead; only a small amount of light was able to penetrate its cover. Traveling without the light of the stars provided them the cover they needed from Boogaran scouts. Without the wolf leading them, it would have been almost impossible to locate Gafney.

Close to an hour had passed before they could hear the soft murmur of the troops coming from the valley floor. Something stirred within Bixby, a feeling of urgency and uneasiness fluttered through his spirit causing him to move faster. They were running out of time and he knew it; if they didn't find his friend right away, he would be lost to them.

The wolf stopped and Tryska waved Bixby forward to where she and the wolf were crouching behind some reeds. Up ahead of them about one hundred paces from where they stood they could see Gafney tied to a tree near the river, hanging limply against the trunk. There was a small fire burning on the ground nearby, and only three soldiers were guarding him.

It was difficult to hear them from where they were, but it sounded like they were fighting over who would get his sword and his boots.

"Let me swim the river," said the Elf girl confidently; I can come up behind him and cut him loose."

"Wait," said Ginzer haltingly, "it looks too easy, what if it's a trap?"

"I don't know," offered Bixby, "I don't think they expect us to come back for him. By now they know that he was once a Gap Warrior fallen from his call, and they will view him as worthless to us, just as they would view one of their own for committing the same crime. They won't be looking for us to return for someone whom they would consider a traitor." Bixby paused for a moment, eyeing his friend slumping against the tree. He looked pathetic to Bixby. A mixture of emotions ran through the Gap Warrior. He had always been at odds with Gafney, even during the good times. "No, I don't think it's a trap," mumbled Bixby as if to reassure himself.

"I hope you're right on this one," said the Dwarf. "I don't fancy getting strung up in a Boogaran camp and having my head stuck on a pole."

"It's time to move," said the Gap Warrior, ignoring Ginzer's statement. "Go ahead, Tryska; we'll wait for your signal. Once you have reached the tree, Folger will take out the ones closest to him with his bow. We'll have to strike quickly."

"Let the wolf shield you and Ginzer," whispered the Elf girl. "She will blend in and cover you from being seen."

Tryska was gone in a flicker as both Bixby and Ginzer walked toward the camp, allowing the wolf to hide them from the view of the guards. The two men held onto the big wolf's fur as it began to vibrate and slowly blend in with the blackness that surrounded them. They were only a few feet away when they saw Tryska appear from behind the tree.

Two of the men were huddled by the fire while the other stood closer to the tree. When Tryska signaled, an arrow flew to its mark, striking the man by the tree in the heart, dropping him to the ground with a gasp. The other two men jumped to their feet, startled, but before they could sound a cry for help, Bixby and Ginzer struck out at them, and they were down before they knew what hit them.

By now Gafney was aware that Tryska had cut him free, and he grabbed his sword lying by the fire. Without speaking, they ran toward Talinor. They were just minutes away when they heard the sounding of an alarm break through the stillness of the night.

"Are you going to make it, Gaf?" asked Bixby, noticing him struggling under the pain of his breathing.

"I'm fine. You set the pace; I'll keep up," responded Gafney sounding irritated with the question.

They were running furiously behind the wolf when suddenly there was a rush of wind and the ground started to vibrate.

"It's the void," shouted Tryska above the wind. "Something is breaching the void and crossing over!" Before them formed a shimmering wall of light, flashing and waving like the ripples on a lake. The middle opened into a dark hole, and four dark creatures with leathery wings and razor sharp talons broke through to their side. The creatures hissed and flapped their wings. The shimmering wall remained for a few more moments, and then a voice came from within the hole, "You cannot have him." It was Gafney. They wanted Gafney, and all of them knew it. Then Folger let loose an arrow. It drove deep into one of the demon's necks; but the arrow melted into smoke.

"Forget it, Folger, your weapons won't work against this kind," shouted Bixby. "The rest of you step back, only Tryska and I..." There was a flurry of wings and one of the creatures was upon Bixby, clawing at him and snapping with its jaws. The swordsman held it back while he swung with his sword as Folger and Ginzer backed away without argument.

Tryska pulled her flute from its pouch and started to play when one of the flying Wraiths darted toward Gafney. As it came down upon him he instinctively lifted his sword to his defense, even though he knew it was powerless against the creature. Suddenly there was a growl and a flash of fur as the silver wolf rammed into the flying beast that was attacking Gafney. The demon's claws tore into the wolf's side, but Keesha did not falter.

Two of the creatures were hovering over Bixby clawing and snapping at him, driving him backward in an attempt to separate him from Gafney. The Gap Warrior glanced at Gafney and then at Tryska who was lying on the ground, motionless, with her flute just out of reach. The distraction provided the opening one demon needed. It slashed out at him, tearing his shoulder, and sending a searing pain through his left arm. Wasting little time, the same demon latched onto him and sent him hurling against a tree. Then two others turned and flew toward Gafney.

Tryska stirred back to life. Shaking the cobwebs from her head, she saw Bixby unconscious on the ground. The Elf girl reached for her flute. Just as she grabbed it, two of the demons latched onto Gafney who was swinging his sword in vain, as it splintered into a thousand shards. The shimmering wall appeared again as two of the creatures pulled a struggling Gafney toward its black center. The melody of the flute was sweet at first, and then it intensified as the look on Tryska's face reflected the same tone of the music she was playing. From out of the wall of shimmering light another form manifested, tall and foreboding, holding something in its hand. Startled by the intruder, the two demons dropped Gafney, and he fell in an unconscious heap to the ground.

Bixby awoke to the sound of flute music and the screams of the flying demons filling the air. He watched in wonder at what he saw next. The new arrival from the void ran toward Gafney where there were now three demons hovering over him. In his hand was a battle-axe that flashed and came to life. Sparks flew off the edge of the blade, and when he reached the body of the former Gap Warrior who was still lying unconscious on the ground, the mystical warrior's blade flew with a grace and force of power driven by the supernatural. With blinding speed he cut through one of the bat demons, and it exploded in a shower of sparks and smoke.

Ginzer and Folger came to Bixby's side. "Who is the one from the void that moves like a ghost?" asked Folger.

Bixby saw the powerful man standing over the fallen Gafney, who was still lying unconscious as the circling demons bore down upon the protector to get to their prey. The mystical warrior set his tall, muscular frame in battle position and let the axe in his hands fly, singing through the air, cleaving and slicing through his attackers. The demons fell one at a time, screaming in angony and defeat. All the while, Gafney did not stir. When the last of the demons had fallen, the Guardian cried out to them, "One Faith!" Then he turned, and ran back into the void, disappearing in an explosion of light.

"Who was that?" asked Ginzer through labored breaths.

"That was Alaniel, Gafney's Guardian," Bixby coughed out the words, pressing through the pain piercing his left shoulder, trying to grasp what he had just seen. Then he looked over at Tryska and saw that she was lying still on the ground with the silver wolf leaning over her, licking her cheek.

CHAPTER 21

When they reached the city gate the guards signaled for them to come in as stretcher-bearers came out to assist them. Gafney had regained consciousness and, other than some bumps on the head and sore ribs that he had suffered while in captivity, there were no serious injuries. When the healers came with the stretcher to take the girl, they saw that Gafney had insisted on carrying Tryska back to the city. Bixby teetered in and out of consciousness. He had lost a lot of blood from his shoulder wound. The guards carried him to the medical tent while Gafney followed, carrying Tryska who was still unconscious. The wolf had killed the one demon and had suffered a wound in its side. At first she hesitated to come with them into the city. She circled around nervously outside the gate before following them inside.

"We need a healer in here," Gafney bellowed at the guards as he pushed them aside to find a place to lay Tryska down. He gently brushed her hair back from her face, and yelled a second time, "Where's a healer?" Ginzer cut back Bixby's jerkin to expose the wound to his left shoulder. Gafney moved over to take a look. "What do you think, Ginzer?" said Gafney, his eyes blazing.

"I'm not a doctor, but I've stitched worse in my time. As long as there's no poison, he'll be all right."

A healer ran into the room, followed by Folger; Gafney waved them over. "Look to the girl first. He'll be all right for now." Bixby moaned and tried to sit up, but he fell back. The pain was too great.

"Hey, what kind of rescue was that?" said Gafney as he leaned over his friend. "You almost got everybody killed including yourself."

"How's Tryska?" asked the wounded Gap Warrior, ignoring his statement as he struggled to look over at her.

"I don't know; she's been out for a long time. The healer's looking after her now."

They heard a whining sound and noticed the wolf sitting in the corner near the cot the Elf girl was lying on, her ears upright, and she was nervously watching the healer as he worked on his patient. "It's all right, Keesha," said Bixby. "She'll be all right." The wolf walked over wagging her tail, put her cold nose on his cheek and licked his face. Bixby reached out to her and gently stroked her silver mane, speaking words to bring comfort to the wolf. She kept looking back at her friend and whining in tones of concern.

Cyle and Choppa burst through the door out of breath. "What happened?" asked Choppa.

Ginzer told them about pulling Gafney out of the camp and how they had battled with the creatures of the void.

"What about Tryska," asked Cyle, cutting Ginzer short, "is she going to be all right?"

"She's going to be fine," said the healer, answering his question as he finished wrapping her head with a bandage.

"I want to know why you didn't take me with you," said Cyle.

"You weren't supposed to come with us," Bixby answered.

"But I could have helped. Maybe this wouldn't have happened."

"I can't tell you why, Cyle, but you were not supposed to be there. My Guardian told me to take Tryska and the wolf. I did as I was told; that's all I can tell you."

Bixby could see the confusion in Cyle's face, reminding him of when he was a young Gap Warrior trying to figure these things out. Back then most of what went on didn't make sense to him either. He remembered feeling like an outsider when the older and more experienced Warriors appeared to always know what was going on. He was sure Cyle was feeling the same way.

"There will be plenty of demons to fight, lad," said Gafney. "Possibly more than you will care to swing your staff at."

Cyle found little comfort in his words. He turned and walked out of the room into the streets, with Choppa following close behind.

"Cyle, wait," Choppa yelled as he ran to catch up with his friend. "What is it? Why are you so angry?"

Cyle turned on his friend with fire in his eyes, speaking with passion. "You were there with me in the meadow; you saw the demon as I did, and we both chose to run away in fear. Why haven't you said anything about it?"

A flash of shame surged in Choppa as the memory came crashing back into his mind of that night when the two of them had run from the Shadow Wraith. He started to answer his friend, but he was cut short.

"I think Bixby knows of my fear, and he's afraid I won't be able to handle it," said Cyle, as he paced and pounded his staff into the ground. "Well, why haven't you said anything?" he pressed Choppa again.

"I...I was afraid all right; more like terrified. I don't know what else to say," said Choppa. He hesitated for a minute to gather his words, then he continued, "Listen, Cyle, since this whole thing started we have battled against creatures beyond our imagination and when the time came, we handled it, and we will handle whatever comes our way next."

"You know as well as I do that the power of those scavs, and the monster at the lake, was nothing compared with the power of the Shadow Wraith we saw in the meadow that night. Those things we fought are puppets to the Shadow Wraiths."

Cyle's words were on the mark. Choppa thought back to the battles Cyle was referring to. Those monsters had powers beyond any thing he had seen before, and yet the Shadow Wraiths were even more powerful. Choppa knew that without the help of the Gap Warriors, they would never have been able to stand against those monsters, especially a Shadow Wraith. "You're right," submitted Choppa. "What do you want me to say? Maybe you are being prepared for what is to come and it wasn't your time yet to face what they just had to confront back there."

Cyle stood there staring at the ground, feeling confused. "They came back torn and beaten," said Cyle, "How could this have happened? How could they have failed so miserably? If it could happen to them, it could happen to me."

"It's not their fault," offered a familiar voice from behind them.

"It's my fault, lad," said Gafney. "When I attacked the demons with my sword it threw off the balance of things; and when it shattered, I was overcome with fear. That fear gave them even more power. They came through the void for me. They wanted to drag me back into it, and leave me there to rot."

"Can they do that?" asked Cyle, confused.

"Only because I once fought as a Gap Warrior and wielded a weapon of power. I had been told it could happen, but I never believed it until last night. The evil in this place is growing, and with it a shift in the balance of things, which brings an increase in the power that fights against us."

"I don't understand," said Choppa, looking confused. "Why won't you help us? We need your blade."

"You are young, and there are some things that are hard to understand."

"That's what people say when they don't have a good enough reason for holding to their convictions," offered Cyle boldly.

"Maybe you are right young Gap Warrior," said Gafney thoughtfully.

"So, what are you going to do about it?" asked Choppa.

"It's too late for me now," said Gafney. "I have lost touch with who I was. I haven't held a weapon of power for years, and I haven't seen or heard from my Guardian for just as long. No, it's too late for me; my time has past. The best thing for all of us is for me to stay away from you. I'm going to head for the front lines and join the fighting there."

"Wait a minute!" exclaimed Bixby. The others turned to see the Gap Warrior approaching them. "You don't know what happened, do you?" Gafney cast a look of confusion his way. Bixby continued, "Earlier tonight when you passed out during the battle, your Guardian was there, fighting to protect you. If he hadn't been there, they would have taken you into the void."

An uneasy look crossed Gafney's face that was difficult to read. Holding onto his stomach, he looked like he would throw up. For the first time, the silence that fell between them seemed awkward.

"How do you know that?" Gafney raised his voice in defiance, stepping backward at the same time.

"I saw him with my own eyes when he manifested out of the void and attacked those two flying demons that were about to drag you through the portal."

"His weapon," Gafney demanded as his voice shook, "what was the weapon that he wielded?"

"It was a double-edged axe with another blade at the bottom of the handle, just like the one you used to carry."

Terror filled Gafney's eyes. He paused momentarily and looked about as if he was lost to where he was, and then without a word, he turned and ran down the street toward the center of Talinor, disappearing into the darkness. Cyle and Choppa stood there staring at him in disbelief at what had just happened.

"What should we do?" asked Cyle.

"Let him go. There's nothing we can do. He's got his own demons to battle. It seems that fear wants to take us all, one way or the other," said Bixby.

As Cyle watched Gafney run away, it reminded him of the time he had run away; he felt no judgment against the former Gap Warrior.

Cyle had been through a lot in the last few weeks. Life was not as simple as it used to be. His life and he himself had changed, and he knew it. He remembered the words of Gruber, his rescuer in the swamp, "Cyle on mission." He smiled as he thought of the little green man.

"Did you find my grandmother?" asked Cyle suddenly realizing he had not asked Choppa about his trip into the city.

"I could only speak with her briefly. They placed her under house arrest because she refused to follow the new faith."

Cyle smiled, "That's my Grandma!"

"She sends you her love and prayers; she even gave me some of her sweet bread to give to you, but I ate it," said Choppa apologetically.

"What about Graybeard, have they arrested him too?"

"No one knows where he is. People on the streets are saying that he's locked up in the castle dungeon."

"As long as Grandmother is safe, she can still pray for us. I can't wait to see her again."

The four Guardians stood at the edge of the void like sentries with weapons in hand, staring out onto Talinor. Melidar, Guardian of Cyle, stood next to Veneda, the Guardian of Tryska, and next to them stood Evan, Bixby's Guardian and Alaniel, the Guardian of Gafney. Each carried a single weapon that was the same as their own disciples, except for Alaniel of Gafney, who carried two axes.

The air around them swirled in wisps of white mist, curling and dancing to an invisible rhythm. One of them spoke, "What of Gafney, will he make it?" asked Melidar.

"It is difficult to say," answered Alaniel. "He carries the weight of shame and is tormented by the sting of grief; both have stolen away many a strong soul." Alaniel could feel the weight of the second axe in his hand as he spoke the words. How he longed to return it to Gafney, its rightful owner. "The Lady Shariana holds great hope for him, and she believes he will make it."

"The Lady Shariana is always hopeful," offered Melidar, "it is her faith that has brought all of us through countless impossible situations."

"The Ancient One does not easily release his grip upon his

Defenders when they falter from the way," said Veneda, her soft melodious voice almost sounded like music on the wind. "The fire of destiny still burns deep within the fallen one; the embers of his faith are being stirred even as we speak."

"Where is the fifth Gap warrior?" asked Evan, staring at his sword as it reflected the light of the swirling void around them, "Is there not one more to join us?"

"There is another," said the voice as it echoed through the void.

"My Lady," spoke Melidar, as the four of them bowed to a knee before the manifesting form of Princess Shariana. A brilliant light shimmered around her countenance as her form completed its definition.

"Your honor of me is appreciated, my noble Guardians. Please stand. There is a fifth Gap warrior, who will stand with the others however, the force of our strategy in this battle does not allow me to tell you who that is at this time. The void has ears that would use that information against our cause. As for now, I need you to hold strong here at the portal between the two worlds. Do not allow any to pass without the right and authority to do so."

"Yes, My Lady," they replied in concert, as they bowed in compliance.

"Talinor is weak, My Lady," offered Melidar, "and easily cast about as a ship without a sail. Today the Defenders will go before the High Council of the King."

"Pray that they will be received back into the service of Talinor," said the Lady as she smiled to offer encouragement. "It is our greatest hope for victory, and the beginning of Talinor's journey back to the One Faith. If they are rejected, then it will cause an even greater weakening in the void that will open the way for darker things to come through. If that should happen, remain strong and fear not; remember that this battle belongs to the Ancient One." As the Princess of the Guardians finished speaking she slowly faded from their sight. Light shimmered in bursts about her form, and then she was gone.

A rushing wind swirled through the void as a new form

appeared before them. It was Gizshra, the dark lord and Prince of the Shadow Wraiths, clothed in a black translucent robe that covered his evil form. The Guardians drew their weapons, holding them ready for battle.

CHAPTER 22

The fighting was fierce for the first half of the day. The Boogaran horde pounded away at the Talinor battle lines; many lives on both sides had been lost by the time the sun reached the middle of the sky.

Stretcher-bearers moved like ants back and forth from the battle lines to the hospital just inside the main gate; a crimson trail of death marked their path. The city of Talinor was swollen with grief at the loss of fathers, brothers and sons. The Boogarans out-numbered them four to one, and just when it looked as if the Dwarves and Tal warriors were making headway at the battlefront, a new wave of Boogaran warriors would stream in like a flood and slash away at their defenses.

Gerrid and Bernard argued over when to retreat to the city. Bernard knew his Dwarves could not take much more of this kind of pressure. The days were long, and the nights for rest were short. Drashkar had enough men to send in fresh warriors and allow the others to rest in shifts, a luxury Talinor did not have. In the end, Gerrid gave in to Bernard, who reasoned that once they retreated to the walls they could fight in shifts, at least until their numbers were depleted. It was a difficult decision even for Bernard. He knew that his men were much better at fighting in open field combat than from the battlements atop a stone wall, but their numbers were dwindling and their strength waning.

By the time Bixby and the others had reached the palace courtyard, a crowd had gathered to see the legendary Gap Warriors, mostly women and children and a few elderly men. The onlookers seemed unimpressed with the appearance of the three of them. Bixby's arm was in a sling and Tryska's head was bandaged. Cyle had disguised himself as a shepherd boy with cloth rags covering his head and face. He appeared insignificant next to the others.

The first thing that Cyle noticed when he entered the area was the rebuilt temple now dedicated to the gods of the Zarish Priests. Worshipers moved in and out of the structure as they passed by on their way to the temple. Two guards appeared at the door of the palace entrance to escort them into the King's War Council Room. They led them up the familiar steps that Cyle had walked countless times before. He was nervous thinking back to his flight from Talinor a few weeks earlier, due to the accusations that he had poisoned the king. He wondered if his disguise would be good enough to fool them.

Inside the War Council Room, everyone was assembled and waiting for King Shandon and his advisor, Darius. The room had changed little since the last time Cyle was here, except for a new banner displaying the shooting star that now covered the eagle crest, which had once hung on the wall above the King's chair. The flags that circled the room still hung from their wooden poles as they gently fluttered in the breeze that blew through the huge open-air windows. Once they carried the image of the great eagle; now like all others, they had been replaced by the same shooting star symbol.

The three of them stood in the middle of the War room surrounded by a semicircle of priests, advisors and guards. When the King entered the room, they all bowed to show reverence. Darius and Jarrod, the Captain of the King's guard, stood on one side of him, and on the other side stood Orom, the Chief Zarish Priest.

Bixby stepped forward to speak, "Your Majesty, may I

speak?" For a moment the King's countenance changed with a look of delight.

"I know you," said the King with a smile on his face, "although the last time we met you were a very young man. Are you not Bixby, master of the fire sword, the one who fought here in our last great battle against the Boogarans?"

"I am he, Your Majesty, and we have come to serve you as we did all those years ago." Whispers filled the room and then quickly died away.

"It is an honor to have you among us Bixby, Warrior of the Gap," said the King. "Many have forgotten your brave deeds from long ago, but I have not forgotten the battle waged by the Gap Warriors. Talinor owes you a debt of gratitude for what you and the others did for us. Tell me, are there only three of you now?"

"Yes, Your Majesty," answered Bixby, "although there is one more that will soon join us in the fight."

"Your Majesty," said the High Priest as he stepped forward, "these Warriors deserve our respect and gratitude for the greatness of their deeds in the past, but if they are to join our campaign, they must fight under the banner of the star."

"Your Majesty," Bixby addressed the Priest and the King, "we will only fight the dark magic under the banner of the eagle. As Gap Warriors we recognize no other gods." Muffled voices filled the room once again.

"Your Majesty, the Priests of Zarish have served us well," said Darius. "They have proven to us that they have the power to defeat the dark magic by destroying the demon in the square at the gate. It is not my intention to speak with disrespect, Your Honor, but we know that these who stand before us have already engaged the dark magic, and it appears as if they fared poorly."

Cyle felt his blood beginning to boil at Darius's words.

"Is this true, have you fought the dark magic and suffered defeat?" asked the King.

"Your Honor, please consider your decision carefully before you reject our services," Cyle responded before he realized what he was doing.

"And who is this shepherd boy that speaks as if he may counsel the King?" asked Darius in an offended tone.

"One who loves and respects the King with all of his heart," Cyle's passion-filled words drove the conviction of his heart as he glared at Darius, remembering the times when the advisor would speak down to him.

"You are a stranger in these courts," hissed Darius. "How dare you claim allegiance to our King?"

"Because your King is my King!" As Cyle spoke the words in defiance to his former teacher, he tore the cloth from his head revealing who he was. The room erupted in gasps.

Darius screamed, "How dare you come back here? You have betrayed the King and his kingdom!"

"Darius, be still!" the King glared at his advisor. As he stood the room grew deathly silent when he gathered his robes and walked toward his former cupbearer. Stopping in front of the young Gap Warrior he reached out and put his hands on his shoulders. "I have missed you," said the King as a tear formed in the corner of his eye. He reached out and embraced him.

"Your Majesty, this is highly inappropriate," warned Darius. The King released his grip on Cyle and raised his hand to silence his advisor.

"Of all of my servants, this one has served me with the greatest of devotion. He has done nothing to harm Talinor or his King; I wish him no ill will."

"Your Majesty, the Priests of Zarish are here to serve you," said Orom. "We have rebuilt your temple and revived the faith of your people. Will you now turn us away?"

"What you say is true, Orom, and I have no intention of turning the Priests away. After all, we had an agreement. As long as you are able to protect Talinor from the Shadow Wraiths, our agreement still stands. Our part of the agreement was to put our trust in you and your faith; so far you have not failed us."

Cyle's heart sank as the King revealed his final decision.

He started to object until Bixby put a hand of warning on his shoulder and spoke softly to him, "The will of a man is not easily changed, and the will of a King is even harder to change."

The King smiled at Cyle and stepped back to stand with his advisors and the Priests before speaking again. "I will not cast these who stand before us out of the city. We will not refuse you refuge from the evil that lies outside of these walls. It is the least we can do for you to honor you for past deeds. You are free to come and go as you please."

"We cannot allow the boy to get close to the King," whispered one of the Priests to Darius. "Affection has a way of turning a heart from its path."

"I have already seen to that," said Darius. "One of their own will bring him to us."

"How have you managed this?" asked the priest.

"Everyone has a price. It's just a matter of whether you can pay it or not."

When the King finished his last remarks, the three Defenders turned to make the long walk back to the tower near the main gate. A blanket of humility hung over them as all eyes watched them depart the War Council chamber. When they reached the palace courtyard, more eyes greeted them with cold stares of indifference as the crowds parted slowly before the Gap Warriors, until three others stepped out from the crowd to join them. Ginzer, Folger and Choppa had been waiting for them. Bixby reached out and put his good arm around Cyle's shoulder and spoke to him in a comforting tone, "Take heart, this is not over yet. A little humility is good for a Warrior's heart."

The walk back through the city streets seemed like an eternity to Cyle.

CHAPTER 23

The tower bell rang out, shattering the silence that covered the city in the early morning hours. Soldiers ran to their positions, chain mail and armor clattering as they made their way to the ramparts. Bixby and Ginzer were the first to reach the top of the tower gate while Cyle, Tryska and Choppa poured into the room right behind them to get a look at the troops.

The mist on the killing fields had not yet settled in to obscure their view. Beyond the Talinor battle lines stood the Boogaran troops and behind them three massive towers rose from the ground, barely visible in the shrouding mist. Hundreds of slaves pulled the towers with ropes, assisted by a giant bog beast on each tower. Surrounding the towers, a second army had assembled. As far as their eyes could see, there was a mass of bodies, greater than Cyle could have imagined. Fear shot through the watchers on the wall as they viewed the massive sea of warriors that had assembled during the night.

"Drashkar has found an ally!" cried Ginzer. "How can we stand against such a force?"

"Many battles are fought against insurmountable odds," offered Bixby calmly as he viewed the sight. "It is the way of war. Anything can happen; you should know that, Ginzer."

"Anything can happen, you are right," said the old Dwarf, "and one thing is sure to happen, many will die and many will be wounded. It is a sad state of affairs we face."

"What will we do?" asked Cyle. "Now that we are no longer needed here?"

"We are needed now more than ever," answered Bixby. "We came here to defend Talinor from the Shadow Wraiths. It would have been better if they had accepted our help, but as you can see things are not always better."

"Then we will pray that their eyes are opened," said Tryska. "The Priests will not be able to give them the protection they need. Until then, we will stand in the gap and fight whatever the Shadow Wraiths send our way."

"Or we will go in after them; either way, we will fight," said Bixby.

Down on the front lines, Somuel's messenger arrived out of breath. Handing the note to Gerrid, the messenger saluted him. After reading it, Gerrid turned to his second in command and told him to prepare the troops to retreat to the walls. Bernard appeared just in time to hear the order.

"The archers on the walls are prepared to cover us as we retreat," said Gerrid to his friend Bernard. "There is a second army assembled out of our view near the towers. If we stay here, we will fall before the sun reaches the middle of the sky."

"You are right, Gerrid," said Bernard ruefully. "But as you know, retreat is not an easy thing for a Dwarf."

"Don't think of it as a retreat my friend. Think of it as wisdom. Prepare your men; when the signal sounds we must move with the greatest of haste."

The soldiers in the rear of the ranks near the gates started to retreat first, edging back slowly at first toward the city gates. Most of them had slipped through unnoticed before Gerrid gave the signal to the bell tower. When the chimes rang out, the men in front made a sudden about-face and started running for the gates.

The Boogarans were slow at first to respond; they had not expected the sudden retreat. However, they soon realized what was happening and charged toward the backs of the retreating warriors. Once the Tals had cleared the firebreak, flaming arrows were loosed into the air from atop the walls. Flaming arrows shot skyward before falling to the oil-soaked fire line to ignite the inferno. Boogaran soldiers caught in the firetrap screamed and ran, while others rolled on the ground as their comrades used their capes to dash the flames from their bodies. The rest of the Boogarans stopped just short of the wall of flames, giving the Talinor army time to run through the main gate to safety. When the last man was inside, they closed the massive gate and barred it shut. The gate was an impressive structure, built of huge wood timbers and covered in iron to hinder any attempts to burn it down.

The sight of the siege towers was draining the morale from the troops; until now they had fought beyond what any man could hope for. Time and again they had held the line on the valley floor for longer than anyone had expected. With the help of the new reinforcements to their cause, the Boogaran army would gain a deadly new momentum.

Later that day, word came through a scout that the Boogarans had hired the Kadiri tribe from the Segron plains. The Kadiri were large nomadic people that kept mostly to themselves but had been known to hire out to fight in wars, if the price was right.

Bernard of the Dwarves stood as a giant upon the walls in his military garb; his metal helmet glistened in the sun. Raising his axe he spoke in an attempt to rally the troops, "Fearless hearts men; we have the advantage of the wall beneath our feet, and we stand in the greatest fortress ever built. We are the Defenders of Talinor, and we will not fail. Our storehouses are full, and upon these walls stands the greatest fighting force ever assembled." Some of the men offered shouts of agreement but not nearly enough. His efforts were appreciated, but they fell short of the results he had hoped for.

"A valiant effort, my friend," said Gerrid. "Had I been a young warrior, my heart would have raged with courage."

"I fear that is the problem," said the Dwarf. "The young are too few, and the old know better than to listen to the ramblings of an old battle-scarred Dwarf."

"That is not true; you sell yourself too short. They respect you, old friend. You are a legend among them. They have watched you these past days as you have held the line against the attacks. No one else has shown that kind of courage against such great odds."

"It will take much more than courage now," said Bernard as he looked at his axe. "We will need a miracle."

"Remember the last battle against Boogara?" offered Gerrid. "The odds were stacked against us then as well. With the help of the Gap Warriors we held our own and won the day."

"We won because we were younger, and we won because we were united under the same faith. There is a growing tide of division that spreads among us. Many of my men resent fighting for a faith they know little about, and the same is true for your men. I have heard them arguing among themselves; it is not good for morale." Bernard turned to face his friend as he sat down upon the wall, resting his battle-axe at his side, "And what of the Gap Warriors? I hear they have been turned away; that does not rest well with me."

"I too am troubled about it, but we must not lose heart. This is our country and our land; if we lose this battle we will lose more than land. Our women and children will be taken from us, and you and I will either be killed or taken as slaves. We have no choice but to fight. If faith will not win the day, then courage will."

"Well-spoken, Gerrid. I can see why you are the Chief Commander of Talinor's military. Maybe from now on you should give the speeches."

"I am a terrible giver of speeches; I think I shall leave that to you, my friend," said Gerrid as he laughed. "As for now, we must decide what to do about those towers. If we allow them to be pushed too close to our walls, it will be the end of us."

"What about fire arrows?" asked one of the young warriors standing by, overhearing their conversation.

"The wood will not burn fast enough," said Gerrid. "They will extinguish the flames before they can burn the towers down."

"Then we need to find a way to encourage the flames," offered the young warrior. "If we can find a way to oil the towers, the arrows will work."

"What did you have in mind?" asked Bernard, his interest peaking. "Remember we have to burn them before they get too close to the walls."

"Slingshots," said the young man as he pulled one from the weapons' bag hanging from his belt.

"What good is a slingshot against a tower?" asked Bernard.

"We will use goat bladders filled with oil. We can launch them over one hundred paces, and they will explode on impact. Then we shoot the arrows."

Gerrid and Bernard looked at one another and smiled. "What is your name, young man?" asked Bernard.

"My name is Micah."

"Well done, Micah," said Gerrid. "I want you to gather everyone together who can use one of those things, and I'll have some of the butchers get the bladders and the oil together. Go quickly. They will be moving those things through the night, and we need to be ready by morning."

CHAPTER 24

Arrows rained down upon the approaching masses as they drew closer to the walls for their initial assault on the citadel. The Gap Warriors watched from the tower gate as the siege on the walls began. Suddenly, from among the enemy ranks scattered groups of warriors broke off to run toward the stronghold. Metal hooks soared over the walls. As the metal clung to the rock, the enemy started its climb upward. Dwarves hacked at the ropes with their axes, severing their hold, and the dark-clad warriors fell to their death.

"It's a distraction," yelled Bernard above the sound of battle, his voice booming across the ramparts. "The towers approach."

Just beyond the attacking horde, a massive bog beast pulled on each tower with the aid of countless slaves, chanting their cadence as they strained to move the giant ziggurats forward. The battle was in full course as volley after volley of arrows rained down on the approaching ranks. While some hit their mark, metal shields blocked others, and the Tal warriors held firm as they immediately turned those back that attempted to breach the wall below.

The slingers were in place awaiting Gerrid's order. "Hold your slings," he yelled as the towers creaked forward. Screams and battle cries continued to rend the air. Gerrid gave the signal and the slings began to twirl above their heads, whining as they spun until they were released on command. Most of them hit their marks, splattering on impact, spraying oil upon the towers. Again they released another volley with the same result. Then the slingers stepped back as the archers moved forward dipping their arrows in pitch and lighting them.

The towers were close now, almost too close. Arrows flew at Gerrid's signal, striking the three towers, igniting flames that raged into the air, consuming all that stood near. The men on the walls cheered while the Boogarans looked on in horror. Many tried in vain to put them out, but the towers were too big and the flames too intense.

Another surge came again from the front ranks, only this time with a greater vengeance. Ladders were raised as men began their ascent, while others climbed ropes. The line of defense weakened at one point as a small group of Boogarans spilled through the breach, hacking and slashing at the men on the walls. Bernard moved in with some of his men, with Micah fighting at his side. The Dwarf and his men held the breach, but soon they were surrounded. Micah had fallen back from the group and was fighting desperately to regain the middle.

From the tower gate, Cyle could see his cousin and the others fighting desperately hold off the assault from the breach at the top of the wall. "I'm going," said Cyle as he ran for the wall to help his cousin. "No," warned Bixby. Cyle stopped short at the door. "That is not our fight; our purpose is clear, we're here to fight another battle."

He looked at Tryska and Bixby with pleading eyes, searching for words, but none came. Then he turned, and disappeared down the stairs.

A Kadiri warrior leapt from the wall and slammed his shield into Micah, sending him back crashing into a post. His head reeling, he looked up just in time to see his cousin's staff slam into the man's head causing him to stagger for a brief moment.

After regaining his footing, the Boogaran raised his sword and brought it down in a chopping arc. Instinctively, Cyle brought the staff up before him with two hands to block the blade. To his surprise, when the metal met wood, the staff held. Spinning to his left, Cyle swung the staff and caught the man in the crotch as Micah looked on in delight. At first a look of surprise crossed the soldier's face, and then sheer agony replaced it. Suddenly there was a rush of movement, and someone flew through the air with both feet banging into the man's chest, sending him over the side with a grunt. It was Bixby. Wincing, he grabbed his shoulder as he gathered himself to stand. The siege had come to a sudden halt; the Tals had pushed their attackers back over the wall and for the moment there was a break in the fighting.

"Come with me, Cyle, you shouldn't be here," Bixby commanded.

"I want to be here," said Cyle defiantly. "I want to fight with my people; besides, I couldn't let Micah down again." Micah looked at him, bewildered by the comment his cousin had just made. Cyle's stomach churned as he realized what he had just revealed.

"What are you saying, Cyle?" asked Micah.

"I was there," Cyle paused, his skin flush with shame, "the night you were captured by the Shadow Wraith and the Boogaran soldiers. I ran…" He looked at the ground. "I ran; I'm sorry," the words came slowly.

"Hey, I would have run too," Micah said as he slapped Cyle on the shoulder and then shook him. "Don't worry about it, Cyle. I hope I never see one of those things again."

"But what about Cree? They killed him."

"There was nothing you or anyone else could do about it; besides you rescued me from Easthold," comforted Micah.

"That's more than enough to make up for it."

"Cyle, we have to prepare for battle," Bixby broke in. "We can't do that if you're up here fighting on the wall. We have to be ready to respond when the demons breach the void."

"He's right, Cyle," said Micah, smiling at him proudly. "My cousin, the Gap Warrior! Who would have ever guessed it? I'm glad it's you fighting those demons and not me." They both laughed although the thought still made Cyle nervous.

"Be safe, Cousin, so we can live to tell our children and their children tales of this day."

"Say a prayer for us, Micah," said Cyle, embracing his cousin before heading back to the tower gate.

The three towers continued to burn sending billows of black smoke that lifted skyward into giant spires, eventually losing their form as they spread a blanketed canopy across the sky. The Boogarans chanted and sounded their war cries. The enemy attacked three more times that day and each time the Tals turned them back.

The massive sea of bodies kept advancing across the valley floor in an unending wave of certain death. If not for the powerful walls of Talinor and the spirited fighting of the Tals and the Dwarves, they would have fallen already.

The smell of death was everywhere, and the medical tents were full of healers fighting to turn the dying into survivors. It had been a treacherous day and, though many lives had been lost on the wall, the Tals had fought courageously and won the day. The Boogarans had lost three lives to the Tals' one. Bernard and Gerrid walked along the ramparts affirming their men for their courage, but it was hard for them to overcome the deepening sorrow that filled the hearts of those who had lost their friends in battle. For the first time in a long time, many of them prayed to the God they had forgotten.

Gafney staggered through the alleyway, his head spinning from the ale he had been drinking for the better part of the day.

Darkness had fallen and the streets were almost empty. He cursed as he stubbed his toe and fell to one knee, feeling little pain due to his condition. "That's it," he said to himself out loud. "I don't feel the pain." And then he thought, yes I do; I feel it, and I'm tired of it.

He sat slumped over with his black hair hanging over his brow, breathing heavily and feeling sick to his stomach. "How did I get here?" speaking to himself out loud again. "How did I let this happen to me?" Then he rocked back in a sitting position on the dirt and leaned against a wall.

The memory of being tied up at the Boogaran camp replayed in his mind. Anger surged through him as he recalled the words of the warlock. "He is no threat to us now." He kept repeating the words in his mind. There was a time when he was a great threat to all that was evil. Lesser demons trembled at his presence, and the greater ones revered his power and skill.

It seemed like such a long time ago when he first made his trek into the Cavern of Lost Souls. He was young, full of faith, and looking for adventure, but it was hard to recall it now. With great effort he tried to remember the reflection in the pool of the cavern. He longed to remember again the image of what he was called to be. If he could only recapture it in his mind, maybe it would give him the courage he needed to go back. It was no use trying; it was lost in the shadow of remembrance now, a forgotten mist. No matter how hard he tried to drag it back into his mind, it would not come clear.

Three gutter rats scampered along the alley wall until they came to some garbage spilled earlier that day. They scavenged through the refuse, chewing at the little pieces of rotted cheese and rancid green meat, feasting contentedly upon their evening meal.

"Pathetic creatures," he spat the words out loud, "you remind me of someone…me. You live miserable lives content to feast upon the leftovers the world has discarded. Only I have a choice; you don't. I forsook that choice long ago." He paused and leaned his head back against the wall. "Has it come to this, now I'm talking to rats?" It surprised him to see the stars overhead glistening against the night sky. A cool breeze kissed his face as he drew air deep into his lungs. He blew it out and said softly to himself. "Where did you go, Gafney? What happened to you?"

A burst of light beamed from across the alley, barely perceptible at first. It brightened and then faded away, sending the rats scurrying for the safety of darker corners. Startled by the light, Gafney reached for his knife, and then he saw a familiar and almost forgotten form standing before him. "Hello, my friend," the Guardian's words were as soft as the smile that crossed his lips. Gafney rose to his feet slowly, lost for words, heart pounding to behold his Guardian who stood before him, fully clothed in battle armor. There were bucklers on his shoulders, a metal breastplate bearing the great eagle, and in each of his hands he bore a double-bladed axe that sparked with life in the moonlight.

"Are you ready to come home?" asked Alaniel. "The battle lines are being drawn, and the voice of your Commander calls out to you."

"I don't know," Gafney struggled to find the words. "I have forgotten who I was; who I am."

"Come to me," said the Guardian. Gafney approached him hesitantly. "Look into the water," the Guardian pointed at a puddle of water in the street, the moonlight reflecting on its surface.

"I see the moon. What of it?"

"Look again."

He looked again, and when he did, the moon dissolved and the puddle turned black. A reflection of a figure appeared on the surface; it was the image of a noble Warrior, strong and full of faith. Gafney swayed as a wave of power flowed over him. His knees grew unsteady and tears creased the corners of his eyes.

"Who is that man?" asked Gafney through trembling lips.

"It is you," said the Guardian, and Gafney fell backward as if dead.

CHAPTER 25

The three towers burned through the night lighting up the killing field. Brok, Nelf and Folger had stationed themselves on the wall near the main gate while Choppa and Ginzer stood just a few feet away. They had been through a lot together and had decided to stick with each other until the end.

Bernard and Gerrid walked the wall until late into the night, encouraging the men. Ginzer finally talked the two of them into getting some sleep, but both of them wanted to sleep on the wall with the other men, and so they did. Tomorrow would test them, thought Ginzer. Drashkar would throw everything he had at them; it would be a miracle if they lasted the day.

When the sun rose over the hills of Talinor, the sky was free of the blanketing mist. The men stood watching as the first rays of light crested the trees on the golden hills. The crisp fall air swirled in wisps upon the fighting walls, bringing a fresh respite from the dreary mist that had dampened their clothes and their spirits. The leaves had turned brown and would soon be falling from the trees to replenish the earth below. All three towers stood smoldering, as a slow reminder of what the day held for them.

Once again, the mist returned to haunt them, seeping into their souls, robbing them of what courage they had managed to cling to until now. War was a new experience for many of the younger ones, and those who had fought in battles before where the dark magic was present were all too familiar with its taunting presence.

A distant horn sounded from the Boogaran camp as war cries rose from their ranks like a distant storm. This was immediately answered by a rush on the wall. "To arms!" cried Gerrid.

"To arms!" echoed the wall commanders as grappling hooks soared over the walls clanging metal on stone as ladders were raised once again for the climbers. Arrows filled the air as metal met metal all along the wall. Men fell in both directions to their deaths as their screams faded to nothing.

The battle continued for most of the day. Gerrid and Bernard continued to fight at the middle of the fray, putting their lives at risk where the conflict was the most ferocious. Their intensity inspired the troops to hold against the never-ending siege of the Boogaran horde. Toward the end of the day there came a lull in the fighting. The warriors on the wall breathed a sigh of relief for the opportunity to rest. A surge of motion came from the ground below, interrupting their brief respite. One of the smoldering towers began to rock back and forth until it tilted forward, crashing down upon the wall into a shower of sparks that brought smoldering flames back to life. It was enough of a diversion to distract the Tal's attention away from the stream of grappling hooks that went flying over the fighting wall. Connected to the hooks was a huge net and at the bottom of the wall the three bog beasts began their ascent. Their twisted forms glowed with supernatural power as they breached the defense on the ramparts. Arrows flew in their direction, but they had little effect on the demonic giants. Others rallied to stop them with swords and axes, but the beasts swatted them away with little effort.

"We can't hold them," cried Gerrid. "Our weapons are not enough."

All at once the three giant beasts leapt from the wall to the ground below, bellowing howls of defiance. The Tals looked on passively as the beasts ran through them and headed in the direction of the palace.

"We must stay to hold the wall," commanded Gerrid, blood-soaked from battle. "It is up to the Priests now to stop them."

Men, women and children fled in every direction to escape their charge, and within moments the beasts had reached the palace square. The Zarish Priests appeared from the temple steps with Orom standing in the midst of them holding his talisman in the shape of a shooting star. The creatures stopped, howling and screaming before them as Orom called his Priests to chant and pray in unison.

Prayers were lifted to the gods of the Priests, to whom they gave their faithful allegiance. The three beasts howled even louder at the sight of the holy men praying, and then something changed. There was a shining curtain of light that shimmered with a translucent quality, and from out of the prisms of light walked three ghostly figures that slowly materialized into the form of two men, one with a sword, the other holding a staff and a small Elf girl holding a flute next to her lips.

The vibration started in Cyle's palms, flowing outward into the shaft. Sparks danced upon its wooden surface as flares of light sprayed to both ends, where he could feel the mounting pressure waiting impatiently to be unleashed with reckless abandon and deadly force.

Enraged by the presence of the Gap Warriors, the three beasts rushed down upon them with deadly intent, slashing and biting. Tryska stood just ten paces away from one of them; raising her flute to her lips, she began to play. The music danced and skipped across the courtyard in a haunting melody. Then there was a displacement of shape and light as a giant silver wolf appeared next to her. Springing forward it attacked the creature that was charging toward the Elf girl. Clamping onto the demon's shoulder with its jaws, the two of them fell to the ground thrashing each other.

Bixby lunged ahead with his sword drawn and sparks flying from its blade. He sliced through one of the creature's thighs. Sparks erupted into a small explosion as it raged against the pain. Flinging itself forward, it sent Bixby sprawling across the courtyard.

Cyle's eyes opened wide as the other beast's claw lashed out at the young Gap Warrior. In one fluid motion he spun his staff to block it, and the force of the blow knocked him to the ground. But he reacted instinctively by rolling on the ground to his left. A new awareness came to him. His training had become second nature, and the realization thrilled him. He continued his roll until he regained his feet and brought the staff around hard against the back of the creature's knee. Power surged through his arms and the staff erupted into the demon. The beast stumbled backward for a brief moment, howling in pain, but it quickly regained its feet.

One of the Priests ran into the courtyard yelling something, but the words were drowned out by the noise of battle. The creature fighting Cyle turned away and grabbed the robed man, throwing him across the courtyard. His careening body slammed into one of the pillars and crumpled to the ground.

Suddenly members of the palace guard appeared with Somuel leading the way. They charged into the courtyard with weapons drawn and swords slashing out at the monsters, but they soon discovered that their weapons had little effect on them. The dark magic was growing stronger and its power was operating at full force in the bog beasts.

"Let them through," hissed the Shadow Wraith, as it pointed to the small breach in the void. Behind him stood twenty winged creatures waiting for the signal to attack while the three Guardians held their position of defense. "The balance of power is shifting; you must let them through."

"Only the five can pass," responded Melidar, "no more."

"Your authority over this realm is diminishing, Guardian," hissed the Wraith. "The humans on the other side have lost their faith in the Ancient One; it's only a matter of time before we all join them." The Shadow Wraith laughed, his voice echoing through the void. Turning to the winged demons, the hooded phantom gave the command and five of them flew through the breach in the void and into the land of flesh and blood.

Chaos had broken out in the courtyard with the presence of the palace guards adding to the confusion of the battle. Half of them had already fallen, and the rest refused to retreat. This was their time and their place to protect. They had been holding back at the palace while the rest of Talinor fought upon the walls to defend the city. It was their responsibility to protect the palace, and they would do so, even if it meant death.

A fissure of light appeared in the midst of the courtyard, opening a breach in the void a second time as five winged demons manifested before them. Desperate to defend themselves, the three Gap Warriors and the wolf moved to the center of the courtyard and stood back to back. Three of the flying demons drove back the palace guard while the other two joined the bog beasts to form a death circle around the Gap Warriors.

"We're losing ground," yelled Bixby. "The balance of power is shifting."

Cyle's heart raced with fear and excitement as he glanced across the yard to see two of the flying demons pushing back the guards, while the others stood encircling them.

"What now?" asked Cyle. "Why aren't they attacking us?"

"They're waiting for the other two to join them," said Tryska. "As soon as they are through with the guards they will be back, and then they will join the others here to try to take us."

The Gap Warriors watched, powerless to help, as the two winged demons bore down on the remaining guards. It was difficult to see the fighting from where they stood, but through the shadows they could hear the men and the demons screaming as wings flapped and blades slashed wildly at the air.

"Can't we help them?" pleaded Cyle, but even as he said it, he knew they would not be able to break free from the demons that surrounded them quickly enough to save the guards. They all watched in horror, straining to see through the shadows, when suddenly a flash of light sparked in the midst of the fray and demonic screams pierced the air, followed by a small explosion of sparks and smoke.

"What is it?" cried Tryska.

Another flash of light shot out and a second death scream rent the air, only this time, cheers erupted from among the guards when out of the shadows stepped a figure barely recognizable in the dim light and swirling smoke. In his right hand was a double-bladed axe upon which sparks and shafts of light danced in deadly rhythm.

"I don't believe it," gasped Bixby. "It's Gafney! He's come back from the dead!"

The Gap Warrior's black locks bounced upon his shoulders as he ran toward his friends, lifting the blade Demon Slayer over his head, and at the same time that almost forgotten force of power filled him with excitement and a renewed sense of purpose. He thought, "It's good to be back." Driving forward with reckless abandon, he lashed out at the nearest bog beast, whirling Demon Slayer through the air at lightning speed, cleaving right and then left. Cyle thought he detected a glimmer of fear in the beast's eyes just before Gafney's blade sliced through its hide and sent it into oblivion.

The others rallied to join him, attacking the beasts and demons with ferocious intensity. Driving them back, their weapons flashed in a deadly display of force. Tryska made the first move as she drew forth the mystical flute, and when she began to play the great wolf attacked the nearest bog beast. Bixby leapt into the air and in one magnificent strike he took off the wing of one of the flying demons, causing it to spin out of control toward the earth where he finished it. Cyle moved with rhythmic motion as one of the flyers struck out at him with its talons. He deflected the strike and rolled on the ground, coming up in one fluid series of strikes with his staff until the creature burst into flames. Only one of the flying demons was left hovering above them. It screeched in terror at the realization that it was alone and flew toward the void, disappearing into the darkness within.

Cheers erupted in the square as the guards waved their weapons to honor the victors who stood breathless in the middle of the smoke-filled yard. Bixby walked over to Gafney and held out his hand; the big man received it firmly. They stared at one another for a moment, "Not a bad day's work for an old man," said Bixby as he slapped Gafney on the shoulder, and the two embraced.

"Two old men!" countered Gafney.

"I think we have a problem," said Cyle, pointing at the Priests who were now joined by Darius.

"Well, well, you've put on quite a show haven't you," said Darius as he walked down the steps of the temple. Cyle could never forget that skinny body and that condescending tone of voice. "Surely this little charade will upset the balance of things. I believe the King made it perfectly clear that you were not to engage in battle with the dark magic." Darius stood there with his arms crossed as if waiting for a reply. "Well, what do you have to say for yourselves?"

"We answer to a higher authority," said Cyle defiantly. Once he had said it, he realized how awkward it felt to speak to his old mentor in that manner.

"We no longer recognize that authority," Darius hissed at Cyle. "Your words show disrespect for your King and for this temple."

"Darius, please, there is no need for harsh words," said Orom, the High Priest; then he turned to address the Warriors. "We wish you no ill will. We are here on a mission by request of the King. If you continue to engage the dark magic, we will not be able to fulfill our part of the agreement."

"We, too, are here on a mission," said Tryska boldly, "and we must fulfill our part. We did not come here at the request of the King of Talinor, we are here at the request of another King, the one we call the 'Ancient of Days.'"

"We have no quarrel against the one you call the 'Ancient of Days,' but our beliefs do not limit us to one source of divine power, for we believe in many sources."

"King Shandon has not broken his agreement with you, and neither have his people," responded Tryska, ignoring his statement. "If Talinor chooses to follow your beliefs, we cannot change that, but as long as there is one among these people who still believes in the old faith, we will remain here, and we will fight to defend this land."

"We shall see about this," barked Darius. "I will be meeting with the King at first light. I believe he will have something to say regarding your defiance." Darius turned and headed up the temple steps mumbling to himself under his breath. "We must do something about the stubborn old woman that still clings to her faith."

She rose from her knees trembling uncontrollably. "It was over, and she could sense it in her spirit. For six hours she had been interceding, deep in prayer, fighting an invisible battle. The exhaustion weighed heavily on her as she walked across the room to get a drink of water. With trembling hands she filled the tumbler and brought it to her lips. She did not know for whom she had been praying, but she was confident that it was related to the battle with the dark magic.

On the counter lay a fresh loaf of bread she had baked earlier that day. After removing the wrapping she placed it on a plate and gathered together some smoked meat and cheese to go along with the loaf. When she opened her front door the guard jumped as if startled by the unexpected movement.

"I have brought you something to eat, Jef," Lena announced as if speaking to an old friend.

"Lena, I've gained ten pounds since I started my assignment here," said the guard as he reached out to take the plate from her. "I will be too big to fight when they call me to the walls." He laughed at the thought of it.

"A little more weight will do you some good. You're too thin anyway; a soldier should be husky and broad."

"A soldier needs to be able to move with some degree of stealth as well if he is to survive."

Jef was young and a little overweight, but as much as he joked about it, he never turned down a meal when Lena offered it to him, and he always ate it with great enthusiasm, which made Lena all the happier.

They had grown to be friends since the time that she had been placed under house arrest. He was there every afternoon until early dawn to guard her, and during his duty they had spent many hours talking together. Jef knew he was testing the limits of his training, which had strict rules about maintaining distance from prisoners. It was hard for Jef to think of her as a prisoner, when in fact they had become such good friends.

It started the night he came to his post carrying a heavy burden. Lena had taken him some food and he had refused it, but she knew something was wrong so she pressed him to talk with her. He told her that his wife had left him and taken the children. She had run off with another man, leaving him devastated. All he found was a note with very little information, just that she had left with their children. He had no idea where she had gone, or whether he would ever see his children again. Lena comforted him with her words and with her cooking.

It was during one of those grief-laden conversations that she offered to pray for him. At first he resisted, for he knew he could be thrown into the dungeons for such a breach of duty. After all, that was why he was guarding the old lady, she had refused to stop praying and renounce her old way of believing. He had embraced the new faith of Talinor willingly because he, like so many others, had fallen away from the old faith. But when she prayed for him that first time, something stirred in his spirit and when he had felt a mystical presence, tears filled his eyes and he sobbed uncontrollably. From that time on the two of them would spend many hours together talking about faith and life's meaning. He preferred the Lady's company to standing alone all night in the dark. It surprised him when he discovered that she was often up during the late hours of the night walking around in her cottage praying. In between her prayers she would come out and talk to him, helping the long nights to pass more quickly. Jef would tell her what was happening at the battlefront, and she used the information to fill her prayers of intercession. He also told her that her grandson was back in Talinor with the rest of the Gap Warriors, and it was reported that he too was a Gap Warrior. Initially, when she discovered that Cyle was a Gap Warrior, she received it with mixed emotions. She had suspected it from the time Graybeard had come to her with the prophecy, and she knew that in time it would be revealed to her. Cyle had done it. He had brought them back, just as Graybeard had prophesied.

CHAPTER 26

At first light the Boogaran horde attacked with a vengeance, screaming their war cry as a fresh wave of warriors assaulted the wall. Ladders were lifted from the ground below as men climbed upward toward the ramparts. The clashing of metal filled the air along with the fatal cries of warriors from both sides as they fell to their deaths. On the ground below the Kadiri pounded the entrance with a battering ram, and each time they connected with the gate the vibration could be felt all along the ramparts. Both Gerrid and Bernard knew that, except for a miracle, they would not last the day. By the middle of the afternoon the fighting had intensified, and although the gate was holding up against the battering ram, the enemy had still managed to breach the main wall.

Micah twisted through a maze of battling warriors, slashing and deflecting blades that lashed out at him from every direction. A thunderous crash rocked the air as the front gate sagged under the pressure of the battering ram. The Tals rallied to the splintered gate to hold it closed, but it was too late. They were breaking through. The gates creaked and moaned as they slowly separated, allowing enough space for the enemy to rush through the opening on to the city streets. The Gap Warriors had returned to the front and joined Bernard and Gerrid in their desperate attempt to hold back the deadly flood sweeping over the Tal defenses.

"Is this it, my friend?" yelled Bernard to Gerrid above the noise of battle.

"If it is, then let us go down together," responded Gerrid. "For Talinor," he yelled at the top of his lungs.

"For Talinor!" yelled Bernard as he raised his axe above his head. At that moment a searing pain pierced his side. When he looked down he saw a spear jutting out of his ribs. At the other end of it was a Kadiri warrior smiling with a look of glee on his face.

The warrior yelled in victory, "I have one of the captains; he submits to my spear." Gerrid pressed through the crowd to reach the warrior. Before Bernard's attacker could remove his spear from Bernard's side, Gerrid was upon him, attacking with a vengeful force that would not be denied, cutting down two other Kadiri. Then he drove his sword through the attacker, bringing him to the ground in a heap.

Ginzer was already there, kneeling over his cousin as blood flowed from his side. "Hold on, Cousin," he pleaded. "This will not be the end of you."

Then Gerrid came to his side as well. Bernard struggled to force his words out, "Give the order to fall back to the palace; we can't hold this ground any longer. Stand me up and leave me, Cousin. I will fight my final battle here."

"You are a brave old fool, I will give you that, but I will not leave you," said Gerrid.

"And neither shall I," cried Ginzer as he and Gerrid grabbed their friend and lifted him to their shoulders while their comrades fought to protect them.

Boogarans and Kadiri were swarming over the walls and flooding through the fallen gate, pushing back the Tals who were yelling for retreat. Suddenly a ram's horn sounded from beyond the wall in the direction of the enemy camp. Both sides ceased their fighting, and for a moment there was a look of confusion on everyone's faces. Again the Boogaran horn sounded. Slowly the enemy backed away, and then began running toward the gate while the Tal army watched in disbelief.

"Maybe we have had our miracle," said Gerrid to his friend

Bernard. Bernard could not hear him.

News of Ashkron's death had reached the Boogaran camp at midday. His father, the king of Boogara had died in his bed. As soon as the news reached him, without hesitation, Drashkar called off the fighting and ordered the retreat of his armies. He then decreed that the rest of the day would be spent in mourning to pay homage to their former ruler. Drashkar, along with the rest of his people would pay his father, Ashkron, the proper respect due a king. Tomorrow, Drashkar would be crowned king, and shortly after that the fighting would begin again. Only this time, he was confident they would finish the battle and take the city. It would be a fitting tribute to his father.

Drashkar felt little sorrow for his father's death for he was old and his sickness had brought him much suffering. Now he, himself, could rest, and tomorrow he would be crowned king of Boogara, soon to be the most powerful nation in the western lands.

"Your Highness," the voice stole him away from his thoughts. Drok Relnik, the warlock, was standing in the entryway of his tent. "Sir, your presence is requested in the woods."

What now, thought Drashkar; the inconvenience of meeting with the Shadow Wraith filled him with angst. "My father has passed on. Can't it wait until tomorrow?"

"I am afraid not, Your Highness. It is a matter of great urgency."

"Very well then, I will come."

When Gizshra, the Shadow Wraith, appeared before Drashkar he manifested as transparent at first until he morphed into a solid form. The future king shuddered in his presence and hated the unpleasant necessity of his services.

"Why did you call off the attack?" the voice came in low vibrating tones from deep within the wraith's throat.

"My father is dead, surely you understand the meaning of respect and honor."

The Wraith snickered from beneath his cowl. His eyes glowed but his face was dark and indefinable. "You are a fool,

Drashkar. Victory was in your grasp. One more moment and we would have been able to breach the void completely," the Shadow Wraith raged against him. "We could have sealed our victory; you would have had all the time you needed to mourn after the defeat."

Anger swelled inside of Drashkar, but he kept it in check. He had learned from his past mistakes not to let it out. "It is our Boogaran custom, and it is my duty to honor my father."

"I told you once that we have little patience for family traditions. It was your own pride of wanting to win this battle as King of Boogara, not family loyalty, that cost us the victory today."

"Tomorrow we shall have victory and then…"

"Tomorrow is forever away from here," spat the demon. "Tomorrow may never come, thanks to your family loyalty. No, tomorrow will not do, we must continue the attack today. There are forces at work here beyond the realm of flesh and blood that you will never understand. The void grows weaker, but there are forces that threaten our ability to open it completely, and if we do not attack now, I cannot assure you victory."

"I know little of the void," countered Drashkar, "but I do know that we have them outnumbered with their backs against the wall, and nothing can change that."

"War is a fickle mistress," whispered the demon. "She can turn on you in an instant and claw your eyes out. You are a fool if you think victory is assured because we have the advantage in numbers."

"I will not fight until the morrow, and that is my final decision," countered Drashkar defiantly.

"Very well," said the demon, "then it is time for you to pay up."

"What do you mean? I do not understand."

"We had an agreement once. You may recall it. I told you that a piece of your soul was required as payment for our help." Drashkar trembled as the demon's words brought his mind back to their conversation. "Only a small piece of your soul. It was the price to guarantee victory, remember?" The demon's words echoed through the corridors of his mind, crashing down upon him. What a farce he thought to himself.

"We could have won this without your help," said Drashkar as the reality of his own words sunk in.

"What you say is true," the wraith laughed devilishly, "but we could not win it without you."

"I release you from your services to Boogara," said Drashkar, as he fought against the numbness that was working its way through his body.

"It is too late for that," the demon laughed again. "I own you; a little piece of soul goes a long way," the demon's laughter filled the glade.

Drashkar tried to run, but his body would not move as terror seized his emotions, choking the courage from him. The hapless king tried to scream, but there was no sound. Another Wraith entered the clearing and approached him, holding out both of his hands and placing them on Drashkar's shoulders until his body began to shake violently. The King's eyes bulged; his body shook violently; and then he dropped to the ground, limp, life draining from him. The demon's aspect faded as it passed into the body of Drashkar.

Bernard's wound would have taken a weaker man, but he was not yet ready to let go. It was too soon to tell if he would make it. The hospital he lay in was filled with the wounded and dying. Blood soaked the ground where the healers and their assistants tended to the wounded, and the dead were carried out in a steady stream. Gerrid had left to attend to the men on the walls while Ginzer stayed with his cousin to try to talk him out of returning to the fight. The two of them argued back and forth until Bernard passed out.

Cyle and Micah had spent the last hour searching for Choppa, fearing that he had been taken in battle. They found him near the main street leading from the city. Cyle was relieved to find his friend unharmed. He asked him where he had been, and his answer was confusing. Choppa seemed nervous when he said something about fighting off the ones that had slipped passed the defenses and into the streets. Before they could talk any further, Bixby interrupted them and summoned Cyle to meet with the other Gap Warriors.

The Bell tower rang out, calling the Tal warriors to arms once again, cutting short the reprieve the weary soldiers desperately needed to regain their strength. Once again the Boogarans were positioning for attack, and Gerrid knew that Bernard was right. They would soon have to retreat to the palace to mount their final defense, and even then, they would only be buying time for the women and children to flee through the escape caves in the mountain behind the city.

Darius had tried all morning to meet with the King, but he had refused. One of the King's advisors told him that he was too busy with military matters. Darius was outraged; this had never happened before. Darius was changing, and for the most part he was unaware of it. It had started when he began to receive advice from the warlock, Drok Relnik. Darius had never had much use for warlocks before, but this man fascinated him. He also knew that if he didn't find a way to stop the Gap Warriors they could hinder the work of the Priests. He had become an avid believer in the ways of Zarish. At first he doubted them, but eventually he came to believe that the Priests were good people, and besides, they had proven themselves worthy opponents against the dark magic.

Drok Relnik had approached him shortly after the Gap Warriors had come to Talinor. The warlock had offered Darius his services, and since Darius was desperate and the price was right, he felt he had no choice. It was Relnik who had suggested capturing the young Gap Warrior, Cyle. The warlock had convinced Darius that the King's former cupbearer was a threat as long there was the possibility of his influencing the King to turn back to the old faith. The darker Darius's heart grew, the greater the influence Drok Relnik had over his thoughts.

Darius also knew that something needed to be done about the old intercessor as well. The King's advisor may have turned away from the old faith, but he could still remember the power of the intercessors back in a time when they were greater in number. It incensed him that the King was unwilling to banish the old woman from the kingdom when the Priests had made it clear that anyone holding to the old faith could hinder the work they were trying to do in Talinor. Something must be done about her, as well. With the King having closed him out as his advisor. He decided the sooner she was dealt with the better.

The warlock had pressed him to move on these matters, because time was short and victory was close at hand. Darius was all too willing to acquiesce to his plan if it would save Talinor. Once they had the boy and his grandmother, the Priests would be appeased and the threat the two of them posed would be eliminated; and, if it became necessary, he would have to find a way to deal with the other Gap Warriors as well.

CHAPTER 27

"The Boogarans are preparing to strike again," announced Bixby as he and Gafney entered the door of the tower gate where Cyle, Tryska and the wolf had been waiting. "The balance of power is still shifting in their favor; we will need to prepare ourselves."

"The wall between the two worlds has grown thin, I can feel the power of the dark magic increasing with each passing moment," said Gafney. "It is only a matter of time now."

"Look to the distance," said Tryska, pointing out the window, "Look into the outlying areas at the edge of the woods; you will see that the scavengers are already gathering." Cyle edged his way to the window to get a glimpse of them slinking in the shadows.

"Does this mean that tonight we will be facing the Shadow Wraiths?" asked Cyle nervously.

"We will face them and whatever they throw at us," answered Bixby. "Until now we have fought the demons that they have sent our way. Tonight we go into the void in their territory, and it will demand our very best," said Bixby.

It was still a lot for the young Gap Warrior to take in. He had had no idea that they would actually enter the void to do battle. He was trying to wrap his mind around all that was happening, and it was happening too fast as far as he was concerned.

"We will all be tested, but we will not be alone as long as we fight as one," offered Bixby. "Have faith, Cyle, remember we have your grandmother interceding for us, and don't forget about the Guardians. They will be doing their part in this conflict."

"Enough talk," said Gafney. "We need to prepare ourselves for tonight's battle. I suggest we take some time to talk to the God who called us here. It's been awhile since I've done that."

Tryska played her flute as the others took to heart Gafney's suggestion. The Silver Wolf stood at the window watching intently as if standing sentry over them. Cyle noticed how beautiful she was. Her fur glistened as the afternoon rays of the sun shone through the open window, sparkling on her silver fur. She seemed so at peace compared with the rest of them.

It had been a long journey, and a lot had changed in the weeks that had passed since he had left Talinor. Cyle believed he was different now. His world had grown and his eyes had been opened to so many things, but most of all he had taken hold of the call on his life and he was ready to live for something far greater than himself.

As he looked around the room, it dawned on him that these people were his friends. Bixby had helped him so many times by answering his questions and giving him the encouragement he needed. From the very beginning he knew he could trust the swordsman; his kind and thoughtful ways had shown him that a Warrior could be both powerful and gentle. He reminded Cyle of some of the images he had seen in the pool at the Cavern of Lost Souls, and he wanted to be like him.

He thought of Tryska and how she had showed him what it meant to have real faith. Even though she was small, the Elf girl had showed great courage at every turn. He admired the mystical bond that linked the Elf girl and the wolf through her flute playing. They had both laid their lives on the line for all of them more than once. Then it dawned on him that was something all of them had in common, they had all risked their lives for one another. It had bonded them in ways that were beyond Cyle's understanding. Maybe it was this kind of friendship that Cyle had admired when he had watched the Tal warriors spending time together.

And then there was Gafney. He hadn't expected a lot from the big man, but as it turned out, he had surprised them all. When they needed it the most, he had fought like a wild beast unleashed, risking his life for them. At times he could be stubborn and impatient, and for a while Cyle thought the big man cared little about any of them, but he was wrong. Beneath that hard outer shell was a heart of compassion; sometimes he just had a hard time showing it. Gafney had lost himself in a world of bitterness and doubt, but now he had found his way home, and it was what Cyle had prayed for. He was thankful that Gafney and his axe, Demon Slayer, would be with them tonight when they entered the void to face the Shadow Wraiths.

From where Cyle sat in the window of the tower gate, he could see both the wall where the Tal soldiers stood ready for the next attack and the field below where the Boogarans and the Kadiri prepared for their next assault. They would scale the wall again and pound away at the gate that the Tals had attempted to repair earlier in the day. As far as his eyes could see there was an ocean of bodies, and when they moved they appeared as shifting sand upon a black shore.

Cyle's thoughts turned to his grandmother. His eyes pooled as he longed to feel her gentle touch. Whispering a short prayer for her, he realized that he might never see her again. The music from Tryska's flute somehow brought a peace to his troubled spirit as it floated through the air, calming his anxious thoughts.

The battle horns of the Boogarans blasted for what they hoped would be their last assault before their final victory. Then came the taunting with insults and jeers rising up from below. Gerrid appeared before his men high upon the ramparts, holding high his sword, with Ginzer standing near by. When he spoke, his words came forth as if carried by thunder. "We are Talinor, and this is our land, given to us by our fathers who entrusted it to us to protect it for our own children. And even though the fates would condemn us to fall this very day, I say that if we are to fall, then let us fall together, defending our beloved land. And as we fight this day, let us fight as though we will live to see the morrow. You and I are brothers, both men and Dwarves, and if one more day of freedom is all we can buy, then let us buy it together as free men." Cheers erupted as weapons lifted into the air, and then Talinor turned to meet the oncoming flood. As the enemy surged forward, pounding exploded at the damaged gates below; metal upon metal rang out in shrill heartless tones. Today, history would be made.

"It is time," Melidar stood at the door, softly glowing as he gave the announcement; the Gap Warriors slowly rose to their feet, awaiting his further instructions. "The demons in the void grow restless. It is only a matter of time now before the breach opens completely. Remember your faith," continued Melidar. "Use all that we have taught you and all that you have taught one another. Tonight we will be fighting with you inside the void, but as you know, our power weakens on this side where flesh and blood reside, and that is why you, and only you can fight the Shadow Wraiths as they breach the void." When Melidar finished his announcement, he turned and disappeared around the corner in a flicker of light.

"What happens if they all break through?" asked Cyle.

"Take heart, young Gap Warrior," answered Gafney. "Battle with your eyes and you will see certain defeat; battle with your faith, and you will see the hope that is required to carry you through."

The four Gap Warriors and the wolf climbed down the tower stairs and into the streets just in time to see a wave of barbarians cut their way through a section of warriors near the crumbling gates. Cyle saw Micah, Gerrid and a group of twenty men attack to drive them back.

Gerrid was yelling from the wall, "Hold them men. Don't let them through!"

Folger and Brok suddenly appeared with swords in hand along with ten other warriors as they dashed to seal the breach, but the numbers were too great as the Kidiri barbarians easily pushed through to force a path into the streets beyond the gates.

Micah, Gerrid and the others were being driven back when a sword cut through the air into Folger. Before he hit the ground, Ginzer and Brok were upon his attacker to finish him.

Ginzer yelled defiantly with his axe swinging wildly, "Hold the line!" But it was no use; they were losing ground.

"We have to help them," cried Cyle as he watched in horror. The Gap Warriors gripped their weapons ready to run into the fray.

"Wait, look over there," cried Gafney, pointing toward the main street leading to the wall. Forty men riding horses, wielding swords, axes and spears, rode full gallop toward the breach in the line.

"It's the Highlanders!" yelled Bixby, holding his sword over his head. He could see the three brothers, Duggan, Gregor and Marcos leading the charge. They drove their powerful warhorses into the barbarians, faltering at first, and then re-gaining the advantage, pushing them backward.

Suddenly a wall of light rose before the Gap Warriors with crystal prisms shooting in every direction. Power vibrated from Cyle's hands into his staff; his heart raced as he gulped to draw in air. Bixby's sword and Gafney's axe, Demon Slayer, exploded. Tryska's flute glowed in her hands as the silver wolf's fur shimmered and sparked with supernatural power.

Bixby motioned, and the four of them ran at the wall, disappearing into the void. A sound came like howling wind with lights flashing, and then there was darkness all around Cyle. A voice spoke from out of the darkness, "Hear my words," it was a familiar voice. "Do you know who I am?"

"You are the Princess Shariana."

"Do not fear, Cyle," said the Princess. "I will guide you; trust only my voice."

As a lit pathway appeared before him, he could hear faint screams in the distance, and then a roar came from ahead of him. Something was moving toward him down the path. His first instinct was to run, but where would he go? He looked for the others, hoping they would soon be joining him.

Whatever it was, it was coming fast in his direction. He held the staff in his hands out in front of his body in the attack position. The thing growled, baring its teeth as it sprang at him. Stepping to his left, he spun the staff around ready to strike and then it vanished, a sinister laughter filling the cavern. "That was too easy for you," said a deep voice. "Maybe we should try something a little more interesting."

Then he heard another voice, "Cyle, come back I need you." It was the voice of his grandmother pleading with him. "I'm in trouble Cyle; I need you to help me."

It was her voice, he was sure of it. Emotions flooded his heart, threatening to take over his thoughts. He missed her desperately, and he wanted to be with her and reach out to her.

"They're coming after me, Cyle. Only you can help me."

He looked behind himself and he could see an opening in the void. Beyond the opening he could see Talinor, and his grandmother being dragged through the streets by a handful of guards. "I'm coming, Grandmother," Cyle yelled out loud. Anger surging, he turned to run toward the portal in the void.

"Cyle, wait," warned the Lady's voice. "Remember what I told you. Listen only to me."

"But my grandmother is in trouble!" pleaded Cyle.

"Who will you listen to, Cyle?" asked the Princess. "The voices of the void or the voice of the one who was sent by the 'Ancient of Days'?"

"Help me, Cyle, help me," he heard his grandmother pleading from beyond the void. Emotions pulled in both directions; turmoil stormed inside of him.

"Remember your faith, Cyle," warned the lady. "Listen only to me. The void cannot duplicate my voice, but it can duplicate the voices of others."

Turning away from the sight of his grandmother, he remembered the words Tryska had spoken to him when he had told her that he was afraid. She said, "When you enter the Gap you must put your faith in the one you serve—the 'Ancient of Days'. If you do, you will discover that the One you serve is all that He claims to be."

"Be gone!" Cyle yelled as loudly as he could. Instantly the image vanished. The void began to shift and change shape around the young Gap Warrior. The voice of the Princess came to him once again, "The others are waiting for you. Follow my voice and I will lead you to them."

He could see shapes shifting in the void around him as the voices started again, or were they his own thoughts? He wasn't sure. My grandmother; I left her alone, just like I left Micah. I'm a coward. Cyle scolded himself as the thoughts tore away at his insides. Maybe they are right, he thought to himself. Maybe I am a coward.

"Those are not your thoughts, Cyle. You must not agree with them," warned the Princess. "If you give them access to your mind through agreement with their lies, they will control you. Now use the authority given you and tell them to go away."

"By the authority of the 'Ancient of Days' I command you to go away," Cyle ordered. There was a rush of wind, and then silence returned.

"Over here," another called out through the darkness that sounded like Bixby. "We're over here Cyle. Follow my voice." Cyle started to move in the direction of the voice, but then he stopped. "What should I do, My Lady?"

"Very good, Cyle, now you are learning." affirmed the Princess. "You may go to them. They are who they say they are."

The darkness parted, and Cyle found himself standing before his friends.

"What took you so long?" teased Tryska. Before he could answer her, she said, "It's all right. It took me awhile my first time out too."

Keesha, the wolf, howled, and the hair stood up on her back. "What is it, Keesha?" Tryska asked, stroking her neck. The wolf started to growl deep in her throat. The void rippled and shifted as the shimmering black form of a Shadow Wraith appeared before them. The intangible presence of evil permeated the air around the Defenders as the skin on Cyle's neck vibrated in response to its presence. Memories of that night in the meadow came flooding back to him. The demon looked at Cyle. Pointing a clawed finger in his direction, it spoke directly to him. "You cannot stand against me. You ran once; you will run again," the words vibrated off its tongue.

When the shame returned, Cyle cursed. He thought he was done with it. The Wraith raised its palm against him and an invisible force slammed into him, knocking him to his knees. Shame pressed in on him again as the staff in his hands flared with power.

"Stand up, Cyle," it sounded like Gafney speaking to him, but he wasn't sure. "You've got to stand up and face this demon. Its name is Shame; I have known it well." Now he knew for sure it was Gafney's voice. "Come, Cyle, we will face it together; this one is here to battle me as well."

Cyle forced himself to his feet, gasping. He looked about to see if his friends were still with him. All of them were gone except for Gafney. "Come, Cyle, we've both carried our shame long enough; I think it's time we destroyed it." Gafney yelled, "One Faith!" His declaration echoed through the void as the demon of shame screamed in agony, recoiling at the words. Gafney ran toward the Shadow Wraith, the blade of Demon Slayer exploded into a savage display of light.

Cyle tried to repeat the words, stuttering and choking. Again he tried, willing them to come. Finally the words stumbled out, "One Faith!" At first they were soft and barely discernable. Again he tried, and this time they came out in a kind of madness and rage, "One Faith!" he called out with a passion driven by a new release of defiant faith. The demons in the void screamed and retched in agonizing pain.

Rising up, he charged to join Gafney in the attack on the Shame Demon. In a panic the wraith waved its hands, calling forth demons from the outer barriers. Two screeching imps with swords flailing launched out at them. Cyle blocked the first assault with his staff. As the blade met wood, an explosion of fire and sparks erupted.

Gafney chopped through the demon that came at him with his axe, and it exploded into a shower of sparks and fire. Then he turned upon the other demon that was swinging its blade wildly at Cyle, who feinted backward to avoid the edge of its blade. Spinning around, Cyle blocked the blow with his staff as more sparks flew. Then he turned in the opposite direction and brought his staff around in a sweeping arc at the demon's head. His staff and Gafney's axe connected with the creature at the same time, exploding it into shower of light.

Suddenly Bixby, Tryska and the wolf appeared, and at the same time four other Shadow Wraiths manifested in front of the Gap Warriors. The Shame Demon laughed and disappeared into the mist, leaving the other four demons behind. Wind reverberated through the void, stirring up a swirling mist overhead and bringing with it another wraith materializing in the midst of the other four demons.

"Gizshra," Bixby whispered his recognition under his breath. The other demons parted around their master in a show respect.

"So, this is the best the Princess could send on such short notice," said Gizshra sarcastically. The other demons snickered softly while the Gap warriors looked on. "The time has come," Gizshra continued. "You must allow us to pass."

"On the contrary, we forbid you to pass," said Bixby defiantly. "If you wish to cross over to the side of flesh and blood, then you will have to pass through us first."

"You forbid nothing!" screamed Gizhra, his voice echoing through the void. Demons could be heard rejoicing throughout the darkness. The great wolf growled, baring its teeth.

"Hold, Keesha," said Tryska softly as she reached out to touch her.

"The people of Talinor have sealed their fate," cried the demon. "They have chosen their path by turning away from the One Faith and in doing so, they have also forsaken the Author of that faith. Your power is fading; you can no longer protect them against our magic."

Gafney boiled inside, and without thinking he found himself lunging at the head demon, swinging Demon Slayer with deadly intent but before he could reach the master demon he hit an invisible wall and was thrown back twenty paces through the air, landing on the ground in a pile.

"You are a fool if you think you can touch me," warned the Shadow Wraith, clearly pleased with his power over the Gap Warrior. Gafney slowly rose to his feet, his powerful body unharmed by the force of the fall.

It was the miracle they had been praying for when the Highlanders, led by the three brothers, Duggan, Gregor and Marcos, had arrived just in time to push back the barbarians to help secure the breach one more time. Some of the enemy had broken through the defense and run toward the palace, but they couldn't worry about that now. The palace guard would have to take care of them.

The victory of the Highlanders had given them another rallying point, raising their spirits for yet another assault against the enemy, but that did not last for long before the Tal warriors found themselves once again fighting desperately to hold them back from a final breach in their defense. With the superior numbers of the barbarians and the main gate only partially standing, it was only a matter of time before the barbarians would break through again, and the next time there would be no stopping them.

The women and children were already leaving the city by way of the escape caves, and many of the warriors had already defected to safer places. By the last count they were down to two thousand at the front and three hundred palace guards, plus some two hundred fresh Highlander warriors, against thousands of the enemy.

King Shandon had been urged by his other advisors to leave the palace, but he would hear nothing of it and insisted on staying to the end. Somuel and his palace guards waited restlessly for the battle lines to reach them, knowing they too would fight to the death defending their King.

"Jef, would you like some bread?" The guard was amazed at the way his prisoner could be so calm at a time like this. Lena had spent most of the morning and afternoon praying and baking bread while the kingdom teetered on the brink of destruction.

"No, thank you, Lena," responded the guard politely. "I'm too nervous to eat anything right now."

"Maybe you should pray with me."

He looked at her surprised by her relentless boldness to draw him in, but the smile on her face always put him at ease. "I...I would like to pray with you, Lena," said Jef tentatively. "Our kingdom is falling and my people have forsaken the One Faith." He paused glancing away, shame masking his face. "I guess

I have forsaken it too. I think I have been a fool long enough; if I'm going to die, I want to die believing in the faith that my forefathers taught me and my kingdom was founded upon, faith in the 'Ancient of Days.'"

"Pray with me then," Lena smiled. "You will be the first one to join me in a long time." Jef seemed to hesitate. "Do you want me to show you how?" asked Lena.

"Well… there's something I never told you in all of our conversations because I was too ashamed."

"What is it Jef? You can tell me."

"My grandfather was an intercessor," tears came to Jef's eyes as he fumbled for the right words. "He prayed for Talinor during the last war. I was only eight years old at the time, but I can still remember some of his prayers as if it happened yesterday." Jef tried to swallow back the tears, but when Lena touched his shoulder, they flowed freely as if a forgotten gate that had been sealed for ages had finally been loosed.

When Jef could speak he said, "Right before my grandfather died he called Graybeard to our home. The two of them anointed my head with oil, and my grandfather, along with Graybeard, laid hands upon my head and prayed over me."

"Jef, can you not hear the Spirit voice of the "'Ancient of Days' calling out to you?" said Lena with passion rising in her voice. "It is time for you to respond to that call and intercede with me in prayer for the Gap Warriors, and all of those that defend the breach against the dark magic."

Lena took the guard's hands, and to her great joy he joined her. For the first time in years she did not pray alone.

The Defenders' weapons exploded with a surge of power that shook them all, causing the four of them to fall backward to the ground. The fur of the silver wolf shimmered and danced as she pointed her nose upward, howling in primal defiance as supernatural energy vibrated all around them.

Cyle's body shook with a violence he had never experienced

before. He fought to rise to his feet, barely able to stand, then fell back again to his knees. Warmth and energy pulsed through his body, and at the same time his staff radiated with an intense vibration, releasing a new dimension of power that made it almost impossible for Cyle to maintain his grip.

"What is it the source of this manifestation?" bellowed Gizshra. The other demons cowered from his wrath.

A new demon manifested before Gizshra, a pathetic looking imp bowing and trembling before him, waiting to be acknowledged. "What is it?" hissed Gizshra, full of impatience.

"Sir… there are now two."

"What?" the lord of the Shadow Wraiths raged at the messenger. "How could this have happened?" The groveling demon shook violently with fright.

"Master…"

"Never mind," said Gizshra, spilling out his wrath upon the pitiful imp, exploding it into a ball of sulfurous flames.

Cyle looked on in confusion; then he turned to Bixby and the others for some answers. Tryska smiled like he had never seen the Elf girl smile before. Then she said, "Another intercessor has joined your grandmother."

The void around them shifted as the demonic beings began to transform into distorted shapes. It appeared as if they would fade from sight, but then new forms manifested. The four Wraiths were transformed into warriors now dressed in full battle armor, each carrying a coal black sword with red flames dancing upon the blades from hilt to tip. Gizshra screamed and the four Shadow Wraiths, along with untold numbers of other demons, attacked in a burst of fury and rage unleashed by the power of the dark magic.

Bixby led the charge, his sword flaring in defiance, slicing into a massive demon that was carrying a ball and mace. The thing screamed as Bixby's blade cut through its leathery skin, but the creature would not go quietly. With sulfurous slime oozing from its side the demon lunged toward him wildly swinging its mace.

In the midst of the chaos Cyle heard Tryska's flute. The music reached deep into his spirit stirring a holy rage deep with in him that welled to the surface. He spun around just in time to see a scavenger, teeth bared, racing toward him. Cyle countered and ran to meet it in the air, driving his staff into its gaping maw. The creature's head exploded and hurled through the air toward another wraith that was moving toward Cyle with his sword in hand. Annoyed by the inconvenience of it all, the Shadow Wraith sliced through the flying scav with its own blade, casting it aside as it fell in two pieces to the ground.

"So, we finally meet," the Shadow Wraith addressed the young Gap Warrior as sinister pleasure creased his smile. "Those pathetic creatures you have been fighting are my pets. Do you really think you can defeat a real master of the dark magic?"

The question took Cyle off guard as he stumbled backward, anxiously searching for something to say in response to the demon's taunts. Then out of the chaos of the battle Gafney ran past him straight at the wraith, planting his shoulder into his midsection. The demon grunted and went flying backward into the surrounding mist.

Gafney looked at the young Defender and said, "Don't talk to 'em kill 'em. If you talk to 'em, they'll just annoy to you."

The fighting continued until Tryska heard the familiar sound of the portal opening behind her, and she saw what she feared most, a powerful Shadow Wraith had breached their defenses and slipped through the portal into the world of flesh and blood. She yelled as loud as she could so the others could hear her, "One of them has slipped through!" She pointed toward the portal where the world of men could be seen beyond the void.

Melidar manifested in the midst of them, and with him was Tryska's Guardian, Veneda, who turned to engage in the surrounding battle while Melidar turned to face Cyle, yelling out a command, his eyes blazing. "Go quickly and find the King. You must turn his heart back to the way. He trusts you Cyle. Maybe he will listen to you." The young Gap Warrior hesitated for a moment, doubt filling his heart.

"It's all right. I will fight in your place," assured Melidar. "We have gained some advantage with the second intercessor."

Cyle turned and ran toward the portal. Running through a swirl of lights, he suddenly found himself running on the streets of Talinor in the direction of the palace. The sounds of battle rang in the diistance, Cyle's heart churned as he searched his mind for the quickest route to get to the King. He knew that the palace would be heavily patrolled, making it almost impossible for him to get past the guards.

"Cyle." He heard the familiar voice, and turned to see Choppa.

"I can't believe you're here," said Cyle exultantly as he ran to greet his friend.

"Where have you been?" asked Choppa, out of breath.

"Never mind that now, I need you to help me get into the palace. I've got to get to the King."

Choppa looked around; then he motioned to his friend, "Come with me, I know a way." The two of them ran toward the palace.

"He'll be in the War Room. Can you get me in there?"

"Just follow me," answered Choppa. "I have an idea." He led Cyle through some narrow back alleys and streets until they came to the edge of the Rainbow River near the center of the city.

"What now?" asked Cyle.

"We follow the river to the palace and then… Someone's coming," Choppa motioned.

Just ahead of them a group of five or more moved through the street, cutting them off from the direction they wanted to take. "Back this way, hurry," urged Choppa. As he turned in the opposite direction, four other men stepped from the shadows closing off their second choice for escape.

Cyle recognized one of the men. It was the warlock, Drok Relnik, smiling as if he had just caught a rabbit in a snare. The warlock looked at Choppa and smiled, "Thank you for a job well done." Cyle looked at Choppa, his heart sinking.

"Choppa, what have you done?" Cyle was sick at the thought of the betrayal by his friend.

"Cyle, you have to believe me. I didn't do it."

"You never know who you can trust, do you," said the warlock, smiling.

The other men approached Cyle and Choppa. "Bind both of them," ordered the warlock. Cyle lashed out with his staff catching one of the men in the chest, sending him backward to the ground. The others pulled long knives and swords as they rushed in on the two of them.

Drok Relnik and his men forced them down the slope with their backs to the river wall. Cyle with his staff, and Choppa with his sword, deflected the blades that lashed out at them. "Hold off," yelled the warlock, his men backed away at the command, "There is no need for the two of you to die. Drop your weapons and we will let you live."

They were out-numbered four to one. Cyle knew they could not last long against these odds. "Come on, kid, drop the staff before I have to gut you," warned one of the men holding a long knife.

Choppa threw down his sword and raised his hands in surrender. "They have us, Cyle. We have no choice.

Cyle heard splashing from behind him and, before he could turn around, something grabbed the back of his tunic, and pulled him over the wall. He plunged beneath the surface, cold water rushed over him as he reflexively gasped for air.

He could hear his captors yelling from the wall above while at the same time something pulled him deeper under the water. Calming himself, he fought against the overwhelming urge to panic. No longer able to hold his breath, he gasped for air as water rushed into his lungs.

Then he broke the surface of the water. Coughing and choking, the young Gap Warrior fought to recapture the air he had lost. Realizing the staff was still in his hand, he tried to maneuver it to fend off his capturer.

"Don't fight," said the voice from behind him. It sounded familiar, but he couldn't place it. "It's all right," the voice gurgled. "Gruber here to help."

"Gruber!" exclaimed Cyle.

"Quiet… men still looking for us."

They had surfaced under a bridge not far from where they had gone under. On the opposite shore they could hear the warlock's men shouting at one another as they desperately tried to find him.

"Stay here. Men can't see us," whispered Gruber.

"Something took him under," said one man to the others. "I saw it. It was some kind of monster."

"Keep looking," commanded the warlock. "He's still here somewhere, I know it."

"Come, we float with current toward castle." Gruber pulled some moss from under the water, "Here, put on head. If they see us we go under water."

The two of them pushed away from the bridge out into the middle of the river. Behind them they could hear Drok Relnik shouting at his men.

CHAPTER 28

"I need your help, Jef," said Lena as she stood up and walked over to her closet. "I need you to take me to the palace temple."

"But Lena, how can I do that?" argued the guard. "I will be disobeying a direct command."

"You prayed with me, did you not? Were you disobeying a direct command then?"

"Well, yes, but, I…"

Lena opened the closet door and pulled out a walking staff, "My bones are aching; I think this will help ease the pain of walking." The intercessor ignored the guard's objections, "Come, we have little time to waste. If we don't act now, there won't be anyone left to disobey."

Jef handed her a cloak to wrap around her and said, "We'll have to be careful."

"Oh, don't worry about that," Lena interrupted, "I've been walking these streets for years after dark, and I've never suffered so much as a scratch. I'll take care of you, Jef, don't worry." Jef laughed nervously.

Anger flared in Cyle at the thought of his friend betraying him, but the evidence was hard to deny. He had always known that Choppa was a free spirit and easily influenced by others. The thought of it angered him. Choppa had been his friend for a long time, but a nagging doubt had always plagued him. He never really believed that he could count on his friend if things got really difficult. Now he knew for sure. When he thought about what had just happened, he remembered how Choppa had acted strangely the other night when he asked him where he had been. He wondered how long he had been consorting with the warlock.

Gruber and Cyle had floated to a place near the palace wall. The moss man knew a way in through a canal that provided water to the castle.

"How did you know about this, Gruber?" asked Cyle.

"Gruber escaped dungeon, remember? This is how Gruber get out."

"I need your help, Gruber. Can you get me near the palace kitchen?"

"Come, we must swim through water tunnel."

The water was cold in the tunnel, and seeing was even more difficult, but the moss man had no problem finding his way through. After a brief swim through the tunnel, they surfaced through the well in the kitchen area.

The room was empty and dark, so they climbed out onto the floor, the two of them dripping with water. Cyle listened for voices and heard no one. "Thank you, Gruber. Once again you have saved my life."

"Gruber glad to help Cyle," said the moss man grinning with an unmistakable look of great pride on his face.

"You need to go now. It won't be safe for you to stay in the castle."

"You be safe, Cyle," said the moss man as he offered his hand to his friend. "Maybe some day we meet again."

"I hope so," said Cyle.

After Gruber slid back down the well, Cyle made his way into the empty dining room. Near the back of the room was a familiar stairwell that led from the wine cellar to the King's War Room. As he climbed toward the King's Council Room a flood of memories came to him. He had walked these steps countless times in the past to perform his humble responsibility of serving wine to the King and his guests. The deep resentment he had felt for being stuck in the role of a cupbearer revisited him. It struck him that the very thing he had hated had now become his greatest asset. If he hadn't been the King's trusted cupbearer, then he would have had no chance of gaining the King's ear. He hoped that the closeness he had shared with the King would be enough to convince him to return to his Faith.

As he approached the top of the stairs, he found that the door to the council room was closed. Carefully he turned the latch and quietly pushed the door open just enough to look in. He saw the King on the other side of the room standing alone by the window. He pushed further and stuck his head in to look around and make sure there was no one else in the room.

CHAPTER 29

With the arrival of dusk, the final assault on the gates began. The once massive structure of iron lay mostly in a fallen heap. The barbarian horde had launched what it knew would be its final push to take the city. Over the walls they poured like mad men as the last of the Tal army fought furiously to turn them back. Gerrid was at the front of the charge, his sword cleaving and slashing through all that challenged. Near the gates Micah had joined a group of Highlanders, along with Ginzer and the wounded Bernard, ready to make their final stand together. Ginzer had done his best to talk his cousin out of this foolishness, but Bernard had stubbornly argued, "If I am going to die, it will be fighting with an axe in my hand. Surely you would not deny me that." Ginzer didn't like it, but he knew his cousin would not be denied.

Suddenly there was one final crash from the battering ram that freed the gate from the remaining buckles, and they moaned as they released their final grip on the walls. The gate was still in the way, but the ram had pushed back an opening big enough to give the enemy the room it needed to send in more fighters.

Micah's blade sliced through a screaming Kadiri warrior, and then three more were upon him. One of their blades tore through his shoulder. He felt the warm blood, but he refused to look at it and pressed forward. Glancing up toward the ramparts he saw the enemy gaining its final ground. Under his breath he prayed, "Forgive us for turning away."

The flags in the War Room bearing the design of the shooting star were a haunting reminder of Talinor's apostasy. And this is where it had led them, to the brink of destruction. More than ever, Cyle resented the new image that had replaced the one of the eagle. After taking a deep breath, the young Gap Warrior stepped into the room to face the King.

"Your Majesty," said Cyle sheepishly as the King turned his gaze from the window to his former cupbearer. At first the King did not appear to recognize him, "Your Majesty, it is I, Cyle."

"Cyle, I'm surprised to see you here. Come in, come in, let's talk."

Cyle could see and hear the fighting in the distance through the window the King was standing at. "Your Majesty, I…I was wondering if I could speak to you about the state of things."

"But of course. I'm so glad to see you," offered the King. "We can talk about whatever you wish. I'm not going anywhere soon."

Cyle felt uneasy with the King's calm demeanor considering his kingdom was on the verge of collapse.

"Sir, your kingdom is almost lost. Most of our soldiers are either dead or wounded, and the women and children are fleeing the city. The main gate is about to fall if it hasn't already. Please, Sir, there's still hope; I beg you to reconsider your alliance with the Priests of Zarish. Surely you can see the emptiness in their promises. The old faith can still be trusted."

"The old faith," mused the king. "Do you really think the old faith can save us now? Look at us. It will take more than faith to rescue us from our enemies."

"Sir, we are not able to use the full force of our faith if you as our King do not return to embrace it. The people will follow you back, I know they will," Cyle tried not to sound like he was begging. "Many of our people are ready to make that step. They just need you to say the word, and they will obey."

"Don't be a fool, Cyle," the King's tone turned against his cupbearer. "It is the end of this kingdom, and you know it."

"This kingdom"… the King's words pricked Cyle's spirit. Why didn't he say, "my kingdom"? Something was wrong, and he knew it. "Who are you?" demanded Cyle, "You're not the King."

"Am I not?" laughed the king. "Then who do you think I am?"

Cyle's palms began to sweat and tingle, and at the same time the power in them sent tiny sparks dancing along the staff in his hands. Suddenly the main door opened as Darius, the High

Priest, Orom, and King Shandon entered the room. The look on their faces reflected shock as they stared at the other king who was standing across the War Council Room.

A stench began to permeate the room, and a strange crackling noise could be heard as the image of the king began to transcend his original shape until, standing before them, was the robed figure of a Shadow Wraith.

"Do not move," demanded Orom, holding out the talisman from beneath his cloak. Fear threatened to paralyze Cyle as he watched the High Priest move toward the Shadow Wraith. Chanting in an unintelligible language, he summoned the power in the talisman on the end of his staff to come forth.

The Wraith laughed hideously at the Priest. "Do you really believe that will help you? You fool, I control the power in the talisman."

The Priest chanted louder, trying desperately to summon the power hidden deep within the object.

"You have served your purpose," hissed the demon as he reached out a clawed finger, pointing it at the talisman. The ball at the top of the Priest's staff began to glow red. Orom's eyes lit up with triumph that was soon replaced with a look of horror. The red glow moved down the handle of the staff until it reached Orom's hands, and then he began to wail and scream in agony. The Priest's body shook in rapid vibrations and the skin on his hands started smoking as the smell of burning flesh filled the air. Screaming and wailing in pain, Orom turned and ran for the open window. Flinging himself out of the opening, his screams could be heard until he hit the palace courtyard below.

Lena rested against her staff as she and her escort arrived at the courtyard. Tired and out of breath, she directed Jef toward the steps of the temple. "We're going in there," she said through heavy breathing. "I need you to come in with me and pray to the 'Ancient of Days.'"

"It has been forbidden," protested the guard. "They will

run us out of there."

Lena walked past him and started her ascent to the top of the steps before calling back to him, "Are you coming or not?"

When the two of them pushed open the temple doors they saw a group of Zarish Priests gathered around an altar with a sculpture of the shooting star. Their chants rose in unison, and the smell of burning incense filled the air. At least thirty other worshipers joined in their zealous invocations to their gods. They prayed passionately for deliverance from the approaching dark magic and the Boogaran horde.

Lena turned to Jef and ordered him, "Stay here and intercede." He started to object, but she ignored him and walked resolutely toward the altar. The staff tingled in her hands.

The altar Priests recognized her at once. "Heretic, you are not allowed in here," one of them yelled, pointing his bony finger at her. "You must leave this place immediately." Lena ignored the warning, and continued to walk toward the altar.

One of the Priests stepped in front of her to block her way, leaving the two of them staring at each other. Lena was the first to speak as the others in the room passively looked on. "You are the ones that are no longer welcome in this place," said Lena defiantly. "I am here to restore this temple to its original form of worship."

"We cannot allow that to happen," replied the Priest coldly. "If you insist upon your present course of action, we will be forced to throw you out of here. We worship here by direct commission of the…"

"And I am here because there will be no King if you continue this foolishness."

"Guards, seize her," ordered the Priest. Three temple guards pressed their way through the worshipers until they reached Lena. Jef saw what was happening and started toward her, intending to intersect them. Lena held the staff in front of her body with both hands. A burst of energy flared outward, knocking the guards and the Priest to the ground.

Jef watched in awe as she ascended the steps of the altar.

Drawing back the staff with both hands she struck the idol of the shooting star sending sparks and flames erupting into the air. The Priests and the worshipers fled, seeking cover from the explosion.

The temple doors opened and another Priest burst into the room yelling frantically, "Orom is dead. His body has been found in the courtyard, the dark magic has taken him…"

The young Gap Warrior's body shivered as the dark magic enveloped him causing him to gasp for air; vomit threatened to rise in him. Through a dense fog he could see the Shadow Wraith laughing at him. Straining to stand up, he leaned on his staff to keep from falling over. An invisible weight pressed him back to the ground. With his stomach still churning and the room still spinning around him, he felt his strength slipping away. His body was lifted off the floor by an invisible force and thrown across the room, slamming into the banner of the falling star that hung from the wall. He winced at the pain as his staff dropped to the floor. Instinctively he reached out to clutch at the banner to slow his fall. Sliding toward the ground he brought the banner with him, tearing it from the holding rings. Cyle grabbed his staff lying near him and looked up to see the eagle carving that had been hidden behind the banner. Below the image of the eagle were the words, "One Faith." The staff vibrated as sparks shimmered up and down the shaft. Then he heard her voice, soft and clear, reaching out to him through all the confusion and fear, "Evil will not let go without a terrible fight; now is the time to stand in the power of the might given you by the 'Ancient of Days.'"

Her words unleashed a well of strength and hope that gushed forth out of his inner being. Rising to his feet he twirled the staff over his head until it came to rest in his two hands, sparking and shimmering with power. The room was clear once again and he could see the Shadow Wraith across the room. Cyle charged toward the demon yelling, "One Faith!" His words echoed off the walls of the War Room as power surged through him and his weapon. He launched through the air striking out at the malevolent apparition that stood before him. Just as he reached it, the thing transformed into a massive warrior clothed in full armor holding a black sword with red flames dancing upon the blade.

The phantom met the young Warrior's charge, swinging its blade in a death arc that left a trail of red flames in its wake. Cyle stepped quickly to his right. When blade and staff collided there was an explosion of blinding light that filled the War Council Room. The phantom Wraith growled at him as it stepped back and started to laugh once again. "Your magic is weak and untested," he taunted. "Do they really think that a mere boy can defeat one of my kind?" The thought did occur to Cyle that this would be the first Wraith he would face without help from his friends. He brushed the thought aside and struck out a second time with a savage assault, hammering his staff into the demon's chest, and sending it back into the wall. Cyle thought he detected a look of concern on the thing's face. Darius and the King tried to leave the room, but the door slammed shut and could not be opened. Then that sickening laughter started again that Cyle had come to hate. "I will have you all before I am done." There was pounding on the door as the King's guards shouted from the other side, trying frantically to push their way in.

"Your Majesty, the time has come to reclaim your faith. Please consider my words before we are finished," entreated Cyle.

"It's too late for that now," screamed the Wraith in defiance. "We have seized this kingdom as our own." Then it struck again with madness unlike anything Cyle had faced before, slashing viciously through the air. The curved blade made contact with the staff over and over again. Each time there were explosive shards of light driving Cyle back. Then the demon's blade flew swift and sure, overpowering the Gap Warrior with a sudden counter move. Catching the staff at just the right angle, it went flying toward the window. Cyle tried desperately to grab at it, but it was no good. Staring in disbelief at what had just happened, his heart raced and his mind searched for a solution to his predicament. Before he could find one, the Wraith warrior was upon him, slamming the hilt of his sword into his chest sending him sprawling into the wall. Lights flashed in his head. As the room spun, he fought to maintain a connection with his world as it slipped away from him. The demon lifted its blade to Cyle's neck. "You're finished playing Gap Warrior, boy," said the demon as a hideous smile creased its lips.

Then something caught Cyle's eye up in the rafters. It was Choppa perched on the edge of a beam. Before he could fully take in what it all meant, Choppa leapt from his perch landed on the Wraith's back, and plunged his blade into the demon's neck. The blade had no effect except to distract the creature. It grabbed Choppa and hurled him across the room. Choppa crashed into the Council table, his arms and legs flailing in all directions.

The Wraith turned back toward Cyle to finish what it had started when it heard the taunts coming from behind it. "Is that it? Is that the best you can do?" cried Choppa defiantly. Blood dripping from his lips and nose, he let loose an arrow from his crossbow. The Wraith turned to catch the shaft in its hand and toss it aside. Choppa's eyes grew as the demon turned upon him. Reaching out for him with its muscular arm, the Wraith warrior seized him by the throat. Choppa struggled to get free as the demon lifted his sword for a final death strike.

By now Cyle was standing on his feet, searching desperately for a way to save his friend. On the wall he could see the words, "One Faith," and then he felt a burning against his chest. It was the eagle his grandmother had given him. His hand closed around the amulet as he prayed for help. With fear for his friend's life still running through him, he grabbed one of the flagpoles displaying the shooting star image and tore it from its standard. Instinctively he spun the pole in his hands as if it were his own, and to his surprise his palms began to tingle as the power surged and lifted through him into the pole. Sparks shot from his hands and danced along the shaft, calling him back to the battle.

The demon was about to finish Choppa when it sensed the

surge in power that emanated from behind it. Slowly the Wraith turned to see the young Gap Warrior standing there with the pole in his hands, and the power coursing through it.

Cyle would never forget the look of terror that appeared on the Shadow Wraith's face when it turned to see the young Gap Warrior charging at it with his staff fully empowered, slicing through the air and hammering it into the demon's head. The Wraith staggered backwards and fell against the wall in a daze.

"Your Majesty, there is no more time left," Cyle pleaded again. "If you do not return to the faith you have abandoned, your soul and your kingdom will be lost before the night is through."

Tears formed in the King's eyes and his hands visibly trembled. For a moment he seemed as though he was lost to the world. He looked at Cyle the way he used to when they would sit by the fire and talk. Then he fell to his knees. Darius tried to bring him back to his feet, but the King pushed him away. Cyle would never forget what happened next. The King looked at the carving of the eagle on the wall, and through tears of agony he cried out, "One Faith!"

The Shadow Wraith shrieked in terror as it returned to its original form. Cyle lunged at it, sweeping the pole through the air. When the staff connected with the robed figure the Shadow Wraith exploded, shrieking and flailing at the air. Then it disappeared into a mist of sulfur. Finally the door holding back the guards burst open as they charged into the room.

The fighting had ceased just after dark the day before, and during the night reinforcements had come into the city. Five hundred more Highlanders and nearly a thousand others from various parts of the province had come to defend their homeland. The battle lines had been pushed back to the open area inside the city walls, and miraculously, the Tals had been able to hold a thin line of defense not too far from where the gates had fallen.

The place was covered in a tomb-like silence. Exhausted warriors were lying in the streets, their spirits drained and their faces devoid of hope. Every spare hand was needed to fight, but even Gerrid and Bernard had lost the fire that once blazed in their eyes.

The distant sound of horses' hooves rumbled from behind them. The men in the streets looked back toward the palace. "It's the King! The King is coming!" yelled the watcher from the tower gate. The soldiers stood to their feet in disbelief as they watched the King riding out in front, escorted by two hundred of the royal guard. The two men riding next to him carried banners bearing the image of the eagle, and among the procession on two mounts rode Cyle and Choppa. The troops stood to attention as the King came to a halt.

"Faithful warriors of Talinor, you have fought with great valor and courage." The King paused to gather his words, tears forming as he looked over the carnage of war that lay before him. "I fear that I have failed you, and all of Talinor. Leaving the One Faith was the greatest mistake of my life, and it may have cost us our kingdom." King Shandon struggled to keep his voice strong, but he knew it was faltering. "I stand before you today indebted to all of you for the sacrifice that you have given to your kingdom. Some have paid the greatest price of all, their very lives. My countrymen, I humbly ask for your forgiveness." Whisperings swept through the crowd in response to the King's show of humility. Shandon pulled his sword from its sheath and held it before them, so all could see it. Upon its blade near the hilt was an image etched in gold and silver of the great eagle. "Today your king requests the honor of fighting with his men and, should you have me, I would ask one more thing-- whether we live or die today, let us unite under One Faith and one God."

Before the troops could respond there was a thunderous crack of lightning that shook the whole valley. Funnel-like winds swirled overhead. The mist and clouds that covered the sky were rent apart to reveal a narrow swath of blue, as bright sunshine shot toward the earth in streams of translucent light.

The troops stood in awe as they observed the phenomenon

in the sky. Then they heard the sound of music, softly at first, and then building as the melody from the Elf girl's flute reached the ears of all below. Her slim figure could be seen silhouetted against the morning sky. She was standing atop one of the tallest towers holding the flute to her mouth and next to her stood the figure of a giant silver wolf.

A screech sounded from somewhere behind the mist, and then a golden eagle appeared, breaking into the blue area of the sky with the sun glistening off its wings.

Cheers lifted into the air along with the spirits of every Tal warrior. "One Faith!" cried Gerrid, and then others joined in until they were all chanting it together. When their voices stilled, the King's voice could be heard sounding the charge, "To arms! To arms!"

The horn from the enemy camp sounded, and they swarmed the gate. Hundreds more washed over the walls in an endless flood of fury and rage. The additional reinforcements and the two hundred men of the King's Guard would only buy them a little more time before an inevitable defeat. King Shandon was right; they would die together united as one.

The Tals were being driven farther back toward the center of Talinor. The ramparts had been abandoned except by the few that had chosen to make their final stand there. The warriors left in the city streets continued their futile stand against the overwhelming tide of death. Gerrid called out orders to hold the front as he battled in the thick of it.

Cyle and Choppa along with Bixby and Gafney had made their way through the soldiers where they found Micah at the center of the front, fighting for his life. Ginzer was also there, ragged and worn from the battle; the patch over his one eye was missing. Near him was Bernard, barely able to move with blood oozing from his wounded side, somehow managing to stay upright.

The Boogarans surged relentlessly forward to break the center of the line where the fighting was now at a fevered frenzy.

Wave upon wave of enemy assaults was turned back as they hit the Tal wall that refused to surrender.

The small band of Defenders fought all along the front line in the battle against flesh and blood, where the mystical weapons of the Gap functioned in the same way as the weapons of those they fought against. The power that once surged through them had faded.

Above the tumult they could hear Gafney yelling out for help. Both Ginzer and Bernard had been struck down and were making the effort to rise again as the axe man fought furiously to protect them. Bixby was the first to respond. He moved cat-like through the fighting to aid his friends. All the while his sword slashed through warriors, rending the life from their bodies, Micah and Cyle followed defending his backside.

Gafney was a picture of power in fluid motion. His blade Demon Slayer slashed back and forth with deadly accuracy against anyone who dared to oppose him, but even the big man who seemed to abound with endless energy was reaching his limit. His movements were slower and less precise, but his heart raged on against the threat to himself and his comrades.

The Kadiri axe man watched from a distance, admiring Gafney's skills and patiently waiting for his energy to wane. Gafney's reputation was legend among the Kadiri tribe, and though legends are often exaggerated, this was one that rang true. Challenging the big man face-to-face was out of the question. He had seen enough to know that he could not match Gafney's skills. Waiting for him to tire would give him the edge and allow him to claim his reputation after killing him. He saw his chance and moved in for the kill.

With his back to the Kadiri, Gafney would not see the blow that was intended for him. The barbarian moved into striking position, filled with elation at the prospect of gaining the killing rights to the powerful axe man. Bixby charged in, but he would not make it in time. He called out a warning to his friend, but it was no use. Gafney could not hear him.

The Kadiri raised his blade high above his head to begin a deadly slash to the back of Gafney's skull. Then something happened that he had not counted on. The wind whistled around him and a phantom arrow found its mark in the barbarian's shoulder. Shock marked his countenance, and then another arrow struck his chest before he fell to the ground. The rushing sound of wind intensified as arrows rent the sky; the Boogarans and Kadiri fell all about them.

"Look to the ramparts," cried Bixby, pointing in that direction. "The Elves are here and they have taken the wall." They rushed into the battle from every direction, releasing volley after volley, their arrows sending a rain of death down upon the enemy below.

Gerrid could feel the tide of battle turning as the Tals pushed the barbarians back to the gate, and rejoined the Elves on the wall. On the hills to the west of the plain a cloud of dust rose skyward as an army of Elves riding on ponies thundered toward Talinor. At the center of the charge was Nephli, the commander of the Elves and to the left of him rode Graybeard, the prophet.

The fighting ended quickly after the arrival of the Elves. The field captain of the Boogarans found Drashkar's dead body lying in his tent. There was little left of it. Torn and shredded, his form was barely discernable. It was as if some unseen force had ripped through his body in an attempt to get out. What he could not have known was that earlier that morning the entity occupying his king's body had sensed that the breach in the void was closing and that the shift in the balance of power was turning against the dark magic. The demon had no other choice but to flee the temple of flesh and blood it had been occupying and return to the void.

When the final retreat horn sounded, the Tal warriors cheered, lifting the banner of the eagle high into the air. Word had spread quickly of the death of Ashkron. The Boogarans would not continue fighting without a king, and the Kadiri would not continue fighting without a king to pay them.

The cheers faded along with the mist, giving way to blue skies as golden rays of sunlight warmed to their faces. Flute music could be heard and its sweet melody reached out to their hearts. The song sounded familiar to the older ones, but to some of the younger ones the tune was unknown. Then someone in the midst of the crowd started to sing along with the melody. The words were muffled at first, and then others joined until everyone was singing together:

> *"At the dawn of time when faith was*
> *born in the heart of the 'Ancient of Days'.*
> *Where comes the source that flows to*
> *all who put their faith in the 'Ancient of Days'."*

Micah and Choppa were soon reunited with Cyle and the rest of the Defenders who gathered around to help Ginzer carry Bernard to the healing tents. The small band of warriors shared tired smiles and pats on the back. The words they wanted to speak to each other gave way to fatigue; there would be time for celebrating victory later.

Graybeard made his way through the crowd until he reached the one he was seeking. Cyle didn't see him approaching, but he felt someone's hand upon his shoulder. He turned, thinking it was his cousin, Micah. Instead he found himself looking into the eyes of the prophet. "You have done well, young Cyle," said Graybeard smiling. "I honor the courage and faith of you and your friends." Cyle was at a loss for words as he stared into the prophet's penetrating eyes while the others looked on.

"How did you get the Elves to come to Talinor?" asked Cyle.

"I told them the truth," responded Graybeard. "I told them that the Gap Warriors had returned to Talinor and that this kingdom would once again fight under the banner of the eagle."

"The Lady of the Guardians told me there was a fifth Gap Warrior," said Cyle. "We have looked for another, but there has only been the four of us."

Graybeard glanced over Cyle's shoulder before speaking, "The one you seek is approaching now."

All of them turned to see Lena walking in their direction; next to her walked the young guard named Jef.

"Grandmother!" exclaimed Cyle. Filled with emotion, he ran to her and she embraced him. "Grandmother, are you all right?"

"Of course I am, Cyle. I had my friend, Jef, to protect me; he's an intercessor."

"Why didn't you tell me you were a Gap Warrior?"

"I thought my Gap fighting days had ended long ago and besides, I had no idea I would be called back into service again."

"But you never told me. Why?"

"I never told you because I wanted to protect you from the evil that was gaining a foothold here in Talinor. You were very young when the people began growing cold in their faith. Fearing for our safety, Graybeard cautioned me not to tell you or anyone else that I had served as a Gap Warrior."

"It seems that Graybeard was right," said Bixby placing his hand on Cyle's shoulder. "It is an honor to meet you, Lena; we could not have won this battle without you."

"You are Bixby of the sword; I remember you from the last battle."

"Yes, and I remember you as well," Bixby motioned for the others to come near. "These are my friends, Tryska, of the flute, and Gafney, of the axe."

"So you are the Gap Warriors that Graybeard prophesied would be brought back to Talinor by my grandson."

"Yes, we are the ones," said Bixby, "and you are the lone intercessor of Talinor."

"Not anymore," said Lena, taking Jef by the hand. "Now there are two."

In the weeks that followed, healers visited Talinor from near and far. Plans were being made to restore the temples to their former state, and the city gates were already under repair. Bernard had survived the wounds he had suffered, but his fighting days were over. His cousin, Ginzer, was trying to talk him into joining him in his new trapping business. Darius was banished from the kingdom; and Gerrid returned to the One Faith with a relentless passion. He sought leave from King Shandon, who granted his request to travel to a land across the sea where he would tell others about the 'Ancient of Days'.

One month after the battle, Melidar visited Cyle in a dream, and the next day Cyle was seen leaving the city carrying his staff. One observer reported that it was glowing. Choppa and Cyle had spent a lot of time together in the month following the battle helping the workers put Talinor back together. Cyle was proud of his friend whom he had never seen work so hard; of course, his food intake also increased significantly. Within a few short days after Cyle had left the walled city, Choppa could not be found anywhere and when they checked his quarters, they discovered that his crossbow was also missing.

"I looked for a man among them who would build up the wall and stand before me in the gap on behalf of the land so I would not have to destroy it, but I found none." Exekial 22:30

EPILOGUE

The knock at the door was answered by the most respected intercessor in all of Talinor. "Hello, Jef, good to see you again; give me just one minute." Lena gathered her robes around her and grabbed a fresh loaf of baked bread, which she handed to her friend. The two of them walked out into the starlit night to begin their prayer walk through the walled city.

"We need to pray with great diligence tonight, Lena," urged Jef. "Somewhere there is a battle raging between the dark magic and the kingdom of light."

"I know there is," countered Lena with a slight smile on her face. "My grandson left for the western regions just one day ago."

In the distance they could hear singing in the temple.

ABOUT THE AUTHOR

Doug grew up in the Central Valley of California where he discovered true adventure at the age of 16 when he found a living faith in God. His mother, Lena (the intercessor), and stepfather, Allan, nurtured the spirit of risk in their four children through tough love and spontaneous adventures. His interests include photography, love of the outdoors, traveling the world and hanging out with the characters in his books

Douglas J. Tawlks

(most of whom he based on some of the amazing friends and family members in his life). Doug lives in Northern California with his wife and best friend, Shari, and his faithful German shepherd, Jasmine. He is an associate pastor as well as the director of the LifeBridge, an organization that combines counseling and inner-healing prayer to bring freedom to individuals struggling to find their destiny.

To inquire about inviting Doug to speak or train for your organization you can reach him at **dtawlks@thelifebridge.org.**

For Information on the Life Bridge Mission you can visit them on the web at **www.thelifebridge.org**.

Don't forget to visit **www.defendersofthebreach.com** to share your own reflections on this book.